JEAN SAUNDERS

UNFORGETTABLE

Complete and Unabridged

ULVERSCROFT
Leicester

First published in Great Britain in 2003 by
Robert Hale Limited
London

First Large Print Edition
published 2004
by arrangement with
Robert Hale Limited
London

British Library CIP Data

Saunders, Jean, *1932* –
    Unforgettable.—Large print ed.—
    Ulverscroft large print series: romance
    1. Love stories
    2. Large type books
    I. Title
    823.9'14 [F]

    ISBN 1–84395–406–0

Published by
F. A. Thorpe (Publishing)
Anstey, Leicestershire

Set by Words & Graphics Ltd.
Anstey, Leicestershire
Printed and bound in Great Britain by
T. J. International Ltd., Padstow, Cornwall

UNFORGETTABLE

Gracie Brown's dream is to become an acclaimed seamstress, but because of her background, she believes that success is an unattainable goal. Then, at the opening of the new Palais, she meets Charlie, a dashing saxophone player. Dancing in his arms, she begins to believe that dreams can come true. But a disastrous fire at the Palais breaks the spell and drives the couple apart. Gracie wonders if she will ever see Charlie again. But he is never to forget the girl he danced with at the Palais, and he pauses on his way to stardom to trace the girl he only knew briefly, but had loved from the first . . .

Books by Jean Saunders
Published by The House of Ulverscroft:

LADY OF THE MANOR
GOLDEN DESTINY
WITH THIS RING
DEADLY SUSPICIONS
A PERFECT MARRIAGE

Jean Saunders began her career as a magazine writer. She has written about six hundred short stories and over eighty novels. She is past chair of the Romantic Novelists' Association, and she frequently speaks at writers' groups and conferences. She is married, with three grown-up children, and writes full-time. She lives in Weston-super-Mare, Somerset.

1

Gracie's heart leapt with excitement as she looked at the newspaper advertisement again. The minute it appeared she had cut it out carefully and propped it up on the mantel-piece in the room she shared with her friend Dolly at Mrs Warburton's boarding-house. The words kept going over and over in her head, like the words of a favourite song.

Grand Opening of the new Palais on Saturday night.
SPECIAL OFFER
HALF-PRICE Entrance Fee for the first Hundred lucky customers.

The fact that the new Palais had been built on the ruins of an old warehouse only made it sound more impressive. Though, according to Mrs Warburton, who didn't hold with two young female lodgers frequenting such a place unaccompanied, it was a danger trap, but nothing was going to stop them. Her book-reading lodger agreed, saying it was like the phoenix rising from the ashes, which made as much sense to Gracie and Dolly as flying to the moon.

Dolly came into their room with her usual crash of the door.

'Haven't you got your glad rags out yet, Gracie? I've been asking old Warby if we could hold the rent over till next week, but she wasn't having any, so we'll have to hope some nice gentleman will buy us refreshments.'

'I told you it was a waste of time trying to get anything out of her! And I'm not sure that *nice* gentlemen are going to be buying drinks for the likes of us. It's more likely to be the other kind.'

'Oh well, you'll have no trouble attracting 'em. You always get the sort you want, and I get left with the riff-raff.'

'No you don't,' Gracie said with a grin. 'You only have to make cow-eyes at the chaps and they come running.'

'That's because I'm not so fussy as you,' Dolly said, openly envious of Gracie's naturally curly cropped hair, while hers was now Marcel-waved into the latest cut, which resulted in rigid corrugated waves marching over her head.

'Sometimes I wonder about you, Gracie,' she added, serious for once. 'You never let on what you want in a bloke. What do you really want out of life?'

2

'Well, not to carry on working in that shirt factory for a start.'

'Nor me. I just want to find a chap to take care of me and get married.'

'And end up having six kids and getting fat and old before your time.'

'What's wrong with that?' Dolly said.

'For one thing I know you don't mean it. You don't want to get fat any more than I do, and I'm not getting married for years and years yet. I want to better myself first.'

Dolly hooted. 'You and whose army? You've been watching too many Valentino flicks. You'll be stuck in that factory, same as me, unless you find a nice chap with oodles of dough. Anyway, it's time we were getting ready for the Palais. It's half-price for the first hundred customers, remember.'

She yanked open the door of the wardrobe they shared, wincing as it creaked on its hinges, and pursed her lips into a perfect Clara Bow shape.

'Now what shall I wear, my pink or my pink?'

Gracie laughed. It was never worth staying huffy with her for long. 'Why not? You look lovely in pink.'

'No I don't. I look like a bleedin' fat blancmange until I strap myself in. It's all right for you. You've got beestings, while I've got melons.'

'Oh, stop being so gloomy. And I don't have beestings either.' She stuck out her bosoms to their full extent and they both collapsed laughing again.

From the floor below, the man who worked the night shift at the laundry banged his stick on his ceiling for them to keep the noise down.

'Stupid old fool, it's only six o'clock,' Dolly grumbled. 'The sooner we're out of here tonight, the better.'

Secretly, Gracie knew she had the same hopes as Dolly. Maybe she would meet Mr Right tonight as well. Providing he was a gentleman with Valentino's looks and charm, and was someone who would respect her.

★   ★   ★

They just made it among the first hundred, which was a relief, since it would have left them skint for the rest of the week if they'd had to pay the full entry price. The place was already crowded, and how it was supposed to cope with a couple of hundred more, they couldn't think. Still, more chance for a squeeze up to some good-looking chap, Dolly reminded Gracie, as long as he didn't paw

4

you to death under cover of being crushed. But Dolly wasn't too averse to that either.

Gracie knew she was too addicted to the Hollywood glamour-boys for her own good. But watching those movies where some dashing chap fell in love with an ordinary girl and made her into a princess was Gracie's ideal. Waltzing around the floor in someone's arms on some fabulous terrace in the moonlight, was her idea of heaven — even if Dolly preferred the latest jazz tunes that were all the rage.

It was a fair bet that the band tonight would play a good selection of dances. A new dance-hall had to cater for all tastes, and with all the publicity there were some big-wigs here tonight for the Grand Opening, gold chains and all. They wouldn't care to be seen dancing the Black Bottom . . .

She became aware that someone was looking at her. She had been gazing at the band without really seeing any of them, apart from the fact that they were setting up their instruments and preparing to strike up the first number.

'I reckon you've made a conquest already, gel,' she heard Dolly shriek in an effort to be heard as they were pushed and shoved on all sides.

Gracie doubted it. Her best blue frock with

the bit of glittery embroidery around the neck and hem was already starting to feel tacky, and Lord knew how it would feel by the end of the evening. Even her long strings of shiny beads began to feel heavy, but she'd been unable to resist wearing them. Nor the cream-coloured button-shoes with heels a bit higher than usual, to make her look taller than she actually was.

'Don't be daft,' she yelled back. 'Nobody's noticed either of us yet.'

'Well, for a start the saxophone player ain't been able to take his eyes off you ever since you came in.'

Gracie's heart missed a beat. She'd noticed him too. You couldn't help it, really. He was the best-looking chap in the band, which was why she thought it highly unlikely that he'd give a second glance to a factory girl. Not that she looked like a factory girl tonight, of course . . .

Nobody could tell how many hours she worked at her machine sewing shirts, and how she'd had to give the ends of her fingers a damn good soaking in olive oil to restore them from their usual pricked appearance.

She risked taking another look at the saxophone player. He wasn't looking her way now, so she could study him more. He had slicked-back hair, very black and shiny with grease which gave him a really sophisticated air like all the band players. They wore white jackets, a flashy little green dickey bow, and black trousers with a green stripe down the outside of each leg. Their shoes were black patent leather. Her dad used to call them 'co-respondents' shoes', until she'd got him angrier than usual by saying he should go to the flicks more, because everybody knew that co-respondents' shoes were two-tone black-and-white.

Her heart missed another beat, because the saxophone player was looking right at her now, and he was smiling, showing the whitest teeth she had ever seen. She gulped, and felt Dolly nudge her arm.

'Smile back, you ninny. Told you he fancies you!'

'Not likely. He'll only think I'm fast. I'm going to get some lemonade.'

Nerves got the better of her. She wasn't fast, and she didn't want to appear to be. She knew what happened to girls who were fast. Boys took advantage of them and the next thing you knew you were up the duff. A couple of girls at the factory had got caught out recently, and it was whispered that they'd been sent away to some sort of detention centre for their own good.

Gracie shivered. She didn't want that to

happen to her, nor to Dolly, either. She was no goody-goody-two-shoes, but one of them had to be sensible, especially on a glamorous night like this when the whole place seemed to be sparkling with colour, and the great ball of lights in the ceiling twinkled like a thousand stars.

'You are a ruddy spoilsport sometimes, Gracie,' she heard Dolly grumble beside her as they fought their way to the refreshment area.

'No, I'm not. If he asked me to dance, I'd say yes, but it's not very likely if he's playing in the band all evening.'

'I s'pose not,' Dolly said, her mind already elsewhere as she saw the two brawny chaps coming their way. 'Aye aye gel, it looks as if we might not have to buy our own lemonade after all.'

The young men wore ill-fitting suits as if they were unused to dressing up. They had red faces and a coarse outdoor look about them — and Gracie knew she was being a snob, when she had no earthly right to be. She was annoyed at her own instinctive reactions, and made her smile all the brighter.

'Hello gels, out for a night on the town, are we?' the first one said. 'Fancy a dance later?'

'Might do,' Dolly said. 'That depends.'

He sniggered. 'Your friend don't look so

sure. Got a bad smell under your nose, have you, ducks?'

'Of course not,' Gracie said, wondering how he could have seen through her so quickly. 'I'm here to enjoy myself, same as you.'

He chuckled, pushing his mate forward. 'This is yours then.'

'You'll have to buy us a drink first,' Dolly said smartly. 'I can't dance until I've had a drink, and nor can Gracie.'

'Gracie, is it? Very Hyde Park. I'm Jim and this is Billy, so what's your name, little lady?'

'Dolly. So do we get that lemonade or not?' she said flatly.

Gracie felt her toes curl with embarrassment. She didn't want to dance with either of them. Jim was a match for Dolly any day, but Billy looked uncomfortable and very out of place. The collar and tie around his neck seemed to be chafing him and Gracie felt a moment's sympathy. But no more than that. If he hadn't wanted to come here, he shouldn't have come.

Her sympathy fizzled out at the way the other one was looking her up and down. Despite her lowly job in a shirt factory she knew she could sometimes appear stuck up — and she sensed that this was one reason why Mrs Warburton had let them have the room at the boarding-house. One look at Dolly, and she knew she'd thought her common — or no better than she should be, whatever that was supposed to mean.

'Stop looking down your nose, Gracie,' Dolly hissed again, when their escorts had gone to buy the lemonade. 'Jim's a bit of all right, and you only need to have one dance with Billy, then tell him to get lost.'

'I'm not looking down my nose at them.'

But she was and she knew it. And she tried not to shudder when Jim thrust the glass of lemonade in her hand and she saw the state of his fingernails, as black as soot. She'd bet a pound to a penny that the saxophone player had very clean fingernails . . .

'So what do you do, gels?' Jim was saying amicably now.

'We work down Lawson's Shirt Factory,' Dolly said at once.

'Blimey. Sewing shirts for soldiers, eh?'

She screamed with laughter as if he'd said something funny.

'Not any more, you ninny. It ain't wartime now, in case you've forgotten.'

He shrugged carelessly. 'Nah, thank God. Some of 'em never let you forget it though, do they? My old man was killed in the war, and my old mum's still going on about it seven years after it ended.'

Gracie was shocked. 'You'd never want to forget, would you? If my dad had been killed in the war, I'd still be upset about it.'

Billy spoke up. 'Jim and his dad hated each other. They had some good old ding-dongs of a Saturday night when his dad came home from the pub.'

'All the same, you wouldn't want your dad to be killed, would you?' Gracie persisted, with visions of the latest Hollywood film she had seen where the poor wounded soldiers came home from the war, clasped in their loved ones' arms.

'You would if you had one like mine,' Jim said grimly, flexing his knuckles.

'So what do you do?' Gracie said, turning to Billy in desperation.

'We're coalmen,' said Billy of few words.

That explained the blackened fingernails that no amount of scrubbing in the bathtub by the fire of a Saturday night would erase. Gracie's dad's were sometimes nearly as bad, though that was from unloading the ships at the docks, not hauling bags of coal around and breathing in coal dust all day long.

'Do you want to dance?' Billy asked. 'I'm not much good.'

And whatever happened to 'May I have the pleasure?'

Dolly giggled. 'That don't matter. You'll be

11

all right with our Gracie. She knows all the latest steps from watching them at the flicks.'

'Shut up, Dolly, and I don't, anyway.'

'Is that right?' Jim said, grinning. 'I thought you looked a bit of a toff.'

'Toffs don't work in shirt factories,' she snapped.

Dolly was screaming with laughter at his remark, while Gracie felt her chin go even higher. It was a daft remark, of course, and she was no more a toff than the shambling Billy, grinning inanely at her now, but she fancied herself a cut above the pair of them. She didn't have to dance with anyone if she didn't want to. Though there wasn't much point in coming to the Palais if it wasn't to dance.

Billy might look a bit soft in the brain department, but she didn't like Jim at all. Jim looked rough and ready, and from what she'd heard about his ding-dongs with his dad, he was handy with his fists as well. He had an air of danger about him, which was just the sort to excite Dolly, she thought uneasily. With any luck they could just manage to have one dance with each of them to repay them for the lemonade and then merge in with everybody else.

'Come on then, Doll,' Jim said, as the band

struck up a lively tune. 'Let's leave these two to think about it.'

'Are you really that good?' Billy asked Gracie glumly.

'Of course not, but we can sit this one out if you like,' she said.

As they struggled through the crowds to the rows of tables and chairs on the balcony above the main part of the hall, she didn't know whether to laugh or be annoyed at his look of relief. But it was mostly relief. She didn't fancy the thought of those sweaty hands clutching her tightly as he tried not to fall over her feet.

Instead, she tried to pick out Dolly and Jim in the crowd of dancers flocking on to the floor now, and to cover Billy's lack of conversation by tapping her feet to the music. From there, they also had a perfect view of the band above the heads of the dancers. And Gracie had a perfect view of the saxophone player.

He wasn't looking at her now, of course. He was too busy playing his music. She had always admired anyone who could play an instrument. It always seemed so sophisticated. And watching the movement of his fingers now, producing that wonderfully rich sound, she thought again that she'd bet a pound to a penny that he never had dirty

13

fingernails. The mouthpiece of the long brass tube of the saxophone was between his pursed lips, and those sensitive fingers caressed it.

By the time the others came back, Dolly was as red-faced as Jim, both from the dancing and, no doubt, by the things Jim was whispering in her ear. Gracie never set herself up to be Dolly's saviour, but somebody had to save her from herself, she sometimes told her laughingly, and got the usual reply:

Oh stuff. You only live once, but sometimes you sound as old as my old granny instead of nineteen, same as me.

'Jim don't live far from us, Gracie,' Dolly said now. 'He delivers coal to the mews around the corner, so it's a wonder we ain't seen him and Billy before.'

'We probably have, but we wouldn't recognize them all covered in coal dust,' Gracie said before she had time to think.

'Hah! Told you she fancied herself as a bit of a toff, didn't I?' Jim said, the smile not quite hiding the gleam in his eyes that said he wasn't too keen on this hoity-toity friend of Dolly's. She might look like the bee's knees, but thank God he'd got the one who was good for a laugh, and Billy would have to make the best of it. After tonight he'd never

14

need to see her again, but that didn't go for Dolly.

This one he'd definitely like to see again, and from the way she'd pressed her cupcakes up against him when they were dancing, he was pretty sure she wouldn't be averse to a bit of slap and tickle.

'Come on, Billy, I'll teach you this one,' Gracie said, deciding that he was probably never going to ask her to dance again, so she might as well take the initiative, even if it wasn't the done thing. Besides, she preferred to get well away from Jim, who was decidedly whiffy now, and it wasn't just what some called poncy aftershave, either.

Billy led her out on to the floor, and by some miracle of manoeuvring she kept him well away from her feet for most of the time. The thought of her lovely cream shoes being all scuff-marked from his size ten clodhoppers was too much to bear. He was doing his best though, and she encouraged him with a smile as they moved around the dance-hall.

'You're wonderful,' he said at last, even more red-faced.

'Why, thank you, Billy,' Gracie said, sorry for her earlier ungraciousness about him now. 'I'm not really wonderful though.'

'You are. Nobody showed me how to dance before.'

She smothered a small sigh. 'We'll have another one later then, if you like,' she said, thinking that this wasn't exactly fulfilling her hopes for this evening. Especially as she glimpsed Dolly and Jim laughing at them as Billy held her carefully away from him so that he could watch her feet and match their movements.

She might have known they were going to be stuck with them. From the moment Dolly's eyes had lit up at the sight of Jim making his way towards her, Gracie knew they were done for. Nobody else was going to break into the foursome and ask her to dance now. And if Dolly thought she had found her love-match in the oafish Jim, she certainly hadn't done so with his mate. But he didn't want to dance very often, so they sat it out while the others got on with it.

It hardly put her in a very good frame of mind, and halfway through the evening the band left the stage, off for a breather, and Dolly and Jim were dancing to gramophone records. Gracie closed her eyes briefly, preferring to listen to the music rather than to Billy's awkward attempts to chat. His offering to buy her another glass of lemonade in this interval had been the highlight of the evening so far, and she sent him off gladly.

'May I have the pleasure of this dance, miss?' a voice said, close by.

She felt a rush of guilty relief, knowing it wasn't Billy's voice, and that at least she might have one decent dance this evening, with someone who didn't hold her as if she was another sack of coal. She opened her eyes quickly, a ready smile on her lips, and then gaped.

The saxophone player, looking just as handsome close to as he had on his exalted position on the stage, was smiling down at her.

'Oh — I — yes, thank you!' She was momentarily as tongue-tied as Billy had ever been. And then he held out his hand to take hers, and she forgot Billy existed as she walked down to the dance floor with the saxophone player, aware of people watching and whispering, recognizing him from the band, and obviously envying the girl he'd chosen to be his partner.

'I've been wanting to dance with you from the moment I saw you come in,' he said, as he took her in his arms.

'Have you?' Gracie asked faintly, knowing this was absolutely the wrong way to react. She should be as cool as a cucumber, like the debs who were pictured in the newspapers, all with their noses in the air and wearing their lovely gowns, and reeking with their daddy's money.

'Don't say you didn't notice me looking at you,' the saxophone player said with an easy smile. 'I couldn't take my eyes off you until I had to. That's the penalty of playing in a band. It's only in the interval when they play gramophone records that I get the chance to dance with a beautiful girl.'

Without warning, Gracie felt madly, ridiculously jealous of all the beautiful girls he'd danced with before.

'I bet you say that to all your dancing partners,' she said.

'Not all of it,' he said, whisking her expertly around the room. 'And I'm being guilty of appalling bad manners, because I haven't introduced myself. My name's Charles Morrison, but everyone calls me Charlie.'

'And I'm plain Gracie Brown.'

Charlie laughed softly, his arm tightening around her waist to steer her out of the way of the other dancers.

'Oh, there's nothing in the least plain about you, Gracie Brown.'

She looked up into his eyes, as blue as her own, and she felt a tingling deep inside her such as she had never experienced before. So this was how it felt when you met the knight on the white charger who was going to sweep you off your feet, Gracie thought weakly. Only in her case, it was the saxophone player at the local Palais who was whirling her around the dance-floor and making her dizzy.

2

'Blimey, you didn't waste much time,' Dolly said. 'You were looking at that bloke as if you could eat him.'

'At least I wasn't fastened so tightly to him that you couldn't put a penny between us,' Gracie said crossly.

'So what? Jim's a real man, not a poncy dance-band player.'

'There's nothing poncy about Charles. Charlie, I mean.'

'Oh my gawd. *Charles*, is it? Going up in the world, ain't you? I bet you didn't tell him you worked for Lawson's Shirt Factory.'

'We were only dancing, not telling each other our life histories.'

But she felt a touch of dismay as she said the words. Charlie — Charles Morrison — was obviously out of her class. He was clever for a start, nimble with his fingers in an artistic and different way from the way she kept her machine going at the sweat shop. She might look the part tonight, and he might think she was a society girl and not a humble shirt-maker. But the thought of her being mistaken for a society girl made her laugh.

'What's got into you now?' Dolly said, pressing more of her favourite Tangee lipstick on to her scarlet lips.

'I was just wondering what Charlie would think if he knew how my old man sweated for a living down Southampton docks, that's all.'

'What difference does that make to a pound of fish?'

'None,' Gracie said, pulling her wayward auburn curls more neatly around her cheeks with a lick of spit. 'Only that he probably meets all the nobs in his job, and I was just a face in the crowd.'

She felt a swift surge of misery at the thought. She really liked him. He could talk nicely, and she knew she had tightened up her sloppy talk when they were dancing. She ignored the memory of her mum saying with a sniff that putting on airs never got anybody anywhere, our Gracie, and it'll only end in tears . . .

'You should think a bit more of yourself,' Dolly went on lecturing. 'I told you he had his eye on you. He never needs to know what your dad does, does he? Tell him you're a duchess, out slumming for the evening,' she invented wildly.

Gracie laughed again. 'I'm sure he'd believe that! Especially if he'd seen me hauling poor Billy around on the dance-door.'

'I suppose a coalman's not good enough for you now,' Dolly said.

'Well, not Billy! Nor Jim, if you want to know what I think.'

'I don't. Anyway, he's good enough for me, and you're a snob!'

She flounced out of the ladies' cloakroom, and Gracie felt her cheeks flame. How could she be called a snob when she worked like stink from morning till night in that miserable sweat shop for a pittance? The only thing that kept her there, apart from the excitement of living and working in London and being independent, was that the girls were allowed to take scraps of material home, and she was skilled at making smart blouses from the offcuts. She didn't need to look poor, just because she was a docker's daughter.

She lifted her chin high and marched out of the ladies' cloakroom to make her peace with Dolly. If she fancied Jim and didn't mind being pawed by those unsavoury fingernails, it was none of her business.

The band was playing again now, and her searching eyes went straight to Charlie. He really was lovely-looking, and any girl would be proud to have him as her young man. For a moment, Gracie let herself dream. And then a classy-looking girl with blonde hair, wearing a black evening dress and long, satin black gloves went on to the stage and began to sing, and Gracie's heart jolted.

'Looks like you've got a rival, Gracie,' Dolly said, close beside her.

Gracie tried not to feel disappointed or stupidly betrayed, when she had no business to be, just because he had danced one dance with her. Just because he had picked her out of the couple of hundred people here, and made a point of coming up to the table where she sat, and asked her in that so-polite way if she would care to dance with him. He probably did that on every occasion. He probably played at ever so many dances, every night of the week except Sunday, and she'd be a fool if she thought she was anybody special.

'Do you want another dance, Gracie?' Billy asked her a while later.

She gave a sigh. He was all right in a dull, undemonstrative kind of way, but he wasn't the sort to make any girl's blood tingle. But he looked at her so hopefully that she didn't have the heart to refuse him.

'All right, but then I'm going outside for a breath of fresh air.'

She had to admit that the atmosphere was becoming claustrophobic. There were too many people crammed into a hall that had seemed large and spacious at first, and now seemed pathetically small for them all.

The air was thick with cigarette smoke, wafting upwards to that great glittering ball of light in the ceiling, creating wreaths and patterns of a peculiar opaque beauty. The smoke made her cough, and crushed in the middle of the heaving mass of dancers she realized she was finding it hard to breathe comfortably.

'Billy, I need some air,' she said, her throat catching.

'All right,' he said, obliging as ever.

They began to push through the dancers. Other people seemed to be coughing too, Gracie realized, and her eyes started to water. It shouldn't be like this on the Grand Opening . . .

Even as the uneasy thought swirled into her mind, people began shouting. Excitement at the occasion turned to mild alarm and then panic. The shouts became screams, and nearing the door, Gracie swivelled around to see flickers of fire appear as if from nowhere.

'Run, Gracie,' she heard Billy shout, pushing her so hard she almost fell.

'Get out while you can, ducks, before you're fried to a crisp,' someone yelled in her ear.

All the doors were suddenly opened, and Gracie was nearly flattened as the mass of people fought to get out of the hall through what seemed now to be minuscule openings. A huge roar sounded behind her, as a sheet of flame was ignited by the rush of air from outside.

Without warning, the beautiful, slowly circulating ball of lights in the centre of the hall came crashing down on the people right beneath it. Shards of glass flew everywhere, and the dancers' finery was quickly sprayed with blood, and worse.

'Gawd Almighty, what's happening?'

Dolly's scratchy voice came to Gracie through the chaos, and she grabbed hold of her friend's hand and almost hurled her through the open door to the welcome air outside. They fell to the ground, in real danger of being trampled by the others following, and the next minute they were hauled to their feet and pulled sideways into a nearby alley. It happened so fast that what had been such a splendid occasion, was now a heaving mass of bodies all trying to escape from the pall of black smoke and flames coming from the building.

Gracie and Dolly were still catching their breath when the sound of fire engines streaking through the night added to the unreality, and they clung to one another in sheer relief that they were alive, even though it became clear that many were not going to be so lucky.

'Bloody good thing we were near the entrance,' Jim said hoarsely, flexing his knuckles in his familiar way, as if to fight the whole damn world if he could.

'The poor buggers who were nearest the band didn't stand a chance,' Dolly sobbed, her face streaked and ugly with tears, her lipstick smeared across her cheeks like a garish clown's face.

Gracie felt her heart stop. Nobody knew what had started the fire, but the Palais had been built on the site of an old warehouse. *Like the phoenix rising from the ashes*, one of their lodgers had said, which seemed like a horrible omen now. But Gracie was remembering that the band had been playing at the far end of the hall, well away from the entrance doors. Charlie Morrison had been playing his saxophone, and it was a sure bet now that he was one of those who had been burnt to a crisp . . . that handsome young man, whom she had foolishly dreamed was going to be her knight in shining armour . . .

'Gawd Almighty, what's got into her now?' Jim asked irritably, as Gracie started keening uncontrollably.

'It's shock,' Dolly said, startled by this

uncharacteristic wailing.

'There's only one way to deal with that,' Jim told her, and Gracie felt a stinging slap across the side of her face.

'What are you doing?' Dolly yelled. 'Have you gone bleedin' mad?'

She pummelled at his chest to stop him, and the next minute she went reeling as he punched her back.

'You silly bitch, can't you see I'm doing it for the best?'

'No. I think you're doing it because you like hitting women,' Dolly raged, pulling Gracie into her arms, and wincing at the pain in her bruised chest.

'It ain't the first time,' she heard Billy snigger.

People were pushing past them to get away from the inferno, not bothering with the four people bunched up against the wall of the alley, and more concerned with saving their own skins as the beautiful new Palais went up in smoke.

'I'm getting her home,' Dolly said through gritted teeth. 'You two can go and stuff yourselves for all I care.'

'Chance would be a fine thing. Tell you what. I'll see you in the park on Sunday, Dolly.' Jim grinned.

'Not if I see you first. Are you loony or

something?' Dolly said, and then yelped as she banged her head against the wall as Gracie jerked out of her arms.

'Don't even think of seeing this lout again, Dolly,' Gracie screamed. 'He's nothing but a bully.'

'And you're such a little princess, ain't you?' Jim sneered. 'Anyway, what goes on between Dolly and me ain't no business of yours.'

'Come on, Gracie,' Dolly said, grabbing her arm and pushing her through the people running out of the alley towards the street beyond. 'We need to get away before they start asking for witnesses.'

They twisted away from the coalmen, but as they reached the main street they were faced with several men asking questions and taking notes.

'We don't know anything,' Gracie yelled in a panic. 'We were dancing like everybody else when the air suddenly got choked and then the fire started.'

'And you are?'

Dolly pushed forward, seeing what all this was about before Gracie did.

'What's it worth for our story, mate?'

'A few bob if it's reliable,' the man said.

'OK then. I'm Dolly Neath and this is my friend Gracie Brown, and we work at

Lawson's Shirt Factory. We was quite near the entrance so we could get out when the fire started — '

'Dolly, they're *reporters*,' Gracie ground out. 'They'll put our names in the papers. Don't tell them any more.'

'Why not? Don't you want to be famous?'

'If my mum and dad get to see any of this, they'll make me go back to Southampton, you idiot.'

'Hold still, girls,' came a voice, and as they stopped arguing, their eyes met a camera flash, and then a few coins were pressed into Dolly's hand before the newspaper men slithered away like the snakes Gracie's dad always said they were.

'*Now* look what you've done,' she raged, but Dolly was looking with disgust at the paltry sum she'd been paid.

'Next time I'll invent something really wild, and get paid properly for my trouble! *And* I'll be looking half-decent for a picture in the paper as well and not like a bleedin' scarecrow — '

Gracie felt alarmed. 'Oh God, my folks will kill me if they see my picture in the paper. You don't really think they'll show them, do you?'

'Nah. They'll be taking pictures of the fire and any toffs who got fried.'

'Oh shut *up*, Dolly. That's a horrible thing to say.'

'Why is it? You got to face facts, and it stands to reason that some of them were done for. 'Specially those near the band — '

She stopped talking at the stricken look on Gracie's face.

'Oh, sorry, gel, I wasn't thinking. But don't worry about your saxophone player. The band came through a door at the other end of the hall to get on the stage, didn't they? Stands to reason they'd have been all right.'

She tried to sound confident for Gracie's sake, when in reality she didn't have any idea of the band's arrangements. It just seemed to make sense on a night when nothing else did. But neither of them wanted to hang around any longer, and they ran down the street until they could catch a tram back to the boarding-house, ignoring the black looks of the other passengers who clearly thought they'd been up to no good.

★ ★ ★

As the next day was Sunday, there would be no reports of the fire in the newspapers yet, and no work until Monday morning. Which was just as well, considering the state of

Gracie's bruised cheeks, and the ache in Dolly's chest where Jim had punched her.

They couldn't keep their discomfort away from the prying eyes of the landlady, though, and during breakfast, she snapped at the two factory girls.

'I don't know what you two have been up to, but let me remind you that this is a respectable establishment, and if you start bringing trouble back here, you'll be out on your ears quicker than blinking.'

'We're not bringing trouble back, Mrs Warburton,' Gracie said, before Dolly could answer back. 'We were caught up in the terrible fire at the new Palais last night, though. Hasn't anybody told you about it yet?'

The bleary-eyed laundry worker, back from his night shift, nodded.

'The girl's right, Mrs W. They say it burned to the ground, and after they spent all that money on it as well. They all said it was courting disaster to build it on top of an old warehouse. Gawd knows what was underneath it.'

Mrs Warburton was clearly displeased at being the last to hear.

'It would be the Lord's work then. I always said such places were dens of evil.'

'More likely to be the work of some more

earthly devils handy with a box of matches,' Dolly said in a loud aside.

The landlady looked at her coldly. 'You should be careful about saying such thing, Miss Neath. Dirt sticks, you know.'

'Daft old trout,' Dolly said, as the landlady went out of the dining-room. 'It's not as if we was smoking cigarettes, anyway.'

Another lodger added his piece.

'You know how particular Mrs Warburton is, and if she thought you girls had taken up smoking, she'd send you packing. It's all right for a man to smoke a pipe,' he added, 'but cigarette smoking is unbecoming for young girls.'

'Blimey, we didn't expect a lecture at this time of a morning,' Dolly said indignantly. 'Sometimes I wonder why I even stay here.'

'It's cheap and cheerful, that's why,' Gracie reminded her.

'I'm going out this afternoon,' Dolly told Gracie, ignoring the comment. 'You can come if you like, but there's a nip in the air, and it'll probably make your cheeks sting.'

'Since when did you become so considerate?' Gracie retorted, then remembered. 'If you're going to meet that Jim, Dolly, you're asking for trouble.'

'What's it to you?' Dolly said defiantly. 'You never met a chap sitting around indoors reading your old movie-star magazines. And Jim's all right.'

'He's a bully and he's the type who's likely to turn into a wife-beater.'

Dolly scoffed. 'Well, at least he's a man with a bit of beef in him, not like a namby-pamby saxophone player. Jesus, Gracie, I'm sorry, but I'm sure nothing happened to him last night,' she added as her friend's lips trembled.

'You don't know that it didn't.'

'You don't know that it did, either, so what's the good of worrying about it? You're probably never going to know, because he's not going to be playing at the Palais again, is he?'

Gracie swallowed. 'I just don't want you to get hurt,' she muttered, even though her mind was still on Charlie Morrison. 'And I can't see anything else happening if you see Jim again.'

'If he gets fresh I'll give you a full report tonight,' Dolly said with a wink.

'Thanks, but I'd rather not know if it's all the same to you!'

By now Gracie knew it was pointless trying to make Dolly change her mind, and watched in exasperation as she took ages wondering what to wear and trying to flatten out some of the stiff waves in her blonde hair, which she had now decided made her look like a bonfire guy.

'At this rate, Jim will think you're never going to meet him, and he'll have given up on you,' she said.

They parted company and Gracie spent her Sunday afternoon poring over her favourite movie-star magazines. Her nerves were still on edge, moping about a man she hardly knew, but who had made such an impression on her. Thinking what might have been . . . She hadn't got over the shock yet, not by a long way, and she didn't have Dolly's ability to put it all behind her so quickly. If they hadn't been near the doors of the Palais at the time, it could have been fatal for them, and they had yet to discover how many had been killed or injured.

She shuddered, realizing she was finding little pleasure today in reading about the doings of her favourite movie stars. It was all make-believe, anyway, and what had happened on Saturday night had been real, raw life. And death.

By mid-afternoon, she knew she couldn't stay inside the boarding-house any longer. With the same sudden need for fresh air as she had felt last night, Gracie thought that if she didn't get out of there, she would become as stagnant as the rest of the Sunday afternoon lodgers.

She wouldn't go to the park though, where she was likely to run into Dolly and Jim. Like a criminal returning to the scene of the crime, she had a bizarre urge to go back to the Palais, to see the damage. Perhaps it wasn't too bad. Perhaps, in their mad panic to get out, they had mistaken a small fire for something much greater. She blotted out the memory of that sheet of flame, boarded a tram and soon realized that people were talking about it in heated conversations, clearly knowing nothing of the true circumstances. Gracie began to feel mildly hysterical, wanting to hit out and say that they shouldn't spread these wicked rumours . . .

The minute she got off the tram and walked the few streets to where the Palais had stood in all its glittering glory, she knew there had been no exaggeration. The acrid smell of smoke reached her long before she got there, and there were other, more sickening smells that she couldn't identify, and didn't care to try. In the starkness of a spring afternoon, the reality looked even worse. Crowds of onlookers gazed at the blackened remains of the Palais, its roof completely destroyed, its framework leaning crazily towards the sky. The effects of fire and water from the firemens' hoses still filled the air with that stifling and nauseating stink.

'Terrible sight, ain't it?' someone said. 'They say dozens of 'em were killed, overcome by smoke or burned to death, or trampled in the rush to get out of the place.'

'Who says so?' Gracie stammered.

'Well, everybody,' someone else said impatiently. 'Stands to reason, dunnit? Not many could have survived in that little lot.'

'Well, *I* did,' she said savagely, angered beyond reason by the callous way he was stating false facts.

A woman nearby nudged her friend.

'You was in there then, was you? What was it like then?' Her voice was eager, ghoulish, wanting to know details Gracie didn't have, and wouldn't have told her if she did.

'Well, if you wanted a quick sunburn, I suppose that was one way to get it,' she replied, her voice harsh. 'What the bleedin' hell do you think it was like?'

'There's no need to be so stuck-up! I was only asking! You young girls think you can say anything these days. You all need a lesson in manners,' the woman said, and turned her back on Gracie in a huff.

She didn't know whether to laugh or cry. Stuck-up indeed, with what she had just said! She normally left the swearing to Dolly, even though she heard plenty of it from the girls and the blokes at Lawson's Shirt Factory, and could cuss with the best of them if she had to. Which went to prove that she was just a factory girl after all, and shouldn't put on airs, just as her mother said.

'Gracie. It is you, isn't it?'

She turned quickly, her heart in her mouth, hoping and praying that the voice in the crowd belonged to Charlie, miraculously saved from the fire and seeking her out, if not exactly on a white charger, as good as.

3

'Billy!' she stammered. 'I didn't expect to see you here.'

The sheer disappointment that it wasn't Charlie hit her like a body blow. For a moment she had really hoped . . .

'Didn't have nowhere else to go. Bit of a mess, ain't it?'

'You could say that.' You could say a lot of things, but you wouldn't get much response out of Billy, who, she already knew, was one of the world's worst talkers. Then, seeing how he was twisting his cap in his hands, she sensed his awkwardness at speaking to her at all.

'Let's get away from here, Billy,' she said abruptly.

You didn't normally ask a young man out, but this was no ordinary young man. This was just — Billy. When he looked even dumber with embarrassment, she went on desperately: 'We could have a cup of tea and a bun in the tea room around the corner. They open for an hour or so on Sunday afternoons. My treat.'

'All right.'

She had only said it on the spur of the moment, and now she knew she was going to be stuck with him. For one awful moment the thought of ever getting married to a man with no conversation was so dreary that she nearly tripped on the flagstones. As his arm went out to steady her, she averted her eyes to hide her feelings. He wasn't dangerous the way she was certain his mate Jim could be, or exciting and glamorous like Charlie. He was just dull.

★ ★ ★

Dolly screamed with laughter when she heard that Gracie had had afternoon tea in a tea shop with Billy.

'You must want your head read, walking out with that dummy.'

'I'm certainly not walking out with him. I was sorry for him, that's all.'

'You want to be careful, Gracie. He'll never leave you alone now.'

'Yes he will, because I told him I've already got a young man, and I was just thanking him for looking after me at the Palais last night.'

'Blimey, I never thought you could tell such fibs. So who's this young man you're supposed to have then? Didn't he ask about him?'

Gracie flushed. 'He's not so dumb. He'd

seen me dancing with Charlie, and he guessed right away that it was him. So I didn't say it wasn't.'

'Oh well, you needn't bother about *him* turning up to put a spanner in the works. He's played his last tune, so you've lost two of 'em now.'

For a moment, Gracie didn't follow — and then she rounded on her friend.

'That's a piggy thing to say, Dolly. You don't know what happened to Charlie, any more than I do, so don't say such awful things.'

'Sorry, I'm sure. Do you want to know what me and Jim got up to?'

'No, but I'm sure you're going to tell me.'

Dolly giggled. 'We had a canoodle under the trees until Jim said we'd better move on before we frightened the horses. Not that there were any horses about, but you know what I mean!' she added with a wink.

'I know you're asking for trouble if you see him again.'

'Too bad, because I'm seeing him next Sunday as well.'

★　★　★

They weren't on the best of terms next morning, to the usual whistles and cat-calls

40

from the men in the packing-room at the factory, and the sniggers from the girls already at work. The owner came towards them almost before they had got the covers off their machines, and thrust a morning paper under their noses.

'What have you two charmers been up to then? I must be paying you too much if you can go dancing of a Saturday night. You won't be paying the Palais any more visits though. You can take a quick look at this, then bring it back to my office. I don't want you slacking all morning.'

His voice was already fading when they looked at the open pages of the morning paper and saw their own faces looking back up at them like startled rabbits in the camera flash. And beneath it, for all to see, were their names, and the details that they were factory girls who'd felt like going up in the world for a night that had ended in disaster.

'Blimey, what a sight I look! What did I tell you!' Dolly screeched, not concerned with anything else.

The other girls crowded round eagerly.

'What happened? Did the place really go up in smoke with you in it?'

'Pretty much,' Gracie said, shuddering at the memory. 'But we were near the entrance, so we got out before the worst of it.'

She felt shivery all over, knowing that every time anyone asked her about it, she would realize again just how lucky she was.

'Was anyone killed?'

'Shut up a minute and I'll tell you,' Dolly bawled, reading quickly. 'It says about fifty people were badly burned and up to twenty died, but it was hard to tell exactly since there were no records of who was there. The dead and injured were mostly trapped by other people trying to reach the entrance doors.'

She snapped the newspaper shut, as Ed Lawson bellowed at them to get on with their work.

'I'd better not read any more, and old Lawson will have our guts for garters if we don't get started,' she said.

Gracie bent over her machine, her face paper-white as the events were relived in her mind. Dolly had no soul, she raged, and then she couldn't think any more. Without warning, she keeled over her machine in a dead faint.

When she came to she was being propped up, and something was being pressed against her lips as Dolly tried to make her drink some water. The only effect was to make Gracie splutter and spill it down her work overall.

'Jesus, gel, you gave us a fright then,' Dolly said. 'Old Lawson came stamping down the room, wanting to know if you was up the duff.'

'What!' Gracie was overcome with mortification, breathing so fast now that she was probably in danger of fainting all over again.

She held herself together with an effort. She wasn't spineless. But she wasn't the sort of girl Ed Lawson was implying either. She was a good girl, a clean-minded girl, and she intended to stay that way until the man of her dreams asked her to marry him.

'It's all right, Gracie,' another girl said easily. 'We all vouched for you, and anyway, we all know you ain't nothing like Dolly here. We just told old Lawson you had a shock from seeing your picture in the newspaper.'

'That's the truth, ain't it?' Dolly said, glaring. 'So if you're all right now, we'd better start some work, or we'll all be for the knacker's yard. You're not going to go off again, are you?'

'Of course not,' Gracie snapped, recovering fast.

'Good, because Lawson's threatening to stop us half an hour's pay for looking after you if we don't look smart.'

The bit of excitement over Gracie soon passed, but not the excitement over seeing their pictures in the newspaper. Dolly was soon preening herself, despite moaning that she could have looked a damn sight better for the cameraman if only he'd given her a chance.

While all Gracie could think about was the effect it would have on her parents — *if* they saw it, of course. There was not much hope of it not happening. When he was sober her dad read the newspapers from cover to cover, and he spent his nightly drinking binges ranting about the useless government, the state of the country and everything else. Her mum never had time to read newspapers, but she learned all that was in them from him.

★   ★   ★

Gracie's faint hopes that he might not have noticed her picture were dashed the moment she got back to the boarding-house that night. The landlady was waiting for her, hovering behind the net curtains as she and Dolly hurried up the steps to the front door, disapproval on her face.

'You know I don't approve of people telephoning my lodgers except in the case of an emergency, Miss Brown, but your father made it plain that it *was* an emergency. He'll call again at seven o'clock to speak to you. I don't intend to run all over the house for you, so please be in the passageway when you hear the instrument ring.'

'Thank you, Mrs Warburton,' Gracie said, resisting the urge to salute, and being as dignified as possible, considering how her heart was racing.

She and Dolly always laughed at the reverence with which Mrs Warburton answered on the rare occasions when the telephone rang. It was the pride of her life since she had had it installed for her use as a boarding-house landlady.

But Gracie didn't feel like laughing now, and once in their room, she rounded on Dolly, her face distraught.

'I told you! He's seen the pictures, and he'll make me go home.'

'Don't be daft. He can't *make* you. You send money to him, don't you? He should be glad you've got a job so you can send a few bob home now and then.'

'And leaves me skint most of the time! I do it for my mum's sake, not his, to give her a few little comforts.'

'What's he do with his money then?'

'What do you think? Boozes it away with his mates.'

Dolly looked at her silently, aware of her bitterness. Dolly had run away from home so long ago she'd forgotten what it was like to care about anybody but herself, but she'd always known Gracie was different, even if she rarely gave anything away about her family.

'Well, I don't know what to say, gel, except that there's no point worrying about it until you hear what your dad's got to say,' she said at last.

'I know. Tell that to the birds, though.'

She flopped down on her bed, aghast at how quickly things had changed. Just two nights ago she had been full of excitement at going to the new Palais. Meeting a dreary coalman called Billy hadn't been the highlight of her evening, but dancing with a handsome saxophone player had seemed so magical she had hardly been able to believe it was happening to her. Prince Charming had nothing on a bloke called Charlie Morrison. Her head and her heart had been full of dreams from that moment on . . . and then everything had gone wrong, as if the wicked witch had decided that this was enough happiness for Gracie Brown, and all those people had died in a terrible fire, because of her . . .

She sat up, knowing she was letting these wild and irrational thoughts get the better of her. The fire had nothing to do with her, and if only that photographer hadn't caught the startled look on her face and plastered it all over his newspaper her dad would never have got to hear about it, and ruined her chance of staying here and ever seeing Charlie again.

But now that the fire had destroyed the Palais, it was highly unlikely, anyway. Even if he hadn't been burned to death, why would he care what had happened to her? If he ever thought of her at all, he wouldn't know where she worked. The paper had just called her and Dolly 'factory girls' and there were dozens of factories in London.

She was awash with misery, and the prospect of talking to her dad did nothing to ease her jitters. He'd never approved of her going to London in the first place, until her mum persuaded him that it was good for a girl to have her independence. Plenty of girls, younger than Gracie, had left home and done their bit in the Great War.

But her independence would all be over now, she thought furiously. She might as well start packing . . .

She went downstairs just before seven o'clock to find Mrs Warburton standing beside the telephone, which she polished every day to gleaming black perfection. All her lodgers knew they risked her wrath any time they received a personal call that wasn't for a dire emergency. It was for business purposes only, every lodger was told grandly when they first entered the house.

When it rang it startled them both, and after a moment or two of speaking into it, Mrs Warburton handed the receiver to Gracie. She took it nervously, and then held it away from her ear as she heard her father's voice.

'You'll know why I'm calling, girl,' he shouted, in the way of a person unfamiliar with a telephone. 'You've shamed us by having your picture in a newspaper with that other young tart. If it wasn't for your mother's condition I'd wash my hands of you.'

'What condition?' Gracie said, ignoring everything else.

He didn't say anything for a few seconds, and she knew the meaning of that daft phrase they used in books. The silence spoke volumes.

When he eventually spoke she could almost hear the tightness in his voice. He was anything but a demonstrative or emotional man, but it was weird how such things became more obvious over a telephone line.

'She's real bad. The doctor don't like the look of her.'

'You had the doctor?' Gracie's voice rose, and she knew it must be serious if he forked out some of his booze money for the doctor's bill.

'I said so, didn't I? Anyway, you've got to come home to look after her, and after this other business, it had better be right away.'

'What's *wrong* with her, Dad?'

'It's a growth on her lungs. You know what I mean. *The other*. She's got six months at most, the doctor says. Maybe less.'

His voice was harsh, hiding his feelings in the only way he knew how, but Gracie was reeling with shock now. Her mother was dying, with the word that nobody ever used except in hushed whispers, and it was more than she could bear. Her thoughts whirled sickly.

'You should have *told* me!' she shrieked. 'I'll be home tomorrow, Dad.'

'Aye. All right, girl,' he said gruffly, and she knew it was as near as she would get to any thanks.

Not that she wanted or expected any. It was her duty to look after her mother, and she would do it out of love and respect. But she wouldn't have been human if she didn't realize it was the end of all her hopes and dreams. Because even if — when — it happened, her dad would still expect her to be the dutiful daughter and look after *him*.

She smothered a sob, aware that the

49

landlady was hovering somewhere near. She could smell the Devon Violets scent, which was a sure giveaway when she was eavesdropping. She could also smell the furniture polish on the yellow duster which would be at the ready to buff the telephone to its gleaming perfection again.

'Have you finished, Miss Brown?'

'Yes, thank you.' She swallowed, willing away those inane thoughts, and tried to be as calm as possible. 'My mother's very ill, so I have to go home. I'll be leaving tomorrow. I'll pay you my rent for the rest of the week once I've been to the factory to collect my wages in the morning.'

The landlady's face was a picture as Gracie swept by and went upstairs to her room, without giving her the satisfaction of any further explanation, though she knew Mrs Warburton dearly liked a bit of gossip to tell about her lodgers. But once upstairs, Gracie burst into uncontrollable tears.

'Oh Gawd, did he give you a bad time, gel? Now you've left home you should stand up to him and not let him treat you like a bleedin' drudge.' Dolly droned on until Gracie snapped at her to shut up.

'If you'd just listen a minute, I'll tell you what's happened and why I've got to leave here tomorrow.'

Dolly gaped. 'I hope it's for a better reason than just seeing your picture in the ruddy newspaper, then.'

'It is. My mother's dying, and I've got to take care of her.'

Her voice broke again, and then she was sobbing out the rest of it in Dolly's arms until the other girl shook her, none too gently.

'I know it's awful for you, Gracie, and I'm really sorry — sorry to be losing you too, come to that — but a fat lot of good you're going to be to your mum if you're crying over her all the time. You've got to be cheerful for her sake.'

'That's easy to say!'

'Well, try to look on the bright side — '

'What bright side? My mother's dying!'

Dolly tried again, uncomfortable with all this talk of dying, but going on doggedly.

'Yes, but at least she'll have you with her, and I suppose that's what she wants more than anything. So you're doing the best you can for her, ain't you?'

Grace grimaced at her logic. 'I suppose you're right, but I'm going to miss you like stink, Dolly! You will write to me now and then, won't you?'

'I'm not much good at letter-writing, but I'll do me best. I'll want to let you know about me and Jim, won't I?' she said.

51

'I don't want to talk about Jim right now, Dolly,' Gracie muttered. 'But — well, if you should hear anything about — about anybody else, you'd be sure to let me know, wouldn't you?'

'The saxophone player, you mean.'

'Or anybody else,' Gracie said, not wanting to let on just how much he had figured in her dreaming for those few brief hours.

She knew how foolish it was. They barely knew one another, but she had danced in his arms, and his music was in her heart, and if she closed her eyes she could picture him as clearly as if he stood right next to her.

'I'd better pack my things,' she said, turning away because it suddenly seemed wrong to be thinking about anything but the enormity of the task ahead of her. But she just couldn't help it, because for those few magical hours she had let herself dream that he was the one . . .

★   ★   ★

The girls at the factory were sorry to know she was leaving, especially in the circumstances. She had to explain her reasons to the boss, and hope he would see fit to pay her what she was owed, while he sat behind his desk like a lazy fat cat. It was demeaning to ask, but she knew she would need every penny to see her mum out in comfort.

She intended to stand firm with her dad too, and insist that he didn't spend all his money at the boozer. She had known the sweet taste of independence, and she was no longer prepared to be a skivvy.

Lawson was more reasonable than she had expected, considering it was a Monday morning when he was never in the best of tempers.

'Right then, girl,' he said finally. 'If you have to leave, then you must. I'll be sorry to lose a good machine-worker, mind, so if you ever want to come back at any time, I'll try to make room for you.'

'Thank you, Mr Lawson,' she muttered.

Thanks for nothing. Despite all his talk, she knew she was no more than a cog in his works machine. By the time she left the office he would already be putting somebody else on her machine and as far as he was concerned, she wouldn't be missed. But he'd paid her up what she was owed, and for that she was thankful. Leaving at a minute's notice, he needn't have paid her anything.

★ ★ ★

Home wasn't far from Southampton station, so Gracie didn't have to splash out on a tram or a cab fare. But walking in the warm sunshine, her bags seemed to have got a deal heavier by the time she turned into the narrow cobbled street where all the houses appeared to be crammed into one long mass. The women neighbours stood outside gossiping in their overalls, the same as they always did in the afternoon, and it was just as if she had never been away.

Most of the menfolk were dockworkers like her dad, and everyone knew everyone else around here, and all their business too. As people nodded and called out sympathetically to her, time seemed to have stood still, and for one horrifying moment Gracie felt as if she was being sucked back into a life she had looked forward so optimistically to leaving behind.

And then she opened her own door and the welcome smells of baking met her nostrils, and her mum came out from the kitchen, smiling.

Gracie dropped her bags and stood dumbly for a moment. She had expected to be confronted by a sickroom and a hushed atmosphere. Instead, at first sight her mum looked just the same, until Gracie realized how thin she was, her face almost gaunt, her arms like sticks; and she saw something like fear behind her eyes.

'Mum!' she said, choked, and was clasped in the older woman's arms.

'Now then, Gracie, I know your father's told you the worst, but we don't talk about it, and we don't think about it.'

The brave words, which were all for her daughter's benefit, were abruptly halted by a racking bout of coughing that left her staggering to a chair.

'What do you think you were doing, baking cakes in your condition?' Gracie said accusingly, because she couldn't think of anything else to say.

Her mother had always been strong enough to stand up to her drunkard of a husband, and now she seemed no more than a shell.

'I wanted to welcome you home,' she was told in a laboured voice. 'I hope you'll stay for a while, Gracie — '

'Don't be daft. I'm home for good now, Mum.'

'No, not for good, love. As soon as all this is over, you're to go back to London. You're not to stay here with *him*. He'll wear you down, the same as he's worn me down all these years, and you're worth more than that.'

'Oh Mum! You should have left him years ago,' Gracie said, not bothering to hide her disgust of her father.

'Women don't leave their husbands, Gracie. Besides, I loved him once, and he gave me you, didn't he?'

The painful coughing started again, and at last she had to give in and go to bed. The effort of baking cakes had been too much for her after all, and once Gracie had put her things in her old bedroom, she glanced in at her mother and watched her sleeping fitfully for a few minutes, her throat catching with sorrow at what they both knew was inevitable.

Then she set about preparing an evening meal before her dad got home from his shift at the docks. This was how it was going to be from now on, she told herself numbly, back where she started, just as if she had never been away, she thought again. And she might as well forget all those foolish dreams about a handsome saxophone player with a lovely smile. Everyone knew that dreams were just for children, anyway.

4

Mick Brown came home from the docks in the early evening, already reeking of beer and bellowing for his dinner.

'Hello, Dad,' Gracie said steadily, hearing her mother's intake of breath at the state of him. He'd never been one for knocking his womenfolk about, but his movements were clumsy and he was unsteady on his feet.

'So you're back,' he snarled. 'Not before time too.'

She smarted at his tone, but for her mum's sake, she wouldn't cause a fuss. 'That's not fair, Dad! I came as soon as I could, and anyway, I'm here now. And we're both going to have to pull our weight in looking after Mum.'

'That's why I sent for you, ain't it?' he barked back.

She stared him out, disgusted by the state of him, but realizing something else too. She hadn't been away from home all that long, but in those months when she had stood on her own feet, she had lost her old fear of her father. In his present condition, she had lost respect too, but she wasn't going to think about that now.

'For pity's sake, you two, don't start arguing the minute you're together,' Gracie's mother said wearily. 'If we can't all get along, what's the point of it all?'

She was stopped by a bout of coughing that left her gasping and reaching for a handkerchief, and Gracie just managed not to yell at her father that this was all his fault. Her mother, the peacemaker, wouldn't want that. So she forced a smile to her lips, resisting the urge to look at the bloodstained handkerchief her mother was trying to hide now.

'Why don't you go and wash, Dad, and I'll put the dinner on the table. It's mince and mash tonight, your favourite.'

It was also one of the meals her mother could comfortably keep down now, as she had learned since coming home. Hiding her heartbreak, Gracie served up the meal and watched as her mother picked at the food, professing that it was lovely, but that she wasn't really hungry.

'She eats no more than a bird nowadays,' her husband said, talking all the while he shovelled the food into his mouth. 'She needs to keep up her strength and she won't do it by starving herself.'

'Leave it, Mick,' Queenie said. 'I'll eat what I need.'

Gracie intervened. 'I've made a blanc-mange. Try some of that, Mum.'

'Just a little, then.'

Gracie was becoming more and more alarmed, seeing now that her mother's behaviour when she had arrived was little more than a sham. This was the real woman, this pathetic, seemingly shrunk little woman who seemed too weary to make any further effort. She resolved to visit the doctor as soon as possible to find out just how long a future her mother really had, and what she could best do for her in the meantime.

At the end of the meal, her father belched and farted at one and the same time, and apologized for neither. It was no surprise to Gracie that her mother decided to go to bed early and left them to themselves. She put the dirty dishes and pans in the scullery sink, trying hard not to bang them about in her growing anger as he watched her with narrowed eyes.

'I hope you were paid all that you were owed from that sweatshop, Gracie. You'll need to pay your way here now you're back. This isn't a charity — '

She plunged her hands into the soapy water. 'Oh, don't worry, I'll do my share, as long as you do yours!'

'What the bloody hell does that mean? And

don't speak to your father in that way. Respect for your elders, my girl!'

She bit her tongue, aware that she was going to have to do it more often if they were all to stay sane.

'What I mean is, Mum obviously needs decent food that she can eat, and regular visits from the doctor. It's all got to be paid for, and you shouldn't be boozing all your wages away.'

For a minute she thought he was going to hit her, and she flinched visibly at the sight of his clenched fists. She had never spoken to him in that way in her entire life before, but she was independent now. At least she had been in London, and although her life might have changed, the spirit was still there.

'When I need a chit of a girl telling me what to do, I'll ask, and you'll be a long time waiting!' he shouted. 'See to your mother and get on with your women's work and leave me to mine.'

He turned and slammed out of the door, leaving Gracie with her eyes stinging. Fighting with her dad was the last thing she intended. Of all times, they should be united when her mother was so ill, and galling though it was, Gracie knew she would have to wear kid gloves when he was around.

The thought was suddenly farcical. Kid

gloves, indeed! They were only words, but when would the likes of her ever be able to afford such luxuries, especially now . . .

'Has he gone, Gracie?'

Her mother's voice made her jump. She wore her dressing-gown and slippers now, and she looked even smaller, her hands paper-white as she gripped the door handle. Coming downstairs again had evidently weakened her.

'I thought you'd gone to bed, Mum. You need your rest . . . '

She waved her hand limply.

'There'll be plenty of time for rest when I'm in my wooden box, and don't start grizzling about that, because we all know that's where I'm heading. I want to talk to you about something important, and I can't do it when he's about.'

Upset at this kind of talk, Gracie led her mother back to the parlour and sat her down in her armchair. Her eyes closed for a few moments while she got her breath back, and then she smiled more resolutely.

'Don't look so sad, my love, we all have to die someday, and I'm quite prepared for it.'

'Oh Mum — '

'I usually come downstairs in the evening when he's gone out again. I like to feel my own walls around me for as long as possible, and not just the bedroom walls either. It's lonely up there, and I like to hear the street noises.'

Gracie swallowed. They rarely used the second downstairs room, except for dusting and visitors. But there was never a more important time for it than now.

'We could put a bed for you in the front room, Mum. You could rest there whenever you liked, and watch the neighbours go by. I'll suggest it to Dad when he comes home. He doesn't leave you alone like this every night, does he?'

'He means no harm, Gracie. It's his way. But it would be nice to be downstairs in my own home as long as possible, and I don't need him snorting and wheezing beside me all night long.'

'I'll see to it then,' Gracie said, furious at her father's insensitivity.

The racking coughing interrupted them again, and to Gracie's untrained eyes, the doctor's six-month prognosis seemed hopelessly optimistic.

'That's not why I need to talk to you,' the sick woman said eventually. 'I've made a will but he doesn't know about it. It's with the doctor, and he'll see to things when the time comes. It's just to be sure that you get my bits and pieces and do what you like with them.

It's not much, but it's for you and not him.'

She spoke slowly and haltingly, but Gracie could see that these were things that had to be said, and she didn't stop her. It occurred to her that her mother rarely referred to her husband by name, and she thought how sad it was that two people who had once loved one another should have grown so far apart.

'I've been paying into a funeral club,' Queenie went on. 'You'll see the little book underneath the rent book in my bedroom drawer. There'll be enough for all that's necessary, and if there's anything left over, you're to have it.'

'All right. So can we stop talking about this now, Mum?' she had to say at last in a strained voice. 'It's too much to take in all at once, and it's not doing you any good.'

'It's all said now, love, so tell me about you. I know you'll be missing London and your friends. Have you got a young man yet?'

The change of conversation startled Gracie. She wouldn't say her mother looked more animated, but it seemed that getting all the funeral business off her chest had relaxed her for the moment.

And the spark in her eyes as she mentioned a young man reminded Gracie that she had once been a pretty woman.

But a young man! No, she didn't have a

young man. There was no one, only two young men she had danced with in what seemed like a lifetime ago. A bumbling, inarticulate coalman called Billy, and a dashing, handsome, black-haired saxophone player in a dance band . . .

'There is, isn't there?' Queenie said, more alert. 'Good. You'll go back to him afterwards, mind. You're not to stay here and stagnate. So tell me about him.'

She didn't want to. What was the point? She would never see him again. She could hardly remember him. He would certainly not remember her. There was a young woman who flirted with him with her eyes whenever she sang with the band. Someone far more glamorous than Gracie Brown could ever be . . .

'He must be nice to put that look in your eyes, Gracie,' her mum was saying quietly now, and Gracie knew she had to pretend, if only to put a bit of sparkle back in her mother's life.

'He's very nice. He plays the saxophone in a dance-band.'

'Bless me!' Queenie said. 'Is that a respectable job?'

Gracie laughed. 'Of course it is. He wears smart clothes, a bow tie and all, just like a real toff.'

And what her dad called co-respondent's shoes, she could have added, but didn't. There was nothing of the gigolo about Charlie Morrison. Not as far as she knew, anyway — and what she didn't know, she would just have to invent for her mother's sake.

'Where did you meet him, Gracie? Was he in the band at the dance where there was that fire?'

There was obviously nothing wrong with her mother's memory, and Gracie remembered that her dad had seen her picture in the newspaper, and that her mum would have seen it too. But the unwitting lead had given her something to tell her now, without bending all the truth.

'Yes, and he was one of the lucky ones who got out safely, just like Dolly and me,' she said, crossing her fingers and praying that it was true.

'Didn't he mind you coming back to Southampton?' Queenie said, but Gracie recognized that her voice was becoming exhausted again.

'The band has lots of engagements all over the place,' she replied. 'It's what they do, Mum, and he's always busy, so I didn't ever expect to see him very often.'

'But he'll write to you, I daresay.'

'I daresay,' Gracie said, overcome with sudden misery.

Her mother was so quiet then that Gracie thought she had fallen asleep, and she crept back to the scullery to finish the washing-up in the congealing water. And then she heard the weak voice again.

'If he's as nice as you say, hold on to him, Gracie. A trustworthy man is hard to find.'

Gracie's eyes welled up with tears again and she dashed them away angrily. A fat lot of use she was going to be to anybody if she fell apart from the first day. And inventing a pack of lies about Charlie hadn't been her intention at all. Saying he was her young man . . . inventing his life for him — and for her . . . hearing his music in her dreams, that rich, mellow sound of his saxophone . . . dancing in his arms in her head, to the music, the music . . .

'Gracie, I'm tired. I think I can sleep now.'

She jerked around as her mother's voice came from the scullery door again, and she wiped her hands on a cloth quickly, before helping her up the stairs and into bed. At this rate the washing-up would never be done, but she didn't care. There were times when other things were more important.

But later, on her own in the small parlour, with only the muted sound of the wireless for company in the background, she closed her own eyes, and thought what a difference a day could make.

This time yesterday she was still in London, still fancy-free, as they called it. Now she had duties that no daughter wanted to perform, even if they were duties that she did with unstinting love. But now she had time to think about Charlie. Unknowingly, her mother had brought him back into her consciousness again. Perhaps he had never really been away, but he had been as unlikely a dream as meeting one of the glamorous stars in her movie magazines. It all seemed so shallow now, compared with the enormity of what the family was facing.

But if filling her mother's days with a few stories about Gracie's dashing young man called Charlie was going to bring her pleasure, who was to say it was wrong? To Queenie, a saxophone player in a dance-band was just as unattainable as any movie star. And he *was* such a beautiful young man . . .

Before she knew it, Gracie was letting her thoughts drift towards the imaginary background she was creating for her mother's benefit. Naturally, she had been properly introduced to Charlie, who came from a respectable family and had encouraged their son to follow his musical talents. His dream was to write songs and have them turned into sheet music for people to buy. One day they might even be performed on gramophone records, and he would be rich and famous. And Gracie would be right there alongside him.

The front door banged, and her father came stomping indoors, his head and clothes wet from a sudden rainstorm, his clothes unpleasant with the smell of damp wool. Uneasily, she saw that he looked none too pleased with himself. He'd wanted her to come home — had practically ordered her home — but they had never got along, and nothing seemed likely to change that now.

'Now then, girl, make us some cocoa and then you and me are going to have a little talk.'

Her heart sank. She'd had enough little talks for one day, and any more soul-searching on her mother's account was more than she could bear.

And although it was probably very wrong of her, she wanted to go to bed with thoughts of Charlie still vivid in her mind, and not the smell of her father's beery breath in her nostrils.

'Can't it wait until tomorrow, Dad? You're in no fit state for talking — '

'Are you saying I'm drunk?' he snapped.

'Well, aren't you? Look at you, hardly able to stand upright!' Gracie snapped back, unable to hide her disgust as he leaned against the table for support.

'Since when did a daughter speak to her father in such a way?'

'When he gave her cause, that's when.'

She stared at him fearlessly. Her months away in London let her see more clearly what a bully he was, if not physically, then always verbally. Always belittling everything she did, and sneering at her gentle mother. And the only way to deal with bullies was to face up to them, not flinch away from them.

'You've changed, my girl,' her father finally growled, slumping down in his chair. 'I'm not sure I like what I see, but providing you do right by your mother, we'll agree to keep our distance as much as possible.'

'That's fine by me,' Gracie said, her head held high. 'Now I'll go and make you a strong cup of cocoa, and there's something I want to talk to you about too.'

Take the initiative, she told herself. *Don't let him browbeat you. And get his agreement to her mother sleeping by herself in the downstairs front room, so she would get some much-needed peace and quiet in her last days.*

'Now then, Dad,' she said a little later,

dumping the two mugs of cocoa on the table in the parlour, and prepared to tackle him all night if need be.

And then she saw that he was fast asleep, snores roaring out of his slackly open mouth. She tiptoed out of the room, went upstairs and found a spare blanket and covered him lightly. Better that he should spend the night in a chair than wake the whole household.

★ ★ ★

Gracie knew she now had to get used to a new routine. The first few days were awkward. They all had to get to know one another again and, apart from doing the daily chores to relieve her mother as much as possible, at the first chance she went to see the family doctor.

He looked at her sympathetically. She was a lovely young girl, and as unlike her brute of a father as it was possible to be. But as he shuffled the papers on his desk, he knew she had a difficult time ahead of her.

'So what exactly do you want to know, Gracie?'

She spread her hands, and swallowed the lump in her throat. He had been the family's doctor ever since she was born, and she was attuned to his mood, and she could see that he didn't want to tell her the worst.

'What you can't tell me, I suppose, Doctor Wilson. That this was all a mistake, and that my mother isn't going to die.'

The breath caught in her throat, just saying the words.

'You know I can't tell you that, don't you, my dear? There's no mistake, and your mother has come to terms with it, and so must you. It's the only way to make it easier for her. She won't want to see gloomy faces for the last months of her life.'

'How many?' Gracie said, so abruptly that he looked startled for a moment. 'Dad said six months, but I've seen the way she looks, and it's not going to be that long, is it?'

'I could lie to you, Gracie — '

'Please don't. Please credit me with being able to deal with the truth.'

'Then three months at most, maybe less. Her heart is weak as well, you see, and either condition could be the one to kill her. I'm sorry.'

'Well, it's not your fault, is it?' she said in a brittle voice. She had asked for the truth, and she had got it. 'I'm sure you'll continue to do what you can for her, and whatever she needs, it'll be paid for, Doctor, don't worry about that. So I'd be obliged if you would come to see her regularly.'

'Of course, if that's what you wish, though it's not strictly necessary.'

'I think it is, if only for Mum's peace of mind, and mine too. She needs to know that people care.'

Apart from my father, she might have added. The ironic thing was she knew he did care, in his own way. He just couldn't show it. And he still expected his wife to always be there and to cater for him. A chattel, no less. And now he expected Gracie to be the same. She hardened her heart against him, thankful that at least she had got her way over her mother's bed being brought downstairs to give her a bit of peace.

She left the doctor's rooms with the need to breathe in fresh air and think. She wandered down to the docks where her father worked, loading and unloading the massive containers that came from all parts of the world. That was the business part of the docks. At another were the huge ocean-going liners, taking the rich and famous to places Gracie had hardly heard about — the glamorous places — taking glamorous people to continue their lives of luxury and pleasure.

Gracie gave a sigh. There was no doubting that when she first went to London there had been such anticipation in her veins. Not that she was going to meet and fall in love with somebody really famous, to be swept off her feet like some beautiful Hollywood film star and live happily ever after ... she was sensible enough to know that life wasn't always like that. Not always. But it could be, for some, and why not her? She had dreams, the same as everybody else.

But now, she was back here where she belonged. It was just as if fate had decided that Gracie Brown had had enough of living in London, as free as a bird, dancing with handsome young men, and being independent in a way no nineteen-year-old girl had a right to be. And it was time she came home and settled down.

'Look out, gel, or you're going to get hurt,' she heard a voice say irritably, and she stepped aside hurriedly as a man pushing a trolley-load of barrels on wooden rollers hurtled past. The smell of beer told her what was in the barrels, reminding her of her father.

She didn't know which part of the docks he worked at, but she didn't want to see him when her heart was full of all the doctor had told her. It was one shock on top of another. Not only did her mother have a growth, but she had a bad heart as well, and if one condition didn't kill her soon enough, the other one would.

She was hardly aware of where she was walking, and when she stumbled on the uneven cobbles she would have fallen if someone hadn't steadied her, and for a minute she thought she was going to be told off again.

'Gawd Almighty, if you ain't a sight for sore eyes, Gracie Brown! I thought you'd gone up in the world since you'd gone up to London, and we were never going to see you again!'

As she looked up into the cheerful face of the young man with the whiff of the sea about him, she gave a small smile of recognition, and the hollow that was her stomach momentarily settled down again.

'I could say the same about you, Davey Watkins. Last time I heard anything about you, you'd run off to sea.'

He laughed. 'I didn't exactly run off, gel, though I did join the Navy to see the sea, as you might say, just like my old dad. And now I'm home on shore leave, and all the better for seeing you — and all grown up and all. So what happened to you? Got tired of the high life, did you?'

'Hardly,' she said, and then her face crumpled.

She'd known Davey all her life, when he was a snotty-nosed schoolkid in short trousers with his socks always half-way down

74

his legs, and his hair an unruly ginger thatch. She acknowledged that he didn't look in the least like that now, and he was looking at her appraisingly too.

'Blimey, Gracie, by the looks of things, it's tea and confession time, so let's go to a caff and you can tell me all about it.'

'I don't know if I want to do any such thing,' she muttered.

She didn't know if she should, either. It was personal business. Family business. And you didn't go telling all and sundry your family business, except to old mates who could be trusted. But he wasn't going to take no for an answer.

In the steamy atmosphere of the dockside caff he went to the counter and ordered two cups of thick sweet tea. Once he had brought them to the table, he sat back with his arms folded. Real brawny sailor's arms they were now, Gracie noted, and not those of the weedy little kid she remembered.

'Come on then, Gracie, tell Uncle Dave what it's all about. I don't get to hear too much gossip these days. Is it hatches, matches or dispatches?'

At his teasing words, she looked at him mutely, and to give her a moment's breathing space she took a gulp of tea that burned her mouth.

At least, she hoped he would think that was the reason for the sudden shine of tears in her eyes.

Noting it, he spoke casually. 'So how's your old man these days? Still swilling the beer, I bet. Remember how we used to hang around outside the pubs of a night, hoping that when any of the old lushes came staggering out, they'd give us a few coppers for some pork scratchings?'

Gracie grinned. She had forgotten such things, but just for a moment she was caught up in a surge of nostalgia. They'd just been kids, the whole unruly gang of them, but they had hung together around the dockside pubs, and there was no fear, no danger, until they were sent off home with the landlord threatening to tell their dads. And them yelling back that their dads were drunker than any of them, and wouldn't remember a thing in the morning.

'Is it something to do with your dad, Gracie?' Davey asked quietly, more perceptive than she thought. But obviously not perceptive enough.

'It's Mum,' she said abruptly. 'I've come home because she's going to die.'

5

'You don't mean it!' Davey said, then added quickly, 'but of course you do. Nobody would make up a thing like that. Blimey, Gracie, that's a real turn up. Poor old Queenie. So you've come home to look after her, have you?'

She nodded dumbly, wishing she hadn't said anything. Once you put it into words it sounded more real. Once you told other people and saw the shock in their eyes it made it even worse.

'Don't start feeling sorry for me, Davey. Mum knows exactly what's happening, and we just have to get on with it as best we can.'

'What about your dad? From what I remember I bet he's not behaving as well as you,' Davey said sceptically.

'We all have to deal with it in our own way.'

'In other words, he's still down at the boozer every night.'

Gracie bristled. It was all right for her to criticize her dad, but she didn't need anyone else doing it and making her feel worse.

'What if he is? It's better than having him moping around the house, and he'll be just as upset as I am when — when the time comes.'

She bit her lips hard, unable to say any more, wanting to get away from his sympathetic eyes.

'Look, I really can't stay any longer, Davey.'

'I understand,' he said at once. 'You'll want to get back home, won't you?'

'Not really.' She hesitated, perverse as the wind. 'Actually, I could do with a bit of cheering up, so how about a walk — or do you have other things to do?'

She felt herself redden, but she had known him since he was in short trousers, and she wasn't trying to flirt with him. He could surely see that.

'Nothing that won't wait,' he replied. 'Where do you want to go?'

'Oh, I don't know. We could take a look at the ocean liners and imagine we're going somewhere exotic and far away,' she said recklessly, willing her thoughts away from her mum's ordeal for the moment. 'I bet you've seen plenty of exotic places in the Navy, haven't you?'

He laughed as they went outside the caff. 'Hardly. Being in the Navy's no joy-ride when you're working in the bowels of the ship in the sweltering heat of the engine-room. You don't even see the sea until you're in port.'

'It sounds horrible,' Gracie said. 'Why do it

if you don't like it?'

'I didn't say I don't like it. Just that it's not all it's cracked up to be, but it beats sticking around here. You got away as soon as you could, didn't you?'

'And now I'm back.' Which said it all.

They walked in companionable silence until they reached the terminal where the ocean liners berthed. There was little activity there now, just one ship in port, awaiting its complement of wealthy passengers. They watched the comings and goings of the ship's company preparing for their next voyage.

'Have you got a boyfriend?' Davey said casually.

She was tempted to spin the same yarn she had told her mother, about the saxophone player called Charlie Morrison. But what was the point? She kept her gaze fixed on the elegant ship as she spoke.

'I did meet someone in London a little while ago, but I doubt that I'll ever meet him again. It's all water under the bridge now, anyway.'

'Hell's bells, Gracie Brown, I never knew you to be so mournful — and I know you've got a lot to be mournful about right now, with your mum being ill and all — but at school everybody called you a right little ray of sunshine.'

'You don't remember any such thing,' she said with a laugh and a catch in her throat, 'and you're only saying it to make me feel better.'

'Is it working?'

After a moment she said, almost in surprise: 'Yes, it is.'

'So come to a dance with me on Saturday night. You can make sure your old man stays home to keep your mum company. My shore leave ends next week, and it would be nice to have a few good memories to take back to sea.'

Gracie's face remained fixed all the while he was coaxing her, and all she could hear were those words: *come to a dance with me.* He couldn't know it, but she was instantly transported to the Palais where she had danced with Charlie and created memories that seemed to be etched in her brain, no matter how foolish.

'What do you say?' Davey went on when she remained silent.

'I'll think about it,' she said hurriedly. 'Come round to our house sometime before then. I know Mum would like to see you.'

She wouldn't say anything more definite than that. She didn't want to go dancing with anyone but Charlie, but she knew how stupid that was. She was hardly going to spend the rest of her life thinking about a chap she had only met so briefly, for God's sake. She wasn't living in the kind of dream-world that only existed in the movies, where miraculous things happened. She didn't believe in happy-ever-afters . . . the hell of it was, that deep down, she wanted to, so badly.

★ ★ ★

'Would you mind if I went out on Saturday night, Mum?' she asked, saying it quickly, before she changed her mind.

'Of course not, love!' Queenie's voice held genuine astonishment. 'You're not a prisoner here.'

'I'll make sure Dad stays home to keep you company,' she went on.

Her mother's laugh ended in a bout of coughing, and they had to wait until it stopped before she could go on.

'I'm well used to that, Gracie, and now I've got my bed downstairs I'll be fine. I can watch the world go by of an evening, and tap on the window if I see any of the neighbours to ask them in for a chat. So where are you going?'

She lay back on her pillow, exhausted after such a long speech.

'Remember Davey Watkins from Leeman

81

Street? He's in the Navy now, but he's home on leave and he asked me to go dancing. You don't mind, do you?'

It was ridiculous to feel like a little girl again, asking permission to go to the shops, but the light in her mother's eyes told her she was thinking differently.

'I remember young Davey Watkins very well. Ginger hair and a cheeky smile. You could do a lot worse.'

'It's only a dance, Mum!' Gracie said, suddenly cross. 'Don't start matchmaking, and besides, I couldn't ever think of him in that way.'

'I know you said you've got a young man, but he's in London — and a saxophone player, Gracie!' Her tone implied that it was a very dubious occupation.

'And a *composer of songs*, Mum!' she said, compounding the fiction.

'Oh well, I'm sure you know best,' Queenie said wearily.

The fight had gone out of her. At one time she would have probed every bit of Gracie's relationship with a saxophone player — or anybody else — even though there was nothing to find out! But now she made token enquiries, and was a semblance of the sparky woman of old. Illness did that to a person, Gracie thought savagely. It ravaged the body, and the spirit too. It was heartbreaking. She turned away abruptly before her mother could see the prickle of tears in her eyes.

'I'll make us some tea. Would you like a biscuit to dip in it, Mum?'

'Perhaps just one. I'm not really hungry.'

They both knew it would either be left in the saucer or the dipping would turn the tea to biscuit soup.

She had composed herself by the time she took the tea into the front room where her mother was dozing on and off by now. Seeing Gracie, she made a determined effort to perk up, and managed to drink some of the tea once it had cooled down. Predictably, she didn't touch the biscuit.

'Mum, I've been thinking. I don't want to sponge on Dad, and it may be months before you get better,' she went on delicately.

Queenie shook her head. 'We both know that's not going to happen.'

Gracie ignored the remark. 'I need to work, Mum, but I wouldn't leave you now. If I can use your old sewing-machine I could take in sewing alterations at home. I'd try not to let it disturb you too much.'

'It wouldn't disturb me! I like the sound of the sewing-machine. It's going to be yours, anyway.'

Gracie swallowed hard. She hated all this

implication of death and what happened afterwards, but she could see it was important to her mother. She was so brave, facing what was inevitable.

'I'll put a card in the grocer's window then, and I'll call myself a London Outworker. Does that sound fancy enough?' she added.

But Queenie had drifted off to sleep now, and Gracie tiptoed out, already composing the words on the card to advertise her skills. She hadn't really meant to call herself any such thing as a 'London Outworker', but if it impressed likely customers it didn't seem such a bad idea.

The old treadle sewing-machine in the parlour hadn't been used since Gracie had gone to London. Her fingers suddenly tingled with anticipation. Doing alterations to garments wasn't the same as making something new, even in the tedium of Lawson's Shirt Factory, but the skill was the same, and it was the work she enjoyed more than anything else.

She felt slightly uplifted. Any money she could earn could pay for the little extras her dad seemed incapable of recognizing that her mother needed. She wasn't going to be useless here, and she had to keep busy for her own sanity and to keep her mind off what lay ahead.

Her father approved of the suggestion — providing his dinner was on the table when he wanted it, and that the parlour wasn't filled with stuff everywhere and bits of fluff and cotton-dust in the air to smother the taste of his food. It wouldn't do Queenie's chest any good, either, he added as an afterthought.

'Don't worry, Dad,' she said sarcastically. 'Nothing will interfere with your well-being. We wouldn't want that, would we?'

He looked at her through narrowed eyes, unsure of this newly independent daughter who no longer flinched when he shouted, and had ideas of her own. His womenfolk were ganging up on him — as far as Queenie could gang up on anybody, he thought with an unexpected pang.

'See to it then,' he said gruffly. 'As long as it don't fret your mother.'

★ ★ ★

After the dance with Davey Watkins she saw him several times before he returned to his ship, but she made it plain to him that it was a relationship that was going nowhere except friendship. Though she couldn't deny he had done her mother good with his nonsense when he had called at the house.

85

She also admitted that it had been a sensible decision to go dancing with him. It had exorcised any foolish dreams she might have had. She could even make a few jokes with him about the local band who weren't up to much, and not compare them with other, slicker bands in London dance-halls. She even reluctantly agreed to answer any letters he sent her from foreign parts.

A month or so later, a letter arrived, but it wasn't from Davey. As Dolly had always told her, she wasn't a great letter-writer. She wrote as she talked, flitting from subject to subject as thoughts came into her head.

Gracie still felt cheered, just to be in contact with her old world again. She had plenty of things to tell Dolly too. She had sent one letter to her friend to tell her the situation when she first arrived home, but there had been no reply, and Gracie had assumed sadly that Dolly had found another friend and that the contact was broken. But now all that was changed.

You'll never guess, gel, Dolly wrote, me and Jim are walking out proper now, and he can be a proper gent when he likes. That's not so often, mind, but I ain't complaining. We went dancing up West the other night, though I had to be extra

86

nice to him for the privilege, if you know what I mean. Jim ain't really big on dancing, and him and Billy only went to the Palais that night on the look-out for a bit of skirt.

They're pulling down the Palais now, but they still ain't sure what caused the fire. Old Lawson reckons it was people smoking, but he'd say that anyway. He's got a new girl in your place now, name of Sheila, but she's not up to much, and I reckon he'll get rid of her soon. He's always shouting that he's lost the best machinist in the place, meaning you, Gracie. We all miss you. Even Billy was asking about you the other night.

Old Ma Warburton's increased my rent until I get somebody else to share the digs with me, but I ain't keen on finding anybody. I always liked sharing with you, so let me know when you can come back. Oh Gawd, I know what that means, and I hope your mum ain't too bad, Gracie, honest I do. I still want you to come back soon though.

Your old friend,
   Dolly Neath

PS. I ain't seen nothing of your saxophone player.

Gracie's smile faded by the time she reached the end of the letter. She really wished Dolly hadn't mentioned Charlie, however obscurely. It brought it all back so sharply. In the same instant, she knew she was glad that she *had* mentioned him, if only to say she hadn't seen anything of him. But what had she thought? That he was going to appear miraculously in whatever dance-hall up West that she and Jim had gone to? Coincidences like that only happened in the movies or in books.

She wrote back straight away, because by doing so it felt as though she and Dolly were sharing confidences again in their poky little room at Ma Warburton's.

Dear Dolly, she wrote, *I can't tell you how glad I was to hear from you. I thought you'd forgotten me. I know it's not that long since I left London, but it seems like years. I'm back in the old routine all right. My dad is still boozing, and Mum's getting worse every day. The doctor's as good as said she won't last out the summer, and I'm sorry if I sound gloomy, but it's not much fun to watch somebody dying and know you can't do anything to help except just be there . . .*

88

Gracie was tempted to screw the letter up and start again. But she and Dolly had always been able to say anything to one another, so she carried on . . .

I'm sure I'll come back to London sometime. Mum wants me to do so, when it's all over. Apart from looking after her, I'm taking in dressmaking alterations, and not doing too badly. Mum likes the sound of the sewing machine. She says it makes her feel she's still in the land of the living.

She paused again, her throat thick and then quickly changed the subject.

I daresay you'll be glad to hear I met an old friend recently. His name's Davey and he's a sailor. We went to a dance before he went back to his ship and he's going to write to me, so it's not all misery here.

I still think you should be careful as far as coalman Jim is concerned, Dolly. I thought he was a bit of a flash card. Remember me to Billy next time you see him — and the girls at Lawson's — and anybody else I know. Write again soon.

Your friend,
Gracie.

She wouldn't go so far as to say *remember me to Charlie Morrison if you see him,* because it seemed unlikely that she ever would. He wasn't *her* saxophone player, anyway. Never had been and never would be. She folded up the letter and put it in an envelope ready for posting on her way to return the alterations she had been doing for someone in a posher part of the town.

It was only by chance that the lady had seen Gracie's card in the grocer's window after seeing someone off on one of the foreign cruises. The words *London Outworker,* persuaded her to leave a message at the shop for Gracie to call on her with a view to doing some work for her and her daughters. Since then she had been recommended to some of Mrs Farthing's friends on account of her fine and speedy workmanship, and there was no shortage of orders.

'Didn't I tell you, Mum?' Gracie had said gleefully. 'It pays to advertise and not to hide your light — or your skills — under a bushel.'

★   ★   ★

Queenie was thankful her girl was finding something to occupy herself, and doing something that she enjoyed. The money didn't matter. What mattered was that Gracie

90

wasn't always watching and listening for the next cough or the next painful wheezing breath. It mattered to Queenie that Gracie could keep her self-respect, and that she wasn't going to kowtow to her father after Queenie was gone, and end up being a skivvy for him. She had got the doctor on her side about that, persuading him to assure Gracie that when the time came, her father wouldn't need looking after, and was perfectly capable of looking after himself.

Queenie was also sure that Mick Brown wouldn't be slow in looking around for another wife-cum-housekeeper to take care of him. He was still a reasonable-looking man, for all his drinking, and had always had an eye for the ladies. They would be flitting around, bringing him home-baked pies and offering to clean the house for him . . .

There had been a time when she would have been eaten up with jealousy and misery at the thought. Now, she knew that none of it would matter when she was gone, especially if it freed Gracie from a life of drudgery, caring for her father.

★   ★   ★

The Farthings lived on top of a hill from where they could look down on the rest of the town. Today, as usual, Gracie had to pause for breath by the time she reached the top. The trams didn't come this far, and most folk who lived here owned a car. The husband was a businessman, and the young daughters, Adele and Edna, were at boarding-school. When they went back to school after a holiday, their mother felt at a loss before taking up her various charity works again, and Gracie suspected it was the reason she spent more time talking to the girl with the sewing skills than she might otherwise have done.

'Come into the conservatory and get your breath back before you show me your handiwork, Gracie,' she said on that warm afternoon. 'You look very flushed, dear, although you have a very good complexion, like my daughters.'

There was a wistful note in her voice but, pleasant though Mrs Farthing was, Gracie had no wish to be thought of as a kind of substitute daughter while her spoiled little girls were away at school. She'd only met them once, and she was glad to conduct her business with the mother when they weren't around. But then Mrs Farthing spoke more briskly.

'So let's see what you managed to do with the girls' dresses, shall we?'

Marriage to a successful businessman

might have given her many advantages, but she had a thrifty streak, and she liked clothes to last as long as possible before they were given away to charity. Gracie had spent a deal of time lengthening Adele and Edna's summer dresses by letting down the hems and adding rows of colourful braiding to disguise the machine lines.

Mrs Farthing was pleased with the result, and gave her more work to take away. Although she was always gracious in passing the time of day, Gracie guessed that she wasn't finding clothes to be renovated or altered just for the company. It was far more likely, she thought cynically, that she saw Gracie as one of her charity cases who needed the extra money.

Whatever the reason, the result was the same, and she walked home with money jingling in her pockets. She planned to buy her mother one of her favourite cream cakes as a special treat, in an effort to tempt her failing appetite.

Her way was blocked at the end of their street by their landlord. Gracie thought him the creepiest of men, a proper Shylock wanting his pound of flesh from his tenants, his face florid and his belly overstuffed, despite the fact that he wasn't even middle-aged. She paid him the weekly rent now, rather than let his calculating gaze assess how much longer her mother was going to be around.

As he barred her way, those eyes were looking her over in a way she didn't like, Gracie thought furiously.

'How's your mother, Gracie? I see the doctor calls fairly often now. Getting near the end, is she?' he said coarsely.

'She's well enough, thank you, Mr Hill,' Gracie forced herself to say.

'Give her my regards, girlie,' he said with a leer. He stepped aside for her to pass, though she felt him watching her all the way down the street.

Her pleasure in buying the cream cake for her mother's treat momentarily fizzled out, then she told herself not to be stupid. Now that she was inside her own home, she could ignore Hill's lecherous manner.

But she couldn't ignore the fact that her mother was looking very sickly today, and the suggestion of eating a cream cake was more than she could bear. In the end her father said it was too good to go to waste, and relished it as a treat after his dinner, while Gracie agonized over how much longer her mother could go on starving herself in this way.

6

Ever since he had learned to play the saxophone and discovered himself to be a natural, Charlie Morrison's ambition had been to play in a dance-band. He had a comfortably middle-class back-ground, and it was thanks to his father's generous disregard for conventions that he let Charlie have his way.

Nothing gave him greater pleasure than to hear the applause when the band finished one of their numbers, or seeing the dreamy looks on the faces of the young girls in the arms of their partners when they played one of their slower tunes. He also relished the excitement of playing the latest jazz tunes.

The older band members teased him that he caressed the buttons on his saxophone in the way some men caressed a woman, but he wasn't concerned with their teasing. He knew he got the best out of the instrument, and the rich warm sound of it never failed to give him a thrill. In his spare time, when they weren't rehearsing, he had written the music for a couple of songs, and all he wanted was someone to write the lyrics . . .

Their singer often remarked when she listened to him playing some of his own tunes that he could make a success of writing music.

'And if only you had the gumption to write the words, Joyce,' he always joked, 'we could make a great song-writing team.'

'Don't I wish we could, darling,' she murmured softly, turning away so that he couldn't hear what she really meant.

In any case, it wasn't as part of a song-writing team that she hankered after him. She might be idolized by more than a few when she sang her soulful songs on stage, but she knew she was never going to be a heartbreaker as far as Charlie Morrison was concerned. Not that she would break his heart — far from it — but she had always known he wasn't for her, and the feeling had been stronger ever since the fire at the opening night of the Palais several months ago.

'Did you ever find your girl, Charlie?' she asked him suddenly, as they were preparing for the evening's session in an out-of-town nightclub.

'What girl is that?'

'Come on, you can't fool me. I know how frantically you tried to find the girl you were dancing with the night the Palais burned down.'

'Oh, *that* girl,' Charlie said casually, and then shrugged. 'Well, I knew she survived because I saw her photo in the newspaper account of the fire.'

'Didn't it give her address?'

'No, just her name, and that she and her friend were factory girls. Anyway, we only had a couple of dances. I was hardly going to scour the whole of London's factories to find a girl called Gracie Brown, was I?'

'Of course not.' Joyce managed to keep a straight face. 'Even though you haven't forgotten a single thing that was in the paper about her, have you? What was her friend's name, by the way?'

'I haven't the foggiest,' he said without interest, and then laughed at her I-told-you-so expression. 'Oh, all right, perhaps I did take a shine to her, but I'm damned sure she'll have forgotten me long ago.'

He hadn't forgotten her though. He could still picture the vibrant colour of her hair, with those endearingly unruly curls framing her face, and her dancing blue eyes. She had a classy look, different from most factory girls, but that was the snob in him, which he quickly squashed. Such things were no longer as important as they had been before the war to end all wars.

He felt himself stir at the memory of holding her in his arms as they danced, and breathing in the scent of her skin. To Charlie, she had the looks of an angel, and was so light on her feet and so in tune with the rhythm of the music as their bodies swayed together that it was as though this was meant to be.

He knew he was a romantic fool, but he'd fallen for her from the word go, and he'd tried hard to track down Gracie Brown, but short of putting an ad in the newspaper or putting a private detective on her trail, he didn't know what else to do. Why would she even remember him? The band had been due to go on the road for some lucrative engagements around the country, and he couldn't let them down by leaving them or acting like a lovesick Romeo, so the chance was gone.

★   ★   ★

Once Gracie had bumped into the landlord, she couldn't seem to avoid him. Her mother had always paid the rent, since then she would be sure the money wasn't frittered away down the boozer. But Percy Hill now seemed to make a point of calling when

Gracie was at home, just as if he watched her comings and goings, she thought uneasily. She thought it was just her imagination, until the next-door neighbour commented otherwise.

Mrs Jennings popped in regularly, often bringing her a dish of potato soup to be warmed up, or a bit of jelly to whet Queenie's appetite. She was as round as she was tall, but she had a good heart, was known to speak her mind, and she had always had a soft spot for Gracie.

'You mind that old devil Percy Hill, Gracie love,' she said, out of the blue. 'He'll take advantage of you if he can, so don't go giving him the chance.'

Gracie began to smile. 'You're having me on, Mrs Jennings. Why would he give me a second glance? He's fifty if he's a day.'

The woman snorted. 'As if that makes any difference to the likes of him. I'm damned sure he'd like to get his hands on a pretty young thing like you. I seen his great gloating face coming out of your house when he collected the rent the other day. Like a pig in shit, if you'll pardon the expression.'

'Language, Lizzie,' Queenie murmured from her bed by the window.

'I reckon your Gracie's heard worse than that since she's been living in London,

Queenie, and I ain't apologizing for it. Don't let that old lecher come near you if you can help it, Gracie. Stuff the rent book under his nose and let him scribble his name on it at the front door when you've handed him the money, then he'll have no excuse to come inside.'

She looked so comical with her arms folded above the great expanse of her belly inside the flowered overall that Gracie had a job not to laugh out loud.

'I'll remember,' she said in a stifled voice. 'You keep Mum company now while I make us all a cup of tea.'

She fled to the scullery, wishing that Dolly was here to share this moment with her. Dolly would have had something to say to Lizzie Jennings about the likelihood of anyone else with a bit of sense in their heads, having anything to do with Percy pigging Hill!

Dolly had been born in London, and thought everybody who lived anywhere outside it had hayseeds growing out of their mouths. And there was none so quaint as the determined, volatile figure of Lizzie Jennings — or the rotund Percy Hill, though there were other words Gracie could have applied to him.

Without warning, she felt a small shiver,

while still certain that Mrs Jennings was being melodramatic as usual. She shouldn't alarm her mother by making her listen to such tales though, she thought with sudden annoyance. The last thing her mum needed was the worry that after she went to meet her Maker her daughter was going to be accosted by their landlord.

By the time the kettle had screamed out that it was boiling and she had taken three cups of tea to the front room she could see her mum was getting tired. Lizzie Jennings was a good friend, even if her busy mouth never seemed to stop working. But thankfully, after she had surely scalded that mouth with the hot tea, she got up to leave.

'You have a nice little kip, Queenie, and I'll pop in again tomorrow.' She looked at Gracie. 'God bless, dear.'

Gracie smiled at her mum. 'Since when did she get so pious? It doesn't quite match her tongue-pie.'

'She means well,' Queenie said. 'But you get back to your sewing now she's gone, Gracie, and I'll doze off to the sound of the machine.'

She made it sound like music. Funny, because it was just the way Gracie always thought of it. Clickety-clackety, clickety-clackety . . .

The sewing didn't pay a fortune, but it helped, and was more interesting than the monotony of making shirts at Lawson's factory. She went to the people's homes to collect the work and took it back when it was neatly finished and ironed. It was a different kind of independence now from London, but it felt surprisingly good to be her own boss, instead of being at Lawson's beck and call.

If only her mother showed any signs of getting better, or even stabilizing, Gracie knew she could be fairly content. But there were no signs of that, just as she knew there couldn't be, nor of her father showing any more understanding than he ever had. She knew he cared for her mother in his own way; he simply didn't have the capacity to show it.

As she worked on altering the flannel skirt for her newest client, her thoughts roamed. Her parents had once been young sweethearts, and there must have been love between them once, the passionate love that produced a child: herself. Making babies wasn't something you cared to think about your parents doing, but they had to have done it, or she wouldn't have existed.

It was so sad to think that such passions died. It surely wasn't what you planned on that day when you first became man and wife . . .

Without realizing it, her fingers had slowed down from guiding the grey flannel material through the sewing-machine, and her foot had stopped pressing the treadle. She was somewhere in dreamland where she was the person in the long white dress, floating eagerly towards the young man at the altar, waiting to put the ring on her finger and make her his wife.

She could almost sense the throb of her heartbeats at the moment when he would turn around and smile at her with love . . . such love . . .

'Oh, Charlie,' she said, with a small sigh of longing, then blew her nose as her eyes became salty with tears.

'Did you call, Gracie?' Her mother's voice came weakly through the wall.

'No, I was just blowing my nose, Mum,' she called back, kicking herself for disturbing her mother — and for what? For a fantasy that would never come true.

She got back to her task, thinking it somewhat symbolic that she was stitching a dull grey flannel skirt that was more in keeping with her lot, than dreams of a filmy white wedding gown.

★　★　★

As if to emphasize that her roots lay here and not in the bright lights of London, she had a letter from Davey Watkins shortly afterwards.

Here I am, Gracie, turning up like a bad penny, just like I said I would, he wrote. I was thinking of you on my ship a few weeks ago. Being in the Navy's nothing like being a rich passenger on one of them big ocean liners you seemed so partial to. We struck a force-nine gale going round the Bay of Biscay, and the ruddy ship seemed to rise up in the water with every wave and then crash down again so hard we thought it was going to break in two.

Gracie's stomach heaved at the very thought, and she went on hastily to the rest of the letter.

It's all calm again now, and we're off the coast of France. With any luck we'll be going ashore for a few hours. I don't expect to meet any French mamselles half as pretty as the ones back home though. You know the one I really mean, don't you? My old mum's not much good at letter-writing, but I bet you are. You were always good at everything at school. If you feel like writing back, the address is at the top of the letter.

And before you think I've gone soppy in my old age, this is all for now so I'll sign off.
Yours respectfully,
Davey.

Gracie felt a stab of alarm. It might read casually enough to some people, telling her of his experiences at sea, but she knew it was more than just a friendly letter, and it wasn't what she wanted. It seemed as if he considered her his girl back home, and she wasn't.

She was just an old schoolfriend, and she didn't intend to be anything more than that. It was obvious from the first part of his letter that he sometimes worked in very hazardous conditions, but that didn't mean he could play on her sympathies to pretend an affection she didn't feel.

Perhaps he had never meant it like that, and it was just an innocent letter from someone far from home. And pigs might fly. She was tempted to write straight back and put him right. Or she could just ignore it for a few weeks, and perhaps by then he would have got the unwritten message.

She dithered so long that a couple of weeks later there was another letter. This time he pleaded with her to write to him, saying it was boring being in the company of his mates all the time, and as most of them got letters from their wives and sweethearts, it would be nice to hear from her if she could spare the time.

'Damn you, Davey Watkins,' she muttered out loud, screwing up the letter furiously. 'You're not putting me on the spot like this!'

She didn't want her mother to know how she felt. Queenie was oblivious to her feelings, anyway, as she sank further and further into a slough. Queenie was glad her daughter had a nice local boy to write to, and no longer wasted her thoughts on a saxophone player she would never see again.

I'm not saying Davey isn't a nice enough young man, she wrote to Dolly, *but I only saw him again for that week when he was on leave, and I'll have to see how I feel when he comes home again.*

She paused, reading her own words. Was she mad? Even to Dolly, she was implying more than she really felt. It was Charlie she wanted, even if she had only met him for one evening, and danced with him so briefly. But it had been long enough for her to fall in love with him — if it *was* love that she felt when her heart thumped like wildfire every time she remembered his name. It was like the song said — 'when you met your one and only . . . '

Still, maybe it didn't hurt to let Dolly think she wasn't having too terrible a time down here. Dolly was still living the high life in London with coalman Jim, and Gracie had too much pride to let her know she was pining over something she could never have. Dolly would have advised her to forget all about Charlie-boy and find somebody new. Which was where Davey Watkins came in . . .

'I expect I'll feel differently when Davey comes home from France,' she went on writing defiantly. 'You can't snub a boy who's doing his bit for King and country, can you? Mum likes him, which must count for something. I'd like to make her last days content by knowing I'll be all right. You know what I mean without spelling it out.'

God, that sounded so bloody noble, and she wasn't at all! She finished the letter quickly before she started to tell Dolly how quickly her mother was failing. Dolly wouldn't want to know about illness. It wasn't that she wouldn't care, but she had never been able to cope with such details. Gracie signed off, saying she might telephone her sometime just to hear her voice, as long as Ma Warburton didn't think it a frivolous waste of money!

The minute she had put the letter into the postbox, she wondered why she'd never thought of telephoning Dolly before, just to hear her chipper voice. The boarding-house phone was supposed to be for emergencies only, but Gracie had always been the landlady's favourite, and she could put it on a bit when she asked to speak to Dolly. There were times when you had to be a bit devious. Not yet, though. Not until Dolly had got her letter and was pre-warned.

She walked back home more jauntily. It really felt like summer at last and it was turning into a lovely day. Maybe her mum would feel like taking a turn to the park around the corner. She hardly went out of doors now, but the sun would do her good, and the doctor had advised her to stay active for as long as she could. She rarely got up before midday, but it was nearly that already.

The minute Gracie went inside the house she heard the sound of high-pitched wailing, and found two strangers in the parlour with her mother. They were large, unkempt-looking men, looking decidedly uneasy and alarmed at the sight of the trembling woman in the nightgown, who was clinging on to the edge of the table for dear life.

'What's happened?' Gracie gasped. 'Mum,

what are you doing out of bed, and who are these people?'

Her heart leapt with fear, but her mother started gasping out a reply.

'They work down the docks with your dad, Gracie. You know he didn't come home last night, but that's nothing unusual.'

She had to pause for the racking pain in her chest, holding her hand to her heart, and Gracie made her sit down before she tried to say any more.

'I'm sorry, miss,' one of the men went on agitatedly, 'but she had to be told, see, and we was sent to do it. They found Mick this morning.'

'Found him? What do you mean, they *found* him? Where was he, then? Dead drunk behind a boozer, I suppose,' Gracie snapped, angry and upset that her mother should have been so frightened, and disgusted with her father that they should be hearing such news.

'No, miss. Just dead,' the other man said brutally, at which Queenie began wailing again.

'For Christ's sake, Bert, couldn't you have made it a bit easier for the little maid to hear?' his mate snarled.

'I'm not a child!' Gracie heard herself shouting, her heart hammering in her chest fit to burst. 'What do you mean — he's *dead*?

How? Are you sure?'

It was a daft question, and she didn't want it to be true. Her head was bursting with a mixture of emotions. She hated him, but she didn't want him dead. She wanted him home and whole, the way he'd been when she was a small girl and he'd bounced her on his knee, before the drink had turned him into the monster he was now. She heard the sobbing in her own throat and smothered it with an effort. Her mother was ashen-faced, and she put her arms around her to comfort her.

The one called Bert tried to defend himself.

'Well, it's sometimes best to come right out with it, in my opinion. It's Mick Brown all right.' He cleared his throat uncomfortably. 'There was a drunken brawl at one of the pubs last night, and Mick was in the middle of it. He must have staggered about and fallen in the docks. The current smashed him about during the night. I'm sorry, Missus, but it took a while for him to be identified properly. The constables say somebody in the family will have to do it too. They've taken him to one of the unloading sheds to clean him up a bit.'

He stumbled on, making things graphic, making things worse. Gracie listened in horror, trying not to imagine her father's body being buffeted about against the concrete wall of the docks for hours on end . . . and then she realized that she would have to be the one to identify him. It would be more than her mother could take. Right now, she seemed to have shrunk down in her chair, saying nothing, just keening softly in that terrible, heart-rending way.

'We was just sent to tell you what's happened, miss. The constables will be coming to see you soon, I daresay,' the other man went on. 'And she don't look too good neither,' he added, with an uneasy look at Queenie.

'Thank you,' Gracie mumbled, though it seemed bizarre to thank people for coming to tell her her father was dead. You did it, though. You went through the motions of being polite, because it was what you had been brought up to do.

She tried to think what to do next.

'Would you ask my next door neighbour to come in, please? I'll get her to sit with my mother while I fetch the doctor.'

They were clearly relieved to get out of there, their duty done. Gracie wondered if they had drawn lots to see who had to do the dirty work, and if they had chosen the short straw.

A few minutes later, while she still held her

mother in her arms, Mrs Jennings came rushing into the house, her face shocked.

'Oh, my poor Queenie! You go and do what you have to do, Gracie love, and I'll take charge here. The poor lamb needs to be in bed, and I'll make her some hot sweet tea.' In an aside, she added: 'You'd better fetch the doctor quick. It looks like there's more need to attend to the living here than the dead.'

Gracie rushed out of the house, tears streaming down her face. She didn't need telling that the news had devastated her mother. Whatever kind of a rat he had been to her in the last few years, he was still her husband, the breadwinner, and she had always been a loyal wife. She would mourn him to the end of her days — however long that might be.

7

Gracie felt as if she had been rushing around like a mad thing for days, when in reality it had only been a few hours. But her whole life had changed again. Her father was dead, and she was still desperately trying to block out the gruesome sight she had been faced with in the unloading sheds at the docks. Whoever — or whatever — that was, it wasn't her father.

Her father was the man who had gone to work the previous day, and left his womenfolk relieved that he hadn't come stamping and hollering into the house at bedtime, reeking of beer as usual. He was the young man who had swung her around in his arms when she was a small girl, filling her head with exciting stories about the big ships that came from faraway places to Southampton docks.

Her father had once been a loving parent who hadn't been consumed with drink . . . and now her mother was racked with guilt, knowing that the relief she and Gracie both felt, was because they no longer had to put up with his moods and tempers. And the guilt was doing Queenie no good at all.

'I've given her something to calm her down,' the doctor told Gracie. 'She's taken this badly, which is only to be expected, and she'll need careful watching. Her heart is further weakened by the coughing and retching from her illness, and this shock is enough to tip her over the edge.'

He never minced his words, and Gracie thanked him numbly. She had thanked the two men bringing them the news about her father, and voicing her gratitude at being warned of a death sentence seemed just as farcical.

The doctor looked at her sharply. 'You must take care of yourself as well, Gracie. You need to be strong for your mother now.'

'I know. I don't want her to go to the funeral, but she's insisting on it.'

'Don't try to stop her,' he said brutally. 'She needs to say good-bye to your father properly, and it can't make much difference in the long run.'

'What does that mean?' Gracie said, hating him for what she knew damn well he meant.

'My advice is to make the most of your mother while you've still got her. Now, about arrangements — if there's anything I can do to help, let me know.'

She could read his mind. They lived in a

poor part of the town; they weren't a well-off family, and if there was no money . . . She lifted her chin. 'I shall see to everything, Doctor. Mum was always thrifty about life insurances, and she's also been paying into a funeral club for years. We shall manage.'

She stopped talking, afraid that her voice would break if she had to say much more. Queenie said the funeral club payments had been intended for the eventual death of both parents, though since the onset of her illness, it was obviously thought that she would go first. Nobody had expected Mick to die yet, especially in such a tragic manner, however ignominious. It was still the loss of a husband and father.

A week later, Mick Brown was laid to rest, and the neighbours rallied round with pots of tea and sandwiches ready for when the two women returned from the churchyard. By tradition, they wouldn't return to an empty house, and the curtains that had been drawn all the week, were pulled back to let in the daylight.

A clutch of Mick's workmates and drinking buddies had been at the graveside, some muttering good words about him, others looking embarrassed and awkward to be there at all. Gracie couldn't help wondering savagely which of them had been involved in the punch-up that had led to her father staggering about in a drunken rage and which had eventually led to his death. But what did any of it matter now? The death had been recorded as accidental, and there had been enough witnesses to vouch for the way Mick had gone lumbering off in the night.

All Gracie wanted was to get this day over. They didn't invite people back to the house afterwards. Gracie had insisted that there was to be no bun-fight, and only the women neighbours who had helped with tea and sympathy would be there waiting for them. And Percy Hill.

'What's he doing here?' Gracie hissed to Mrs Jennings, when she had got her mother settled in an armchair with a cup of tea.

'We couldn't keep him out,' Lizzie said resentfully. 'Calls it his duty to pay his respects to one of his tenants, but he's no more than a bloody leech, pardon the language, casting his eye over his property, and making sure the rent will still be paid now your dad's dead and buried.'

Gracie flinched, wishing she didn't make it sound so final. Which it was, of course. No matter how solemnly the vicar intoned the words about life everlasting, and our brother Mick being sent to a higher place to be with his Maker, and all that religious stuff, it didn't change anything. You were still dead and buried.

She swallowed a sob, turned around and cannoned straight into Percy Hill, coming out of the parlour. His hands went out to steady her, and she was thankful she hadn't yet taken off her costume jacket so that she didn't have to feel the pressure of his fingers on her bare arms.

'Steady now, Gracie. We don't want two accidents in the family, do we?' he said in his cloying voice. Even when he was trying to be sympathetic, which she presumed he was trying to be now, he still had that nasty little calculating gleam in his eyes.

'Thank you for calling, Mr Hill,' she said, keeping her voice distant. 'My mother and I are bearing up quite well in the circumstances.'

That was what you said, wasn't it? Even when your heart was breaking, and you wished this oaf and his like to Kingdom Come, you said you were bearing up quite well in the circumstances.

'We'll be fine with our neighbours now, thank you,' she went on pointedly, hoping he would take the hint. 'Women need to be together at a time like this.'

He pressed his hand over hers. It was

clammy and moist, and she had an enormous job not to fling it away from her.

'I understand, my dear. Just remember that you have a father figure in me, and if there's any little thing I can do for you, you only have to ask. I'll leave you now, and I'll be along to see you at the end of the week.'

For the rent money, of course. The blood money. For a moment, Gracie felt a violent urge to laugh out loud at his hypocrisy, and really thought she was going to do so. And how would that look on the day of her father's funeral!

But once he had left the house, the women relaxed, and began the custom of telling their own tales about the deceased, and their own shared experiences of child-bearing and deaths in an attempt to cheer up her mother. It was an odd kind of therapy to Gracie, but it was what they did, and it seemed to work, so that by the time they were at last alone, her mother had a little more colour in her cheeks and was actually smiling at some of their anecdotes.

But it was short-lived, and in the next weeks Gracie had more to worry about than the regular visits of the landlord, as Queenie went downhill rapidly.

'I know Dad's death was an awful shock to her, but he led her such a life, that I thought she'd start to relax by now,' Gracie told Lizzie Jennings.

'It often happens,' the neighbour said sagely. 'You may have thought they didn't get on, Gracie, but all married couples find their own pattern of living, and this was theirs. Now that he's gone, she misses his tantrums and his yelling. They may have been a long time past the lovey-dovey stage, but I remember what it was like when my old man passed over. Me and him never had a good word to say about one another, but when he went it was like losing my right arm.'

She made it sound like an exclusive sisterhood to which only widows belonged, and Gracie supposed that was exactly what it was. You couldn't understand it because you had never experienced it. She shivered, knowing that she didn't want to, either.

'Is Percy Hill pestering you, Gracie?' Lizzie said out of the blue. 'I've seen him in the street more than usual lately.'

'He's called in a few times apart from collecting the rent to enquire after Mum. I suppose he's only being considerate.'

Lizzie snorted. 'Considerate, my aunt Fanny! He knows damn well that your mum's days are numbered, and once you're left on your own he'll have his eyes on more than this house if you know what I mean.'

'I don't want to talk about it, Mrs Jennings, and I wish you wouldn't keep reminding me. I'm sure it's all nonsense, anyway.'

She was referring to Percy Hill, but she also didn't need reminding about her mother's condition. It was becoming all too clear to her that Queenie was a very sick woman and that she was unlikely to last out the time the doctor had suggested.

'Just remember that all you have to do is knock on the wall when you need me,' Lizzie said, taking no offence.

She didn't say 'if', just 'when', and since they both knew it anyway, Gracie nodded, feeling her heart heavy.

She was too busy caring for her mother and continuing with her sewing jobs to worry about anything else. There was no other money coming in now, and the insurance policy on her dad's life would dwindle away soon enough, so she needed the work to keep up the payments on the rent.

There had been another letter from Davey Watkins, but she had merely answered it with a terse note to tell him the news about her father and to say she would write again when she felt able. It was the least of her concerns.

Then came an indignant letter from Dolly, who, of course, had no idea of the traumatic events in Gracie's life in recent weeks.

What's happened to you, gel? Dolly wrote. *I never thought you'd be so stuffy as to forget your old pals. You said you was going to phone me and give old Warby a fright, but I'm still waiting. I hope it don't mean your mum's feeling worse, or that the worst has happened. Anyway, to cheer you up, I thought I'd let you know that me and Jim are still going strong. That's a turn-up, ain't it? Bet you thought I'd have ditched him by now. He's all right, if a bit of a rough diamond, but I don't have to tell you that, do I?*

We went to the Empire Exhibition at Wembley a couple of weeks ago, and fancied ourselves among the toffs. Some of the stuff there would make your eyes pop out. There was a band playing on the bandstand in the park, and people were dancing on the grass, so it was quite a hoot. Me and Jim had a bit of a dance too, and we're going to go again sometime.

Hurry up and phone me like you said, or write to me sometime, or I'll think you're getting too big for your boots what with your own little business and all.

Your friend,
Dolly Neath.

Gracie gave a wry smile as she finished the letter. Her own little business indeed! Perhaps she had bumped it up a bit in what she had told Dolly about her sewing commissions, but that was for the sake of her pride as usual. She loved her mother and she didn't want anybody feeling sorry for her in having to come back home to care for her.

She knew very well why she was letting her thoughts ramble on. It was simply to avoid the other sentence in Dolly's letter that she had written so carelessly. The bit about seeing the band in the park, and people dancing on the grass in the warm sunshine, and the pictures it sent to Gracie's mind. If she closed her eyes very tightly, she could imagine herself being there, whirling around on the sweet-scented grass in someone's arms, with the sound of the music high on the summer breeze. It wouldn't be Charlie's arms that held her, of course, because he would be taking his place on the bandstand, his lips on the mouthpiece of his saxophone, his fingers caressing the buttons and producing that wonderful sound.

'Gracie, can you come in, dear?'

The sound of her mother's reedy voice shattered the illusion at once, and she went into the front room almost angrily — not at her darling mother — but because she still couldn't rid her mind of Charlie Morrison's image, when she knew there was no future in her dreams of him.

'What is it, Mum? Can I get something for you?' she asked, trying not to notice how painfully thin her mother had become. She had eaten little enough before, but since Mick's death she had gone completely off her food. What she did eat, she rarely kept down for long.

'Another tablet, please dear,' Queenie whispered.

'Is the pain very bad?' Gracie said, her fingers opening the packet so nervously she nearly scattered them all over the bed. They both knew it wasn't time for her to take another pill, but if she needed it, it seemed cruel to deny her the temporary relief it gave her.

'It's tolerable,' Queenie said, as she always did. Which Gracie interpreted as meaning that it was bloody bad.

Queenie retched on the tablet as she tried to swallow it, and spilled half the glass of water on to the bed as her hands shook uncontrollably.

'Never mind, Mum. I'll crush another one for you and put it in a little drop of water,' Gracie told her, and fled to the scullery, her own hands shaking at the task. With every day that passed, her mum got weaker, and she could see her slipping away as the pain and the illness ravaged her.

There were times when she found herself resenting her father for what was assumed to have been his quick death, and was immediately full of shame at the thought. But how long could this go on? She longed to keep her mother alive for ever, but she couldn't bear to see her becoming so frail.

'You're a good girl, Gracie,' Queenie said, when she had finally got the crushed pill down, and lay back on her pillow. 'I don't know what I'd do without you. But remember what I said. When all this is over, go back to your friends in London and start a new life.'

'Mum, I don't want to hear this kind of talk!'

'I'm not afraid to say it, love. We both know I'm dying, but you've got all your life in front of you. Don't settle for second best.'

'You mean Davey Watkins, I suppose?' Gracie said, without thinking.

'Him, and a house like this. I want better things for you, Gracie.'

Gracie felt choked. 'I didn't have better things in London, Mum, sharing digs with Dolly and working in a sweatshop! Besides, there are so many memories here. This is where I was born, no matter what kind of a house it is.'

'And it's where I'll die, but I don't want that for you. Promise me, Gracie, that you'll always strive for better.'

She was starting to look exhausted from so much talking. Blue shadows had appeared around her lips, and Gracie was suddenly alarmed.

'I'll promise anything you like, Mum, as long as you get some rest now. I won't do any more work today — '

'Don't be silly,' Queenie said wearily. 'You know I like to hear the sound of your sewing-machine.'

'All right, as long as it doesn't disturb you.'

She bent down and kissed her mother's forehead as her eyes closed. The rise and fall of her chest was so slight now that it hardly made a movement beneath the bedclothes. Gracie watched her briefly before tiptoeing back to the parlour and the blouse she was working on for one of her clients. It was difficult to do anything for a few minutes though, because her eyes were so blurred with tears. It was hard to concentrate, but the lady in question wanted the work done urgently.

By mid-afternoon the blouse was finished and neatly ironed, and no one would ever know it had been altered, Gracie thought with satisfaction. A smile curled around her lips as she remembered Dolly's remark about her own little business. Fat chance. But there was a small circle of ladies in the town now, willing to pay for her services. Word had spread that she was a reliable, excellent seamstress. It was hardly a business, but it was a thriving little sideline.

The smile faded, knowing it had better be something more than that if she was to survive on her own. Her dad's insurance money wouldn't last for ever. When her mum went, there would be a life insurance payment due for her too, but that was too upsetting and ghoulish for Gracie to think about.

She glanced in at her mum and saw that she was sleeping peacefully, and then she wrapped the blouse in tissue paper before parcelling it carefully in brown paper. She took off her work overall, combed her hair and put on a lick of lipstick before she put on her cotton gloves and left the house. She prided herself on looking as neat and tidy as possible before entering the best town houses.

She came away carrying a bolt of cotton material and a pattern for a child's frock. It gave her such a fillip to be making something new, and this time it wasn't just one article to make. There was a private nursery school in the upper town, and the little girls were all to wear identical clothes. Gracie was commissioned to make them for a lovely fat fee. It was something to make her heart sing, and to make her mother proud.

She felt so joyous she decided this was the perfect time to telephone Dolly and give her the latest news. She must tell her about her dad too, she reminded herself guiltily, knowing she hadn't been able to do that yet. But Dolly had always been one for the living and not the dead, and she'd be pleased that Gracie was finding work in such a backwater as Southampton. Gracie grinned, hearing Dolly's dismissive voice in her head, when in reality, everybody knew that Southampton was an important shipping area. In Dolly's mind, though, the world began and ended in London.

Gracie went into the house quietly, but Queenie was still sound asleep, and she looked so peaceful that Gracie was reluctant to waken her, even though she was bursting with her news. Instead, she spent a little time spreading out all the pattern pieces on the parlour table and studying the detailed instructions. Then she thought about what to make her mum for supper that would be tasty and enticing. Beef tea seemed to be the most palatable lately, Gracie thought with a sigh, but at least there was some nourishment in it, so that would probably be the best idea.

The knock on the front door made her jump. She answered it quickly, praying it hadn't disturbed her mother. Though such a thought seemed almost tragic. She would be getting all the rest in the world soon enough.

'Oh, I'm sorry, Mr Hill, I forgot it was rent day. I don't have it ready yet.'

'That's all right, my dear, I can wait.'

He was inside the house before she could stop him, right behind her as she returned to the parlour, and she kept her back to him as she opened the bureau drawer where the rent money was kept, her fingers flustered and her heart beating faster than usual.

She could hear his wheezing breath behind her. He was perspiring in the heat of the summer day, and the smell of him was rank. Gracie was already planning to sprinkle a good few drops of lavender water about the room the minute he was gone.

'Here you are, then,' she said, turning round with the book and the money. She hadn't realized how close he was, and his hand closed over the rent book, enclosing hers inside it. He didn't immediately let her go, and although she wasn't exactly pinned against the bureau, she felt as though she was.

'Please let go of me,' she said. 'I assure you the money's all there.'

'I'm sure it is,' he said smoothly. 'Your mother was always a regular payer, despite your dad's little vices, and I'm sure you'll be the same in due course.'

Gracie flinched. 'I think that's in very bad taste, Mr Hill.'

Although enraged at his callousness, she didn't raise her voice, because the last thing she wanted was for her mother to hear her wrangling with this oaf.

He let her go so suddenly she felt weak with relief. He counted the money and marked the rent book without another word, and then he smiled sweetly, if sweetly was the word for the smile of a waiting snake.

'Don't worry, girl. I'll take care of you when the time comes. You'll always have a roof over your head, providing you pay the piper.'

He left her, and she sagged against the bureau. She couldn't doubt the meaning in his voice. It wasn't just the rent money he was after. It was her. It was just as Mrs Jennings had said, even though she hadn't really believed her. Percy Hill was *old*, compared with her, and why would a young girl, not yet twenty, want his fumbling hands on her, and his fat lips slobbering over her? She shuddered, willing the thought of it away. And then she did what she'd intended and wafted the room with lavender-water to be rid of his smell.

Remembering what she had been about to do, she set about making the beef tea for Queenie. Once she had seen that she drank at least a little of it, she would have something to eat herself, and later she would go down to the newsagent and use his telephone and call Dolly. If anything was guaranteed to make her laugh, it was talking to Dolly. And she could make light of the fact that old Percy had taken a fancy to her, and cut it down to size.

Half an hour later, when she had calmed down properly, she took the tray into the front room and set it on the small table, preparing to spoon-feed Queenie herself if necessary, to make sure she took some nourishment. She put a smile on her face as she turned to her with the cup of beef tea.

The woman in the bed hadn't stirred. The blueness around her mouth had spread, but the lines in her forehead had smoothed out. In sleep, she was free from pain, which was why Gracie was always so loath to waken her. She replaced the cup on the tray and watched her for a few moments more, then she stroked her hand, and pressed her lips gently to her cheek.

'Oh Mum,' she whispered.

8

'It was a lovely way to go,' Mrs Jennings remarked. 'She never felt nothing, did she? A stroke, the doctor said, just went to sleep and never woke up again. It was a blessing really, considering the pains she went through with the other, and a sight better than fishing your dad out of the drink, all smashed to pieces.'

'You're such a comfort, Mrs Jennings,' Gracie murmured, wondering if there was ever a woman with a bigger heart and less tact.

'That's what neighbours are for, ain't it?' Lizzie said, not seeing the irony. 'Take another sip of medicinal brandy to keep your spirits up, lovey. And you don't have to worry no more about your mum and dad. They'll be up there together now, all nice and cosy.'

Gracie looked blank. 'Up there?'

'Up with the angels, gel,' Lizzie emphasized, her face reddening, ''Course, they might still be at each other's throats, but that's just the way they carried on. It didn't mean nothing. I ain't too sure about such things as angels, mind, but you got to believe in something, or what's it all for.'

Gracie took a quick sip of the brandy the woman thrust at her, trying not to notice the way it stung her throat and fuzzed her senses.

'You think Mum and Dad are up there together, then, Mrs Jennings.'

'Well, I ain't saying your dad went to the other place, despite all his drinking and hollering fit to wake the dead. You wouldn't want that for him, would you?' she went on uneasily.

Gracie gave an unexpected laugh, and immediately squashed the sound. But right now the house was so full of the scent of lavender that she imagined her mum was laughing at the thought as well, instead of lying stiff and cold in the front room, waiting for the laying-out woman and the undertakers.

'I can't imagine anything worse than for my mum to have to spend the rest of eternity with my dad,' she snapped.

Lizzie Jennings glanced around the room, as shocked as if she had been struck by lightning — or fearful that Gracie was about to be struck down with something even more powerful for such blasphemy.

'Gracie, you shouldn't say such things. Have a talk with the vicar — '

'What for? You know very well that Mum skivvied for Dad all her life until she got too ill to do so, but he was never around when she needed him the most, so why would she want to be with him now?'

She heard herself saying the brutal words, hardly knowing where they came from, nor if she really believed them. They simply had to be said, to ward off the reality that within a few short weeks she had lost both parents.

'Would you like me to stay here with you tonight?' Mrs Jennings said, going off on another tack. 'You shouldn't be alone in the house with — well, with your bad memories and all — '

'I don't have any bad memories here, Mrs Jennings. Thank you for the thought, but I'd like to be left alone for the next few days until the funeral's arranged. Anyway, I'm not alone. Mum's here.'

★ ★ ★

There was no pleasing her, Lizzie Jennings reported to anyone who would listen. Not that she could blame the poor girl. What she'd gone through lately was enough to send anybody off the rails — and the sooner poor Queenie Brown was decently planted six feet under, the sooner Gracie could start thinking for herself again. But they had to respect her wishes to be alone with her mother in the house until Queenie was screwed down.

So there were only the visits of the laying-out woman and the undertaker's men, and once Queenie was lying in her coffin ready for burial, the front room was reverently closed.

Although if they had seen Gracie's feverish activity over the next few days, they might have been more alarmed for her sanity, as well as being scandalized that she could behave in such a way with her mother lying cold in the next room.

But there were children's frocks to be made for the nursery school in the upper town, and there would be a decent fee at the end of it. And contrary to what people might think, keeping busy was the only way Gracie could hold her thoughts at bay from the horrific change to her circumstances. She needed to keep her hands and mind busy, to hear the constant whirr of the sewing-machine, with the knowledge of how her mum had loved hearing it, and knowing that she, of all people, would understand.

She worked each day and long into the night, cutting and pinning the cotton fabric to the pattern pieces, and stitching each little frock with all the love and care as if it was for her own child. It was the way her mother had cut and pinned and stitched for her when she was a little girl. There were memories tied up in every action. It was a labour of love as well as profit, and by the time the day of the funeral arrived, she was so tired she could hardly see straight, and the neighbours murmured how sad it was that such a young girl had to deal with all of this.

To her relief there was no sign of Percy Hill on this occasion, and the neighbours went quietly from the house afterwards, sensing her mood. She seemed numb and had no wish to talk to anyone except to thank them for being there.

As soon as the door closed behind the last of them she continued with her sewing task. She had worked so hard that she had hardly given herself time to weep or mourn, and she didn't stop until the entire set of frocks was finished, pressed, and stacked neatly for delivery. Then she went into the front room, preparing to strip the bedclothes off the bed and restore the room to normality. She pinched her nostrils together as she did so, knowing it should have been done days ago. The imprint of the coffin was still on her mother's bed, and she stared at it silently for a few moments, her throat closing. Then, without warning, she found herself lying prostrate on the bed while she cried her heart out.

* * *

'You've done an excellent job, Miss Brown,' the wealthy client exclaimed. 'And so speedily too. You must have worked day and night.'

Gracie said: 'I enjoyed making the frocks, Mrs Anstey, and once I had made one I wanted to get all of them finished.'

'I admire your diligence, but you look pale, my dear, and you have dark shadows under your eyes. You must take care not to overdo it, but since you've proved to be so reliable I insist on paying you a little extra for your trouble.'

'It's very kind of you, Mrs Anstey,' Gracie murmured. 'Thank you.'

She felt a sudden need to be out in the open air. The house was as stifling as a hothouse with the sun beating in through the long french windows, and the heavy, ornate furniture that seemed to make it even more claustrophobic. And the lady's voice was receding further and further away . . .

'Are you feeling a little better, Miss Brown?' she heard her saying anxiously. She discovered that she was sitting on one of the elegant armchairs in the drawing-room and that a glass of water was being pressed to her cold lips.

'You fainted, my dear,' Mrs Anstey

continued. 'As I suspected, you've been overworking, and much as I'm delighted to have these little garments finished so quickly, you're much too thin, and I'm surprised your mother doesn't keep an eye on you.'

Gracie looked at her mutely, her face filled with anguish. Five minutes later, Mrs Anstey was still holding her hand and passing her handkerchiefs and listening to Gracie's hysterical words about her father dying and then her mother, and how she had needed to work to keep herself busy.

'And you've had to deal with all this by yourself?' the lady said sympathetically. 'Don't you have friends or family to help you?'

'I have good neighbours,' Gracie whispered, ashamed of herself for breaking down. 'But I needed to work to keep myself from thinking.'

'But work merely delays the grief that we all have to go through. My advice is to grieve properly for your parents and give yourself time to recover before you think about working again. Now then,' she said, more briskly. 'I shall pay you for the work you've done, including the little extra I promised you, and then I shall send you home in my car.'

'Oh, but that's not necessary!'

'Of course it is, and I won't take no for an answer.'

⋆ ⋆ ⋆

If she had been up to registering it properly, she would have been tickled pink by the neighbours' expressions behind their net curtains as the chauffeur-driven car rolled smoothly down the street and stopped outside Gracie's house. As if she had been used to such luxury all her life, she thanked the man graciously as he touched his cap, and went into the house with a wild urge to laugh, feeling like royalty.

'How about that then, Dolly Neath?' she said out loud, just to break the silence in the house. Just as if Dolly was right there, eyes open wide with envy, gawping at her luck. She couldn't bear the sound of silence, where every creak of the floorboards seemed magnified, and she still expected to hear her mother's weak voice calling out to her as soon as she got inside the house. Quickly, she turned on the wireless set for some disembodied company.

As always, coming in from outdoors, her thoughts were momentarily disjointed. She should telephone Dolly. She still hadn't done it, nor answered her last few letters. Dolly would think she was getting too stuck up to bother with her now, when nothing could be further from the truth. It was just that the longer you put something off, the harder it was to put it into words. She'd thought it would be easier, but it wasn't.

As yet, until today, when she had poured her heart out to Mrs Anstey, she hadn't actually had to tell anyone her news. It had passed by word of mouth among neighbours and friends who had known the Brown family all their lives, and a week after the funeral Davey Watkins's mother called to pay her respects.

'I've let my Davey know what happened,' she told her. 'I daresay you may not have felt like writing to him, but he'll want to send you his love.'

'Mrs Watkins, Davey and I are just friends, and nothing more,' Gracie said.

If it was being brutally frank, she couldn't help it, and she was too weary to care, but Mrs Watkins looked none too pleased at this stark response.

'That's between the two of you, Gracie, but you should never shut friends out at a time like this. You never know when you'll be needing them.'

'I don't mean to offend you, Mrs Watkins, but I have a young man in London, and

Davey knows all about him.'

She rambled on in embarrassment, knowing she shouldn't continue the fantasy about a young man in London, but thinking it was the only way to quench the matchmaking gleam she could see in the woman's eyes.

'I see,' she said at last. 'Well, Gracie, I always thought you were a nice girl, and you and my Davey would have made a go of it, I'm sure. You'll be going back to London now, then?'

'Oh, I expect so. There's things to sort out here first though.'

There were things she hadn't even begun to tackle yet. Things she had been putting off until she felt better able to face them.

Mrs Watkins seemed to read her mind.

'If you want some help with sorting out the used clothes for jumble sales, you let me know. It's a sorrowful job to take on by yourself, and I'll be glad to take it all off your hands.'

Gracie couldn't get rid of her quickly enough. The old hag, she thought furiously, already seeing how she could make a few shillings in her rummaging. She had forgotten Mrs Watkins's eye to the main chance when scavenging for jumble-sale collections.

She had no doubt his mother would also be telling Davey a thing or two about how she considered Gracie Brown much too hoity-toity for him now, so he might as well forget her. She sighed, but it was probably all to the good, and she certainly hadn't wanted to give him any false ideas.

But his mother had inadvertently reminded her that there was work to be done. She and Queenie had made no more than a token attempt at packing up Mick's clothes and possessions, and now she had her mother's to do as well. The church would be glad of them, and she would ask for the clothes to be distributed far away, in some foreign mission or other.

Although the thought of some poor dark-skinned natives sweltering in her dad's old waistcoats and mufflers and hobnailed boots in the hot sun was enough to make her smile.

In the end, she enlisted the help of Mrs Jennings to help her sort through it all, giving her a few small keepsakes, though none of her mother's clothes. She couldn't have borne seeing any of the neighbours appearing in them, and thankfully most of the women in the street were much larger than her mother's slight frame, so wouldn't have expected to inherit any of them.

'What will you do now, girl?' Lizzie said at last, when everything was packed in

141

cardboard boxes ready for the vicar to collect.

'Do?' Gracie said vaguely.

'Well, will you want to keep on paying rent to old fart-face, or will you go back to London? There ain't much to keep you here now.'

'I've still got some sewing orders to complete, and it would feel as if I'm deserting Mum if I left straight away, even though she was always urging me to do so when . . . when the time came.'

'Well then. You should do as she wanted.'

'Are you trying to get rid of me?' she asked, with the ghost of a smile.

'Lord love you, Gracie, that I ain't! You're like a breath of fresh air around these miserable streets.'

Gracie laughed out loud now. 'I hardly think so, when I've had a face as long as a fiddle all these weeks!'

'Nobody would have expected anything else after all you've gone through, duck, but you're still the prettiest girl for miles, and it's a wonder to me that you ain't got more than one young man sniffing around after you.'

Despite the compliment, she didn't exactly make her sound an attractive proposition, Gracie thought, but she knew her heart was in the right place. And then she saw her face grow more serious.

'Whatever you decide, Gracie, be sure to keep your door locked of a night.'

'Nobody locks their doors around here, and there's nothing worth stealing!'

She glanced around. The furniture was old and none too special. The only precious thing, in Gracie's opinion, was the old treadle sewing-machine that had done such good service over the years, for her mother and herself.

'I ain't talking about possessions,' Lizzie Jennings went on. 'I'm talking about something more valuable than that. You just remember what I said about Percy Hill, and don't give him an ounce of encouragement.'

For once, she spoke in riddles, but Gracie knew exactly what she meant. She flushed, but she hardly thought a landlord, regardless of how most people thought him a leech, would do anything to violate that position.

'I'm hardly likely to encourage him, Mrs Jennings. And I'm sure he'd never look at me in that way. I'm less than half his age.'

'Since when did that ever stop a man? But I've told you what I think and given you my advice. And remember, you only have to bang on the wall with the broom handle if you need anything and I'll soon sort out the likes of him.'

She looked so comical with her arms

folded over the enormous bosom inside her flowered overall, her chin stuck out so far that the hairs on it caught the light, and her lips clamped together so tightly that they all but disappeared into her cheeks, that Gracie had a job not to laugh out loud.

'I'll remember,' she said in a choked voice. 'Now, I think I'll go and let the vicar know we've got all this stuff ready for him.'

She was still smiling when Lizzie reluctantly left her, and to her surprise she actually found herself humming a little tune as she washed up the teacups. She knew Queenie would have been just as tickled as Gracie at the thought of the neighbour, ready to take on all comers, and she so longed to be able to share the moments with her. Her heart lurched with sadness for a moment, and then she squared her shoulders. Life had to go on, however trite that sounded, and she had to go on with it.

★   ★   ★

Dolly wasn't a brilliant letter-writer, but it was so long since they had communicated now, that Gracie knew she must have taken the huff at not hearing from her for weeks. The summer was turning into a lovely autumn, and it was already early September when Gracie wrote to her. The more she thought about it, the more she knew it would be impossible to speak on the telephone without breaking down. She couldn't bear that, but she did long for some contact with her old friend, so a letter was the only way to tell her what had been happening.

If they did speak, at a time when she was still feeling so vulnerable, she knew Dolly would be all genuine sympathy one minute, then overcome with embarrassment, and then begin to cover what she considered soppiness by telling of her own doings about herself and coalman Jim, and finally insisting that Gracie should come back to the Smoke right away and put it all behind her. Gracie could imagine it all so clearly. So it definitely had to be a letter.

She wrote the news about her parents briefly, saying she would need to stay in Southampton for the time being to sort things out, and she would think about her future when she had got her breath back from all the sorrow of the past weeks. The words sounded stark and almost callous, but she knew it was better than to reveal all the emotional upheaval she had gone through. Dolly wasn't good with emotional upheavals, any more than she was good with illness, but once she had got the news out of the way,

145

Gracie knew she was just what she needed to pull her out of her depression.

'*So that's why I haven't written before now, Dolly,*' she finished. '*Please write and tell me everything that's going on. I miss you a lot, but I've got plenty of work down here, enough to let me pay the rent on the house, anyway.*'

She ended the letter quickly, because it sounded as though she was living in luxury, having a house to herself, when in reality, it was little more than the backwater Dolly had always thought it was. The town was splendid in parts but not here. Not in the dockworkers' shabby back-to-backs where the walls were so thin that nothing was private from the neighbours. Without her mother there to make it a home, Gracie was seeing it as it really was, and it was only out of stubborn loyalty to her memory that she stayed.

There was also the useful bit of money she was making from her sewing, although it didn't really come to much, and there had only been one good commission with the children's frocks. When winter came and she had to buy coal for the fire, people might not have so much work available for a London Outworker, and things might look even less rosy.

Gracie shivered, wondering if she was

being foolish in staying. Queenie had made it clear she didn't want her to, and now that the life insurance money had been paid, it would surely be right to move on.

But where would she go? Back to Lawson's Shirt Factory? She didn't think so. Back to Mrs Warburton's boarding-house? Much as she enjoyed Dolly's company and didn't want to lose her friendship, it all seemed like a backward step.

She wasn't sure she could face the sympathy of the other lodgers, either. If she went back to London, she would have to find other digs, and other work. And before she committed herself, the best way to do that would be to go and take a look around. In her heart, she knew it was not so much a matter of if, but when.

She got a letter back from Dolly shortly afterwards. It was what she had expected, cautious at first, saying how sorry she was about her mum, then saying she was no good at the soppy stuff, but just to cheer Gracie up, she hoped, she told her that she and Jim had been to have another look at the Empire Exhibition.

'*Honestly, Gracie, you ought to see it before it closes at the end of October. If you must stay in the back of beyond, there's nothing to stop you coming up to London for* a day out. I daresay old Warby would put you up for a night and we could have a good old gossip. Not that I'd be telling you all the saucy bits about me and Jim, mind.'

Here it was, Gracie thought resignedly, glossing over the rest of the letter and her enthusiasm about her coalman. As for Dolly telling her all in the darkness of their old shared bedroom . . . she wouldn't want to hear it, and she didn't want to imagine it. The memory of those black fingernails at the Palais was enough to make her shudder. As was the memory of other fingers caressing the golden shaft of a saxophone . . . except that in that case, it was a different kind of shudder.

But at last she telephoned Dolly. One reason was the growing idea in her mind about looking for somewhere new to live; and a second was curiosity about this Empire Exhibition in the park that Dolly thought was so wonderful.

Once the operator had put her through, she had to listen to Mrs Warburton's gushing sympathy over her mother. Predictably, Dolly had informed everybody at the boarding-house. But eventually Dolly's chirpy voice came through.

'Blimey, gel, you sound quite posh,' she said with a chuckle. 'Must be from meeting all them toffs you're working for. So when are

148

you coming back?'

'Not yet, but I might come up on Saturday for the day to see this exhibition. Do you think Mrs Warburton would let me stay in your room overnight?'

''Course she will,' Dolly yelled in delight. 'You just get here as early as you can on Saturday. It's time you started enjoying yourself again, gel.'

9

As the train steamed and snorted into
Waterloo station, it felt weird to be enveloped
in the hustle and bustle of the crowds, the
guards blowing their whistles, the flower-
sellers offering their sweet-smelling blooms
nearby. As soon as Gracie left the station, she
breathed in the familiar smells of the city, a
world away from the dockland area of
Southampton. For a moment her head
rocked with the noise of the traffic and the
congestion of trams and taxi-cabs and
horse-drawn drays fighting their way through
the streets. It was weird . . .

But to her surprise, she acknowledged that
it felt more like home than Southampton.
Hearing the cockney accents; the street
costers bellowing out their wares; the
newspaper boys yelling out the headlines; the
warmth of it had nothing to do with the
balmy September air, but more to do with the
revival of her spirits at getting away from so
much sadness that had haunted her recently.

She caught the first available tram that
went near Mrs Warburton's, and walked the
rest of the way briskly. The trains didn't run

on Sundays, so she intended to ask if she could stay an extra night. Then, when Dolly had gone to work on Monday morning, she would take a proper look around. If Dolly had any idea of her plans, she would press her to move in with her again, and Gracie knew it was time to strike out on her own. Real independence wasn't sharing a room in someone else's boarding-house. Besides, there was another little idea simmering in her head. An idea that made her nerve-ends prickle with anticipation.

But first, she had to endure Mrs Warburton's voluble commiserations over her sad losses, as she called them. It was a relief when she and Dolly could retreat to their old room, flop down on their beds and take stock of one another.

'You don't look too bad,' Dolly said at last, after the initial awkwardness of getting to know one another again.

'Did you expect me to have grown two heads?'

''Course not, but you know what I mean. It must have hit you hard to lose both of 'em in so short a time.'

'You have to get on with it, don't you? You can't spend your whole life crying over things that can't be changed.' She swallowed hard, then looked sharply at Dolly, lying on her bed with her hands clasped behind her head now and staring at the dark spots on the ceiling.

'Anyway, I may not look too bad, but I can't say the same about you. What's up? You and Jim haven't had a falling-out, have you?'

'Nah. We have our ups and downs, but we're all right.'

'Well then?' Gracie demanded.

'Well nothing,' Dolly said crossly. 'What's this? Twenty questions?'

'I've hardly asked any so far, but if you don't want to tell me — '

'There ain't nothing to tell.' She swung her legs off the bed. 'Are you going to unpack, or are we going out? You're here to enjoy yourself, ain't you?'

Something was definitely wrong, or at least, not quite right, thought Gracie. Dolly was always bursting to tell her every last detail of what went on between her and her latest beau, usually far more than she wanted to hear. The last thing she had wanted to know about was her courtship with coalman Jim and his black fingernails . . . she might not want to hear it, but it was very unlike Dolly to keep it private.

'I'll unpack my stuff later. I haven't brought much anyway,' she said quickly, not wanting to antagonize her from the off.

'I hope you've brought your glad rags for tonight then.'

'What's happening tonight?' Gracie said, with a horrible premonition.

'Jim's got tickets for a nightclub up West and Billy's coming too, so get rid of that long face. You've been out in the sticks for so long you've probably forgotten how to dance, but me and Jim make a cracking show at the Charleston now and you'll be all right, providing Billy don't fall all over your feet.'

Gracie groaned. She didn't want this. Hadn't anticipated it. There had hardly been the time or the inclination for dancing except for a village dance with Davey Watkins . . . and the only important time she had got properly dressed up to go dancing, she had met Charlie Morrison at the Palais . . .

'I can't go anywhere like that. I haven't brought anything fancy, Dolly — '

'Don't matter. You can borrow something of mine. Now, are we going to this bleedin' exhibition, or aren't we!'

*　*　*

They caught the Metropolitan railway extension to the station at Wembley Park, and Gracie was thankful Dolly hadn't suggested

153

meeting Jim and Billy already. They would face that hurdle later. The exhibition itself was enough to take in, with its vast pavilions lavishly bedecked with flags, the interiors displaying features from all parts of the Empire.

'You'll like the Chinese street, and the Ceylon pavilion with the collection of pearl necklaces. It's enough to make your eyes pop out, Gracie,' Dolly announced. 'They've made a copy of old Tutenkhamen's tomb as well, and it's really creepy. Come *on* — what are you hanging about for?' she said, as they were swept along by the crowds flocking out of the station towards the entrance now.

'I thought I saw somebody I knew,' Gracie said, floundering.

But of course, it couldn't be him. Wouldn't be him. Why, out of all the world, would a tall young man with black, slicked-back hair, and sensitive fingers that caressed a saxophone that made music to tease the senses, appear as if conjured up by magic?

She shook her head. There were dozens of young men with black, slicked-back hair. It was the fashion, and she was being totally stupid to think that in coming back to London, she would find him again. She hadn't consciously thought it, but she knew that in her dreams, she certainly had.

She ignored such futile hopes and threw herself into enjoying the magic of the day instead. Walking around the massive site was hard on the feet, but before they gave up on the pavilions and went out to the amusement park, they visited the doll's house that had been presented to Queen Mary.

'Blimey, if you believe all it says in the leaflet, the cost of this would have built a whole townful of ordinary houses,' Dolly complained, by the time they had examined every room in the ornate little building. Leading architects and craftsmen had made every detail correct; each room was expensively furnished, and the four bathrooms included running water from the taps and flushing toilets.

'Flushing toilets for a plaything!' Gracie exclaimed. 'There's many a real place that doesn't have those, nor proper bathrooms. And the books in the library were written by famous authors! You'd think they had better things to do.'

She was quite depressed by the opulence of it all, and by the exhibition in general. Everyone knew it was one life for the rich and another for the poor, but this only emphasized it. And for two girls who scratched for a living, they were more than thankful to get away from it and take a breather in the beautiful gardens and then go on to the amusement park.

'Jim and Billy are meeting us here,' Dolly said as they sprawled out on the grass. 'He's taking me for a few trips on the caterpillar. You'll like it, Gracie, providing it don't rattle your brains out.'

'I'll stick to the sideshows, thanks very much,' Gracie replied, cross at being made part of a foursome that was destined to last all day and all evening too.

She was watching the band assembling on a rostrum nearby. She knew it wasn't *his* band, but just seeing a band was enough to make her heart turn over at hearing the brass instruments start up.

'Hello babe!' she heard a voice say, and the next minute Jim was giving Dolly a bear hug and Billy was shuffling awkwardly.

'We thought you was never coming,' Dolly said. 'We're just taking a breather before we go on the rides.'

Jim grinned. 'She's a rum one for the caterpillar,' he said to Gracie by way of acknowledging that she was there. 'It's a wonder her guts ain't turned inside out, the number of times she goes on it.'

Dolly laughed hysterically as if he'd made a corker of a joke, but after they had been walking around for so long, Gracie was too tired to see the funny side of anything.

'Sorry about your mum and dad,' Billy said, sitting down heavily on the grass beside her. 'Must have been 'orrible, both of 'em going like that, 'specially the way your dad went.'

'Yeah,' Jim said in a noisy aside to Dolly. 'Pity 'e couldn't swim!'

Gracie glared at him. Insensitive swine. She couldn't think what Dolly saw in him. His looks were dark and gypsyish, but he always seemed to have money to flash around, and Dolly never minded having a bit of it spent on her.

The trouble was, blokes like Jim usually expected something in return.

'You coming to the dance wiv us tonight, Gracie?' Billy said, red-faced.

She turned to him with a sigh. 'It looks like it,' she said shortly. 'Otherwise I'll be sitting on my own in my room all night.'

She was still peeved about them. She'd thought it would be just her and Dolly, going out together, having a laugh about the goings-on at Lawson's Shirt Factory, or the sayings of the old boys at Mrs Warburton's boarding-house.

Instead of that, she'd be going dancing up West, and wishing she was anywhere else as she moved around the floor in Billy's sweating embrace, and wincing as he tried to do the Charleston with his two left feet. She shuddered.

'So are we going to the funfair or aren't we?' she snapped, thoroughly out of sorts.

'Blimey, gel, what's rattled your cage?' Dolly said in surprise. 'I thought it was me keen to get there.'

'I just want to do something,' Gracie said. 'I'm fed up with sitting about.'

'You have to excuse her,' Dolly said to the men as they all stood up and brushed the grass off their clothes. 'She's still feeling bad after her folks died.'

Gracie strode ahead, crosser still at having Dolly apologize for her to these two oafs. She was truly starting to feel hot and edgy among all these crowds, and was wondering why she had come. A moment later they had to step hastily aside as a party of elegant young men and women swept past them. She instinctively admired and envied the cut and style of the women's shimmering dresses — and knowing exactly why she was here, her spirits rose.

Once they reached the vast amusement park and Dolly and Jim headed off for the caterpillar, the double-track mountain chute, and the other hair-raising rides, she was thankful that Billy was content to be her faithful shadow at some of the sideshows.

They threw balls at the coconut shies; tried in vain to pin the tail on the donkey; then threw darts on to a board full of playing-cards to try and win a fabulous prize or two, and ended up with their arms full of rubbish that could be bought at the market for a few coppers.

'You're much more fun to be with than Dolly,' Billy told her when they had bought some lemonade to cool down.

'Am I?' she said, smiling at the antics of a fellow with a mechanical monkey on a stick entertaining a group of excited children.

She hadn't felt as if she was much fun a little while ago. There was a large assortment of souvenir tea-caddies and biscuit-tins on one of the stalls, and without thinking, she was wondering which one to buy for her mother. It had given her a nasty jolt in her stomach to think she had forgotten, even for a moment, that her mother wouldn't need anything like that ever again.

'She always wants things,' Billy was going on.

'Who? Oh, Dolly. Well, everybody wants things, Billy,' she said, no longer listening to him properly, and having a job to remember what he'd been saying.

'Yeah, but it's not what Jim wants,' he said, and something in his voice made her stop watching the screaming children so vacantly and look at him properly.

'What do you mean?'

'Nothing.'

'Yes you do. What is it that Dolly wants and Jim doesn't?' she demanded, giving him all her attention now.

He looked uneasy. 'What all girls want. Getting hitched and all that stuff.'

'Oh, I see.'

She relaxed. Whatever Dolly might think about it, if Jim didn't have any intention of marrying her, that was all right by Gracie. She couldn't think of anything worse than getting tied for life to that bullish fellow.

'They're coming back from the rides now, and I reckon even Dolly's had enough,' she told him with a grin. 'She looks green.'

When the others reached them, she said cheerfully: 'You're not going to throw up all over us, are you, Dolly?'

Dolly's answer was to retch violently, but as people nearby glanced her way in disgust, Jim laughed loudly and thumped her on the back a few times, and said she should take more water with it if she couldn't stand the pace.

'Oh Gawd, I think it's time I went home, or I'll never be any good for dancing later,' Dolly finally gasped. 'We'll see you two charmers at the club tonight. Come on, Gracie, let's go for the train before I really disgrace myself.'

160

Gracie needed no second prompting. Going dancing was still furthest from her mind, and she'd have thought Dolly would have gone off the idea as well. But within a couple of hours Dolly was egging Gracie to try on one of her frocks for the evening.

'You were always bigger than me in the bust department,' Gracie protested. 'Anything of yours will just hang on me.'

'It'll just look fashionable, so stop your objections. You didn't think we'd just be sitting around like two old maids all the time, did you?'

'I don't know what I thought,' Gracie said, looking at the small selection of frocks Dolly had spread out on her bed now. 'Certainly not to be going anywhere with boring Billy. And I'm still in mourning, remember.'

'You're not still hankering over that trumpet player, are you?' Dolly said, ignoring any thoughts of dying and mourning. As far as Dolly was concerned, you were a long time dead, so you might as well make the most of living.

'He's a saxophone player, and no, I'm not.'

'Thank Gawd for that, but if you were, you don't have a cat's chance in hell of seeing him again if you carry on living in the sticks. So when are you moving back here properly?'

'I don't know. I'm still thinking about it.'

'Bleedin' hell Gracie, what's there to think about? You ain't needed at home any more, and I miss you. I ain't never had a friend like you.'

Since she rarely stated her feelings out loud, her voice was belligerent.

'You'll be the first to know when I've decided. Can I borrow this cream frock then?' Gracie said, changing the conversation quickly before they started bickering, and knowing the signs of old.

Dolly shrugged. 'You can have it if you want to alter it a bit. It's much too tight on me now anyway.'

'It never used to be.'

'Well it is now. You can borrow my tortoiseshell beads to go with it too if you like. Try it all on, then we'll persuade old Warby to make us a cup of tea.'

She could be as changeable as the weather sometimes. Gracie had always thought the cream frock was one of Dolly's favourites. It was a sleeveless style with a low waist but if it was too tight now, Dolly apparently couldn't be bothered to alter it herself. She would have done, once. She was as skilled as Gracie in that respect. But that was before she took up with coalman Jim, and before he occupied most of her time.

'How do I look?' she said, once she had

donned the frock and twisted the long rope of tortoiseshell beads twice around her neck.

'Very nice, if you like beanpoles,' Dolly said listlessly. 'Now take it off, and let's go downstairs and holler for that tea. I'm parched.'

After the fun of the fair, Gracie was parched too, but the very act of trying on something different and seeing how well it suited her, had sent a sliver of excitement running through her. It was so long since she had dressed up and gone anywhere, and she couldn't mourn for ever. Not out loud, anyway. The feelings she cherished for her mother — and for her father, come to that — would always be there, but they didn't have to blight the rest of her life.

⋆   ⋆   ⋆

It was like old times, getting dressed up for the nightclub that evening, apart from the moments when she had to blot out the memory of the night of the Palais fire. Even Dolly wasn't totally insensitive about it.

'Bit different from the last time, ain't it, Gracie? It was a few days after the fire that you got the phone call from your old man and had to pack up and leave, wasn't it? What a night that was, too.'

163

'It's all in the past now and I doubt that they'll ever get to the truth about how it started,' she said, not wanting to think about that night any more than she had to. Not all of it, anyway.

She pulled her wayward auburn curls into shape, and pinched her cheeks to put a bit of colour in them while Dolly was pressing far too much rouge into hers. She was much paler than she used to be. Gracie's dad always said that burning the candle at both ends was no good to man nor beast — and much notice he had ever taken of his own advice, Gracie thought bitterly.

'What happened to that sailor you was seeing?' Dolly said suddenly. 'You ain't mentioned him since you came back. If you don't think about saxophone Charlie no more, have you set your sights on the other one?'

'Me and Davey Watkins are just friends, though his mother would like to think otherwise,' Gracie said.

'There you are then! And if he's away at sea a lot, you'll have to make the most of it when he comes home on leave, won't you? You know what they say about sailors, Gracie,' she added with a wink.

'I *told* you — '

'I know, and the moon's full of cheese,'

Dolly said, laughing as if she had said something hilarious. 'Are you ready? You look a treat, by the way.'

'So do you,' Gracie said generously, though Dolly had definitely put on a bit of weight. It suited her, even though it wasn't strictly fashionable, and she had spent a lot of time squeezing herself into a cotton brassière to flatten her chest.

★   ★   ★

Tonight was going to be an ordeal. Just walking into the brightly lit nightclub with the music playing was enough to make Gracie's heart thump. Jim and Billy were waiting for them, and they pushed their way through the crowds to find a table on the circular balcony overlooking the dance-floor.

'Lovely, ain't it?' Dolly breathed in her ear, as the men went off for some refreshments. 'You are going to enjoy yourself, ain't you, Gracie?'

'Of course I am,' she said, forcing a smile, and willing her eyes away from the band. Just as if he would be here. Just as if pigs could fly.

She danced with Billy a few times, but since he didn't seem to mind sitting out, it suited her well enough to watch everyone else on the dance-floor. Dolly and Jim were always in the thick of it, and once the music changed tempo from the slower tunes to the frantic Charleston, they hardly saw them for the next hour.

'I thought Dolly was exhausted this afternoon, after all those rides at the funfair,' she said. 'But she'll do herself an injury if she's not careful.'

'Jim likes his girls to be lively.'

'His *girls*? He doesn't have more than one, does he, Billy?'

'Nah, 'course not. Not at the same time,' he said hastily.

'That's all right then.' For a minute Gracie thought he was implying that Jim was playing fast and loose. For all Dolly's airy-fairy ways, she knew she really fancied Jim, and she wouldn't want to see her get hurt.

Much later, she admitted that the whole evening hadn't been quite the ordeal she had expected. It was like falling off a bicycle, or so they said. You had to get on and ride again to get over your fear. By the time they returned to the boarding-house and crept upstairs, they undressed and crawled into bed, exhausted.

It had been a long day, especially for Gracie, after travelling from Southampton. She was nearly dropping with sleep, and not even the novelty of being back in her old room again would keep her awake much longer, but she was still looking forward to their after-lights-out chats, when secrets were shared.

It was familiar territory, after all, she thought, with a rush of gladness. The constant noise of the London traffic throughout the night was as soothing as the sound of birds singing to a country-dweller.

She moved her head sideways on the pillow. In the slivers of moonlight shining in through the small square of window, she could just see the mound of Dolly's curled-up shape beneath the bedclothes.

'You're not going to sleep yet, are you?' she whispered.

There was no reply for a few seconds, and the next thing she heard was a regular, rhythmic snoring coming from Dolly's bed. So much for sharing secrets then. With a small sigh of regret Gracie turned her head away from the light, and was asleep in seconds.

10

Dolly was glad she was staying an extra night. At least, that's what Gracie thought she said from the jumble of her bedclothes on Sunday morning.

'But if you think I'm getting up at the crack of dawn, forget it,' the voice continued blearily. 'I can't face breakfast, but don't let me stop you.'

With that, she rolled over again and buried her head beneath the blankets to escape the sunlight now streaming in through the window. It was a waste of a lovely day to be lying in bed, but Gracie had no objection to spending time on her own. Yesterday had been fun, but today was different, and being alone was probably the best way to decide whether she really wanted to live here again.

It no longer felt as if she would be deserting her mum or betraying her memory. Queenie had always urged her not to stay in Southampton, especially if it meant looking after her dad and becoming a drudge for him. That situation had changed more tragically and quickly than any of them had expected, but the result was the same. Gracie had nothing to keep her in Southampton, and everything to make a new life for herself. And it wouldn't be sewing shirts for Ed Lawson, she thought determinedly.

Mrs Warburton welcomed her down to the breakfast table and fussed around her as if she was a long-lost relative.

As she went out to fetch the eggs and bacon, Mr Taylor winked at Gracie.

'Treats us like schoolboys, she does, but her heart's in the right place. So what are you and Dolly doing today?'

'She's not up yet, but I'm going to the park,' Gracie said, before she had time to think.

She hadn't actually decided on anything, but it seemed as good a place as any to take advantage of this lovely September day.

'You all look as if you could do with some fresh air too,' she added cheekily, addressing the lodgers.

'What, come with you and cramp your style?' one of them said with a cough and a spit into a grubby handkerchief. 'You won't want old codgers like us hanging around a lovely girl like you with all them young bucks around.'

'I'm not looking for a husband, Mr Daley,' she said, trying to ignore his unsavoury implications. And she hadn't actually invited their company.

'If I was forty years younger I'd snap you up myself,' he answered.

'You'd have to play the saxophone first,' said a voice behind them, and they turned to see Dolly, not exactly at her best, but clearly thinking she should make an effort since her friend was only here for a short time.

'What's all this about a saxophone?' said Mrs Warburton, clearing a space on the table for the toast rack.

'It's nothing,' Gracie said, suddenly annoyed. 'I knew somebody who played in a band once — well, not exactly *knew* him — I only met him once, and I'm not likely to see him again.'

'She just lives in hopes,' Dolly added with a sly grin.

Mrs Warburton gave an impatient sigh. 'That's as may be, but do you want breakfast or not, missy, because I've got church to go to and I'm not going to be cooking all day for the likes of you.'

'I don't want nothing.' Dolly was scowling now. 'I just came to tell Gracie that I'll go for a walk too.'

★   ★   ★

'Are you all right, Dolly? You look a bit seedy,' Gracie said a while later, when they had left the boarding-house behind and were striding out towards the park, their arms linked.

'I had too much to drink last night, and I'm not sure what Jim was putting in my glass,' Dolly said with a grimace. 'Dancing the Charleston didn't help the way my guts were turning upside down after all those rides on the caterpillar either. I'll be all right, but the smell of old Warby's greasy cooking was the last straw.'

She sounded really down, Gracie thought, and she needed to hear something to cheer her up.

'I think I might come back to London quite soon, Dolly, but I shan't come back to Mrs Warburton's.'

Dolly stopped walking so suddenly that she nearly pulled Gracie over.

'Why ever not? Where will you go, then?'

Gracie laughed at her indignant expression.

'You've practically answered that for yourself, haven't you? All that greasy cooking, and living in the company of those old blokes, nice as they are — well, it's not my idea of living — nor yours, I'd have thought.'

'Are you going to ask old Lawson for your job back? I know he'd have you like a shot.'

'I daresay he would, but I'm not going back there, either.'

They were through the gates of the park now, and the grass was sweet and green, the late summer flowers in full bloom, filling the air with their heady scent. People were milling about, dressed in their Sunday best, and from the smiles on their faces it seemed as if the sun was bringing out the best in everybody.

'So what are you going to do then?'

Gracie gave a small sigh. Her first instinct not to say anything until her plans were definite had obviously been for the best. It was only because she thought Dolly needed cheering up that she had abandoned this on the spur of the moment, and now she was stuck with it. She spoke quickly.

'I might look for a room to rent somewhere and set up on my own, doing alterations or making new garments to order. It worked all right in Southampton, and there's more money to be made here — '

She couldn't get any further before Dolly was squealing at her.

'That's a cracking idea. Why don't we do it together?'

Gracie was taken aback. It wasn't what she'd been planning, even though the plans were still so vague, and she hadn't really got any further than moving back to London and doing what she was good at.

'What? A kind of partnership, you mean?' she said with an uncertain laugh. 'You and me, throw-outs from Lawson's Shirt Factory?'

'We ain't throw-outs,' Dolly said. 'You left because you had to look after your mum, and I can leave any time I like. What do you say?'

'I say I think you're crazy,' Gracie said flatly. 'We know nothing about business, and what I'm thinking about is just to take on a little sideline work to keep body and soul together, not competing with fashion houses.'

'Why not? Why ever bleedin' not?'

'Be realistic, for God's sake. I've got to do this on my own, Dolly, and that's the end of it. I'll be starting from scratch, and later, if there was enough work coming in, maybe we could think about it, but for now, I *need* to be on my own and to do things my way. Too much has been going on in the last couple of months for me to rush into anything like you're suggesting.'

'You don't want me any more, then?'

'Oh, don't be daft. Of course I want you. You're like a sister to me, as well as my best friend,' Gracie said, hugging Dolly's arm, 'but I need to do this by myself, to prove something, I suppose, and don't ask me what it is, because I don't know.'

Dolly laughed.

'I always said you was a crackpot, Gracie Brown.'

But the prickly moments had passed, and Gracie breathed a sigh of relief. It was funny, though. Spelling it out in words had clarified her mind in a way she hadn't expected. She *did* need time alone. Her parents' deaths couldn't be forgotten in a week or a month, and she needed to rebuild her life in her own way. Perhaps it was only when both parents were gone that you really felt as though you were an adult. There were no other relatives above you, and no one to help you stand on your own two feet but yourself.

She shivered, brushing aside such deep thoughts as the sound of music came towards them over the soft air. Today wasn't a day for philosophising. Ahead of them they could see rows of deckchairs and beyond them a bandstand. Musicians were playing bright tunes suitable for a Sunday morning in the park, and despite herself, Gracie's heartbeats quickened.

'It won't be him, Gracie,' Dolly said.

'I know, but we can still go and listen, can't we?'

'You ain't never forgotten him, have you?'

Gracie was tempted to say that of course she had, but Dolly knew her too well.

'No, but I'm not wasting my life thinking of something that's never going to happen. In the end I'll probably settle for Davey Watkins and be a sailor's wife.'

She didn't know why she said it. She certainly didn't mean it. She just wanted to stop Dolly looking at her with that pitying look in her eyes that said she was being a damn fool to hanker over a saxophone player, because there were plenty of other blokes in the world.

'Yo ho ho then!' Dolly said. 'I thought you were holding out on me. Has he asked you yet?'

'To marry him, you mean?'

'Well, what else would I mean?' Dolly said mockingly. 'You ain't — you *know* — done the business with him. Have you, Gracie?'

'Of course not! I wouldn't be that stupid. Now shut up about it and let's go and listen to the band.'

And of course it wasn't Charlie's band. She'd never imagined that it would be. The saxophone player was sixty years old if he was a day, and he wasn't nearly as good as Charlie, but that was probably just her opinion. All the same, if she closed her eyes, it wasn't difficult to imagine it was his music she could hear in her head.

'I still reckon you've got it bad, but I hope your sailor-boy's worth it,' Dolly whispered as a parting shot, watching her, and was immediately shushed by other people trying to listen to the music.

The band played a selection of rousing patriotic songs; *Land of hope and glory* and *Jerusalem*, then a good smattering of popular songs, though nothing that would outrage older listeners on a Sunday morning, and, to end with, some traditional sea shanties. Dolly nudged Gracie as the concert ended.

'I reckon they played them sea shanties just for you, gel, to remind you of your Davey. What's he like, anyway? Tall, dark and handsome?'

'Oh yes. Valentino to the life,' Gracie said, heavy with sarcasm. 'As a matter of fact he's quite good-looking, but when you've known somebody practically all your life, you hardly notice it, do you?'

'So when are you seeing him again?'

'I don't know! When he's home on leave, I suppose, that is, if I'm still around. If I've moved back here, I won't be seeing him at all, will I?'

'Never mind,' Dolly said giving her arm a squeeze. 'You're a lovely writer, Gracie, and I bet he likes getting letters from you.'

'I daresay. So can we shut up about him now?'

And despite what Dolly might think, she had no romantic feelings towards Davey Watkins and never would have.

★　★　★

She left London early on Monday morning, having decided that she didn't need to look around for a place to rent just yet. There would be time enough for that when she had sorted out everything at home.

Her parents' life insurances had been paid out promptly and thanks to her mum's foresight in paying into the funeral club each of them had been given a decent send-off. But there were still papers and letters to sort out in what Queenie always called her business drawer.

Mick had always scoffed at it, saying she was getting above herself making such a fuss about keeping every bloody receipt as if they were gold dust — but Queenie had confided to Gracie long ago that if she didn't keep money for the gas and coal bills and suchlike away from his prying eyes, he'd booze the lot away. And keeping receipts had always been a matter of pride to her, to prove that the Brown family could pay their way.

After the deaths, although Gracie had dealt with the necessary insurance policies, she hadn't had the heart to empty the drawer properly, but she knew it had to be done. She couldn't break the final ties with home until she did so. She also realized that there could be unpaid bills. Because of the pain and the drugs her mother had been forced to take during her last weeks, Queenie had been vague about so many things. The only thing she had insisted on with what little animation she could summon up, was that her daughter shouldn't stay in Southampton.

Once Gracie had returned to the house she opened all the windows to rid it of the stale smell of being unoccupied, even for so short a while. Not that the varying smells that wafted from the dockside were any too savoury, either, and it was soon preferable to close the windows again. But not before more than one person had noted that the Brown girl was back.

Much later, having unpacked and made herself a sandwich and a pot of tea, she opened the business drawer purposefully. There were no surprises, just the rent book and the large envelope that said simply 'Bills and Receipts.'

Gracie tipped them out on to the parlour table, startled to discover that they went years back. Uneasily beginning to agree with her dad she saw that this had become something of an obsession, though some of them made interesting reading. Halfway down the pile she found another envelope. The sight of nothing more than her own name on it made her heart jolt and then start to beat painfully fast.

Queenie hadn't been an educated woman, and if this was going to be what was called a letter from the grave Gracie wasn't sure she could bear to read it. But how could she not? It had been meant for her, and written some time ago, she guessed. So perhaps Queenie hadn't written it in her last months when she knew she was dying, but a long time ago.

The thought made it easier for Gracie to slit open the envelope, and then stare in complete disbelief at the contents.

'Cooee, is anybody home?'

Without waiting for an answer Mrs Jennings came bustling into the house after a peremptory knock on the door, as she had always done while poor Queenie was alive. She'd seen no reason not to do it now.

With one swift movement, Gracie covered the contents of her mother's letter with the larger envelope and managed to stuff the whole lot back into the drawer before she turned with as natural a smile as she could manage.

'My goodness, you gave me a fright, Mrs Jennings!'

'I'm sure I never meant to do any such thing, duck. I was just wanting to make sure you was all right after your jaunt to London, and to bring you a dish of mutton stew and dumplings for your dinner.'

'It's very kind of you — '

'Think nothing of it. You could do with a bit of filling out, and you young girls don't do much cooking for yourselves, do you? So did you have a good time with your friend, and ain't you glad to be back from all the noise and the smoke?'

She paused for breath, but at least her rambling had given Gracie a chance to catch her own breath while still mulling over her discovery. Never in a million years had she expected her mother to have done something like this without Mick's knowledge. And one thing Gracie *was* sure of. It was definitely without her father's knowledge.

'It was very nice to see my friend again, Mrs Jennings,' she murmured in answer. 'And good of you to bring me in the stew. I'll enjoy it later, I'm sure.'

She hoped the neighbour would take the hint that she wanted to be alone, but she might have known it was too much to ask. Eyeing the brown earthenware teapot on the table, she asked Gracie if there was another cuppa in the pot.

'I'm sure there is,' she said with a sigh, telling herself not to be ungracious in wanting the woman out of here as quickly as possible. But it was another half-hour before Mrs Jennings was replete with two cups of tea, brushing down her apron for biscuit crumbs, and leaving her alone.

Gracie turned the key in the front door behind her, not wanting to be disturbed again until she had got over the staggering amount of money inside the envelope marked 'Gracie'. It wouldn't be huge in many people's eyes, but it was to her, and would have been to Queenie. Quickly, having been unable to do so when she had been interrupted she scanned the letter folded around the notes.

I been saving this over the years for you, Gracie love, she read. *Your dad don't know nothing about it, and I know you'll open this before he does. So do what you like with it, and remember, it's for you and not for him.*

Your loving mother.

Her eyes were blurred with tears when she came to the end of the poignant little note. Perhaps Queenie had had some long-ago premonition of dying before her husband, and she hadn't wanted him to get his hands on the little nest-egg she had hoarded for her daughter. As fate had turned out, Mick had died before Queenie, and now they were both gone.

It took a while for Gracie to get over what she had found. She took the precious envelope of money upstairs and hid it under her mattress, as if she thought she was about to be robbed in broad daylight. Which was ludicrous, because when had Gracie Brown ever had anything of value to steal? Besides, the daylight was fading now, and she would soon draw the curtains and shut out the night, and decide what this new-found wealth was going to mean.

A rap on the front door made her jump again. She peered out of the bedroom window but couldn't see anyone. It was probably Mrs Jennings coming back to reclaim her dish, but Gracie had been too keyed-up to eat any of the mutton stew yet, and wasn't at all sure that she could have faced the heavy dumplings.

She ran downstairs and opened the door, knowing that the woman wouldn't go away until she did so. Wanting to feed her up, thought Grace with a rueful smile. The smile faded as soon as she saw who was standing there.

'Well now, Miss Brown, we were forgetting something last weekend, weren't we?' came Percy Hill's oily voice.

She knew at once what he meant. She had forgotten the rent money, and she should have given it to Mrs Jennings to pay him while she was away.

'I'm sorry, I'll get it for you now,' she said, flustered and turned away.

He was right behind her. She could feel his breath on the back of her neck. The words seemed to ooze out of him.

'Things can't be easy for you now, my dear, but if you're having trouble paying, there's always another little arrangement.'

Before she could think, he had pulled her back towards him. His arms were around her body and his hands seized her breasts greedily. They squeezed her tight, tweaking her nipples between his fingers and thumbs until she gasped out with shock and pain. And then one of his hands slid downwards, yanking up her skirt and thrusting his hand up her leg towards her inner thigh. She opened her mouth to scream, but he was too quick for her. While his right hand probed, his other one left her breast and fastened itself over her mouth like a vice.

'Now then, my beauty, don't tell me you ain't been angling for this ever since you came back,' he panted. 'And don't tell me you don't know what it's all about, neither. I always wondered what you got up to in London, and I wouldn't mind betting you learned a trick or two to whet a man's appetite.'

Gracie tried desperately to clamp her legs tightly together, but she could already feel the hotness of his probing fingers. She sobbed in terror, punching back at him with her elbows, but when she opened her mouth to scream, his fingers were instantly inside it, pumping in and out in a mockery of fornication.

He was thickset and bulky and she knew she couldn't get away from him unless she did something desperate. If she hadn't been too far away from the drawer with the kitchen knives in it, she knew she would have done for him.

At last she managed to struggle free. She let her hand drop to where she could feel the great ugly thing inside his trousers prodding at her. Without a second thought she grabbed it hard and twisted. He howled with pain as he staggered back. She rushed to the wall and banged on it, screaming and yelling for Mrs Jennings.

'You bitch!' he shouted, doubled up with pain and clutching himself. 'You bloody whoring little bitch. You won't get away with that!'

Seconds later Mrs Jennings's outraged voice came at them both as she stormed in through the front door.

'What the bleedin' hell's going on in here?'

It only took one look at Gracie's terrified face and at the uninvited visitor. She didn't need to say any more. Without waiting for an answer, she grabbed the teapot from the table, and threw it and the contents at the landlord. As it hit the floor it smashed to pieces. Percy Hill was left spluttering and hollering with hot tea and tea leaves streaming down his face and clothes.

'Maybe that'll cool you down, you bastard,' Mrs Jennings yelled at him.

'You bloody madwoman. I'll get you out of this street before I'm done,' he screamed, turning on her furiously.

'You and whose army! I'll see you up before the magistrates if you try turning me and my old man out. I'll make sure the neighbours know what you did to this little maid, and you can whistle for your bleedin' rent money.'

The two women watched him blunder out,

and as Gracie stood silently sobbing she realized Mrs Jennings was laughing.

'Don't worry, my duck. Everybody knows what he's like, and they'll all have heard the rumpus. They'll take one look at him as he gets off home and they'll know what's been happening. He won't bother you again.'

As she finished speaking, they could hear the catcalls and hissing in the street, and Gracie knew the woman was right. She was still too shocked to get any enjoyment out of it, though, and she saw Mrs Jennings look at her sharply.

'He didn't really hurt you, did he, lovey? You know what I mean. You don't want the doc to come and take a look at you, do you?'

'No, it's not necessary. I think I hurt him though.'

The memory of his howling flashed through her mind, and she gave a trembling smile.

'That's better. Now, I won't take no for an answer, Gracie. You didn't want me stopping with you the night your ma died, but I'm stopping here tonight. I can sleep on the sofa perfectly well. No arguments, all right?'

'I'm not arguing,' Gracie mumbled, and then her legs turned to water, and she was enveloped in the neighbour's arms.

11

Before she went to bed, Gracie scrubbed herself until her skin felt raw, to rid herself of the taint of Percy Hill's pawing. Her nerves were in shreds, but she was weirdly comforted by the regular sound of Mrs Jennings's snores from the parlour below. She had left London that morning, undecided about her future movements, and now two things had happened to decide it for her.

In the sleepless hours of the night, when every small unexpected sound could make her jump with fright, she kept her mind occupied by thinking about anything but the memory of that hateful man, knowing he would probably have succeeded in his vile intention but for the intervention of Mrs Jennings.

Weak tears ran down her cheeks. The neighbour had warned her about Percy Hill, but she had never expected such a vicious attack in her own home. She had never taken the warnings seriously; now she knew how foolish that had been.

The other, totally unexpected happening was the amount of money her mother had been squirrelling away for her all these years. The money that would enable her to get out of here, find a decent place to live, and start her own business. She tried to think positively about that future.

She would need to live in a decent part of London if she wanted a good clientele. An area where there were children of moneyed parents who would pay well for well-made clothes for their offspring . . . and her interest in making them had definitely been stimulated by her recent commission. She tried to concentrate on those thoughts, and by the time a pearly dawn light had begun to filter through the darkness, she knew the time had come. She fell into a deep, exhausted sleep, and awoke with a start when Mrs Jennings brought her a cup of tea.

'Oh, whatever time is it?' she mumbled, disorientated.

'Never you mind the time, duck. You just stay there and drink your tea. I've got a saucepan of porridge warming nicely in the kitchen, summat to stick to your ribs and make you feel better.'

'Thank you,' Gracie said weakly, not sure whether she felt like laughing or crying at the image it created. Lizzie was watching her carefully as if she was a piece of precious porcelain, and she realized she was starting to feel somewhat better — even without the porridge sticking to her ribs.

'I'll drink my tea and get up,' she said. 'Then I'd like to talk over a few things, Mrs Jennings, unless you've got to go.'

'Bless you, no. Jennings can take care of himself for a few hours. You just think of me as the next best thing to your ma, if it's not impertinent to say so.'

'It's not at all,' Gracie said huskily.

Half an hour later, feeling more like herself, she went downstairs and forced the dish of porridge down for politeness' sake.

'Now then, gel,' Mrs Jennings said, leaning forward, arms folded; the concerned neighbour — and a prize gossip, Gracie reminded herself.

Gossip would be useful for letting the rest of the street know what a rat Percy Hill was, but presumably they all knew that. But Gracie didn't want everyone knowing about the money she now possessed. So she had to be cautious.

'If I give you the rent book and the money that's owing, would you see that Mr Hill gets it, Mrs Jennings?'

''Course I will, lovey. If you want to let me keep the book and let me have the money each week, I'll pay him with ours, then you won't have to see the toerag at all.'

'Thank you. And you know Mum wanted me to move back to London sometime, don't you?'

'Don't let that bastard scare you out of your own home, Gracie!'

'He's not,' she said quickly. 'But there's nothing to keep me here now. I've got friends in London, and my old job is always open to me,' she invented quickly. Though it wasn't really an invention. The option was there if she wanted it.

'Oh well, I suppose you know best, but I'll be sorry to lose you, Gracie.'

'I know,' Gracie said, swallowing the lump in her throat, 'but life has to go on, so I'll give you the rent book and the money, and then I've got things to do.'

And good neighbour though she was, Gracie hoped she would take the hint, and stop looking as though she was a fixture for the day.

★   ★   ★

Later that morning Gracie walked purposefully to the homes of her best clients. Although they all showed surprise at her request, none of them refused her.

'I shall miss your cheerful smile as well as your expertise, Miss Brown,' Mrs Farthing said, 'but I wish you every success in your venture.'

It was the same everywhere, and Gracie was flushed and embarrassed by the time she had finished. But by then she had a small collection of references signed by some of the most reputable ladies of the town. Whether she would need them she didn't yet know, but they were always useful to have.

Her next call was at the newsagent's where the card advertising herself as a skilled London Outworker was still in the window. She asked him to remove the card now, and bought a London newspaper instead.

Reading it minutely at home, she felt a surge of nostalgia at the photographs about the Empire Exhibition, due to close at the end of October. That day in London had been so perfect, and Wembley was growing and becoming a fashionable area now. It would attract people of quality. It was where anyone who wanted to make a success of life might do well to start a new business.

The tingle of excitement inside her grew. She turned quickly to the pages at the back of the newspaper. There were advertisements of houses for sale and rooms to let, and she studied them carefully, pencilling a circle around anything that looked suitable for her needs, and eventually she sat back, with her head spinning. So what now? All the adverts had box numbers, a few details about the furnished rooms in question, and stating that the property was in the Wembley area. So she had to write some letters to request more details.

It was a good idea, anyway. In a letter she could say exactly what she needed without getting flustered on the telephone, and without the embarrassment of simply turning up and having to say it wasn't suitable at all.

She started to compose the letter right away, and when she was satisfied, she read it back carefully, trying to see it through someone else's eyes.

Dear Sir, she wrote.

I am requesting more details about the rooms you have for rent. I am a professional seamstress with a number of references, and would be using the rooms for my work as well as living-quarters. Please reply as soon as possible and let me know when I may come to view the property.

Yours faithfully,
Grace Brown (Miss)

It looked brisk and efficient, and describing herself as a professional seamstress was truthful enough. She copied the letter six times, filled in the box numbers on the envelopes and went out to post them before she got cold feet.

But she squashed the feeling at once. She could do this, and she *would* do it. As soon as she found a place to live, she would move back to London — providing they all replied. And providing they thought her a suitable tenant.

Her heart sank for a moment. Queenie had loved the sound of the sewing-machine whirring night and day, but not everybody would. Remembering the clatter of the machines at Lawson's Shirt Factory, where they all had to yell at one another to be heard, Gracie knew that. But she wouldn't let that deter her, nor take away the anticipation that she might be on the brink of a new life.

Meanwhile there was furniture to be sold. Everything here was dear and familiar, but she couldn't take any of it to London. She was unsure what to do about her mother's treadle sewing-machine, which had done such good service, but she ignored the sentimental attachment she felt. It would be a heavy thing to transport to London, and she could always purchase a more modern one when she saw what space she had in the new place.

She was convinced that there was a bright and shining future ahead of her now, and a new life meant a new everything. The night when Percy Hill had come here with evil intent had besmirched the happy memories of her childhood in this house, and she would be glad to leave it behind.

★ ★ ★

It was amazing how quickly things changed when fate gave them a helping hand. Gracie considered fate had been on her side from the moment she saw the money her mother had saved for her. Even Percy Hill's attempted rape had motivated her to leave Southampton and do what she had been dithering about. The local saleroom people had taken most of the furniture away and would probably pay her a pittance for it, but that didn't matter so much as getting everything sorted out.

It had been a treat to see the look of astonishment on the neighbours' faces when the saleroom van had come trundling down the street and taken most of Gracie Brown's belongings away.

'What's going on, Gracie?' Lizzie Jennings exclaimed, bustling into the house as beds and mattresses were being carried out. 'Your rent's been paid up regularly, duck — '

'I'm getting rid of things I don't need, Mrs Jennings. I only need a bed to sleep on and a chair to sit on, and I'll let you know when I'm leaving.'

The treadle machine went next, and the neighbour's eyes widened.

'Well, now I know you mean it, Gracie. I never thought you'd part with that old faithful. Even Jennings quite likes the sound of it of a night.'

Gracie turned away, unable to bear seeing the removal men loading it on to the van.

'I can always get another one.'

''Twon't be the same,' Mrs Jennings said. 'There was a lot of love gone into that old machine — '

'I know, and talking about it only makes it worse,' Gracie said, her voice wobbling a little.

The neighbour had got the information she came for and left Gracie alone. It was bad enough seeing all her past go out of the door and into a furniture van, without having somebody putting into words what she was trying hard not to feel.

Several weeks later the replies from the box numbers began to arrive. Two said the rooms had already been let. Two more said they weren't suitable for business premises, and the last two gave her the Wembley addresses and asked her to call as soon as convenient. Gracie immediately phoned Mrs Warburton and asked if she could stay for a couple of nights.

'Lord love you, Gracie, of course you can. Dolly's at work now, but I'm sure she'll be happy to share her room. You always kept that little madam in order,' she finished, half-way between a chuckle and a sniff.

Gracie smiled, not sure anyone could keep Dolly in order. She didn't particularly care to be thought the more staid one of the two, either. She was the one who was striking out on her own, not Dolly Neath. And at not quite twenty years old!

She packed a few things quickly, full of quivering excitement now, and told Mrs Jennings she would be away for a few days. There was no need to say anything more definite yet, but the neighbour was keeping a motherly eye on her now ever since the incident with Percy Hill. Gracie was touched by it, even though it was in danger of smothering her.

But once on the train for London, her spirits rose. This was an adventure of her own making, and it gave her an enormous sense of achievement, even getting this far. It also made her appreciate how much independence a little money could give you. She had never had any to speak of before, but now she had a post office savings account, and she intended using it wisely.

Dolly was still at work when she reached the boarding-house, and as Mrs Warburton clearly thought she might be planning to move in permanently again, Gracie quickly put her right.

'I'm here to see some people on business,' she told her grandly, hoping she wasn't giving herself too many airs.

But the landlady nodded sagely. 'I always said you were wasted at that shirt factory. You've got the looks and manners of a young lady. Folk notice those things, and respect you for it.'

Percy Hill hadn't respected her for it, Gracie thought, then pushed him out of her mind as easily as if he was a gnat to be swatted out of existence.

Dolly wasn't so flattering. She was in a funny mood, Gracie decided, and she didn't mean funny ha-ha either. As soon as Dolly saw Gracie's things on her old bed, she stared at her suspiciously.

'What's going on? Are you still keeping secrets from me?'

'Why do you say such daft things? Are you keeping secrets from me?'

'I don't have any secrets.'

'Well, neither do I.'

They were almost at loggerheads the minute they'd seen each other, but it was none of her doing that Dolly seemed irritable and ready to pick a quarrel.

'What's up?' Gracie said at last. 'Have you and Jim fallen out?'

Dolly glared at her. 'Me and Jim are all right, same as you and your sailor-boy, I presume.'

'Don't you want to know why I'm here?' Gracie asked next, refusing to comment on Davey Watkins.

Dolly shrugged. 'I know you'll tell me in the end.'

She was being mean and hateful, deflating all Gracie's excitement. But since she didn't know anything about it yet, it was easy to overlook it.

'I've come to look at some rooms to rent in Wembley. And before you ask how I can afford it, I've been saving my earnings in the post office and my mother left me some money. Besides that, there's another reason why I have to get away from Southampton. A more unpleasant reason.'

It all came out in a rush. She hadn't meant to mention Percy Hill at all, but now she had started she knew Dolly wouldn't leave it alone. The astonished look on Dolly's face when she had mentioned renting rooms in Wembley and then the even more astonishing fact that Gracie's mother had left her a bit of money, was quickly replaced by concern.

'What's happened? Has Davey Watkins let you down?'

'It's nothing to do with him. Let's just say the landlord tried to get a bit too friendly, if you get my meaning.'

'Blimey, Gracie, you don't mean he tried it on!'

'Yes I do, and I don't want to talk about it.'

'Gawd, no wonder you're all hot and bothered. What's he like? Not one of your movie star heroes, I take it?'

Gracie lashed out angrily. 'For pity's sake, Dolly, he tried to *rape* me, but for your information he's a loathsome fat pig, and fifty if he's a day. Now shut up about it. Do you want to come and look at these rooms with me tomorrow or not?'

Tomorrow was Saturday. Many sweatshops stayed open six days a week but Ed Lawson liked his weekends at home and wouldn't let his girls work there unattended, so that meant free days for all of them.

Dolly was still gaping at her. 'Big enough for two, is it?'

'I *told* you I have to do this alone — '

'All *right*! You don't half jump down

peoples' throats lately, Gracie!'

So would you if you'd had to fight off a bastard like Percy Hill.

★ ★ ★

The trains to Wembley were still packed with people going to the Empire Exhibition, but the street they were looking for had a row of small shops and businesses. People would come here for shopping, but when Gracie found the rented address, one look at the sign over the downstairs business decided her.

'What's wrong with this?' Dolly asked, seeing her face.

'I'm not living above a butcher's shop,' Gracie said flatly. 'Can you imagine a good class of people bringing work for me and having the smell of dead meat in their noses? It would get into the materials and ruin me before I even started.'

'A good class of people!' Dolly mimicked. 'Are you sure you ain't getting above yourself, gel?'

'I'm being sensible,' Gracie snapped, 'but if you're not going to take me seriously I'll carry on by myself.'

'Oh, all right. So where next? I don't feel like traipsing around all day.'

Gracie consulted her small street-map. 'It's

not far. What's up with you, anyway? You used to walk for miles.'

'It's nothing. Let's find the place and then we can go and find a Lyons and have something to eat.'

'You should have had breakfast at Warby's like I did.'

'Couldn't face it. I've given up breakfast, anyway.'

'Afraid of getting fat, are you?' Gracie said with a grin.

'Something like that, beanpole.'

Gracie's enthusiasm was waning fast. She had had such high hopes of finding a place instantly, and after the first four replies had been no good, she had expected to choose the best one between these last two. But working above a butcher's shop was definitely out, and even Dolly had retched at the smell of blood wafting towards them, so now there was only one possibility left. And if that didn't turn out to be suitable . . .

'Oh!' she said softly, as they finally found the last street. It could be more accurately described as a tree-lined avenue with a small selection of shops.

'Does this suit you, your highness?' Dolly said with a grin, recovered from the effect the smell of animal blood had had on her.

'It's probably too good to be true. The rent

will be out of my range, and it'll be above an undertaker's or something,' Gracie answered, betraying the fact that from the outside it looked simply perfect.

'Blimey, more dead meat,' Dolly said brutally, 'but you'll never know until you find out. What's the number?'

They found it half-way down the street. The ground floor was a discreet little shoe-shop, and the window displays were elegant and fashionable. Gracie pushed open the door, her hands trembling, anticipating the worst, but praying for the best as she told the elderly man behind the counter she had come to see Mr Foster.

'You're speaking to him,' the man said. 'And you must be Miss Brown. Come through to the back room while we have a chat with my wife.'

The gods were definitely smiling on Gracie Brown, she thought later. The Fosters lived at the extended rear of the premises, and didn't use the upstairs rooms as Mrs Foster was lame and could no longer manage the stairs.

'We want someone else living in the house, to keep the rooms aired and occupied,' she was told, when they had been given tea and biscuits, and had had a thorough discussion with the couple. 'We're prepared to charge a nominal rent for the right tenant. A young business person is ideal, and you said in your letter that you are a professional seamstress, Miss Brown, and will work at home, which suits us admirably. I'll show you the rooms, and then we can discuss it further.'

Dolly was still sniggering over Gracie's describing herself as a professional seamstress by the time Mr Foster left them alone to inspect the rooms. There was one bedroom with a window overlooking a garden, a sitting-room, a small boxroom, and a bathroom. There was a separate entrance to the upstairs apartment, so no one had to go through the shop to reach it.

'Blimey, gel, have you fallen on your feet! Providing he don't charge the earth, o' course, despite what he said.'

'I don't care what it costs. It's perfect,' Gracie breathed, already seeing herself installed here with her own bits and pieces and the new sewing-machine she was going to buy. 'I want it, and I have to have it.'

'Sounds more like a feller than a place to live,' Dolly said with a grin.

'You would say that, but I just want to make a success of what I do, however small it is, and to do it by my own efforts.'

'I never knew you was so ambitious, Gracie,' Dolly said in a slightly more strangled voice.

'Neither did I, until now.'

Gracie was completely charmed by the prospect of living here. She and Dolly wandered through the rooms separately. They were already furnished, and the Foster couple were well enough off to have carpets on the floor instead of the lino Gracie was used to. It was a real touch of class, she thought happily, and if that was being snobbish, she didn't care.

In her mind she was already adding personal touches; the framed photo of her mum and dad's wedding; the poster of Valentino from one of her movie-star magazines that would hide a dark patch on the bedroom wall; the crochet doylies her mum had made that would go on the sideboard; the little boxroom that would make an ideal working area . . .

She became aware of strange noises coming from the bathroom, and wondered briefly if the plumbing wasn't all that it should be. Perhaps nothing was this perfect after all. The door was not quite closed, and she looked around for Dolly to ask what she thought. When she couldn't find her she had a sudden suspicion, and pushed open the bathroom door.

Dolly was bending over the lavatory, heaving and spluttering into the pan. Her face was bone-white as she pulled the chain quickly, but not before Gracie realized she had just been very sick.

'Good Lord, Dolly, what's wrong?' she said in alarm.

Dolly wiped her streaming eyes with shaking hands.

'Ain't you worked it out yet, Gracie? Even you can't be that dumb!'

12

All Gracie could hear was her friend's rasping breath, and all she could see was her frightened face, as shock hit her like a blow between the eyes. How *could* Dolly have been so stupid? And presumably with coalman Jim and his black fingernails. She gave an involuntary shudder.

'I know what you think of me,' Dolly said shrilly, 'and don't think it's not what I ain't been calling myself ever since I suspected.'

Gracie put her arms around her, feeling her trembling body, and knowing now why she couldn't face Mrs Warburton's fatty breakfasts, and why she had made all those cryptic comments about putting on weight.

'Come and sit down and get your breath back,' she said at last.

'Do you think that will make it go away?' Dolly said, still in that strange harsh voice which held such underlying terror. But she let Gracie take her back to the sitting-room and sit her down.

'Stay there while I go and speak to the Fosters. I'll tell them you're feeling unwell and we need a little longer to decide about the flat.'

She also had to ask about the rent for this fairytale place, but it hardly seemed right to mention that to Dolly just now. She fled downstairs, did what she had to, and then went back to where her friend was gazing into space.

It was so bloody unfair! They had always been such good pals. Now she was on the brink of this great adventure, and Dolly was going through hell. And all because of that bastard Jim and his lecherous ways. She ignored the thought that it took two to make a baby, and that Dolly had always been a reckless flirt, giving men the wrong idea and making herself seem like a tart.

'What does Jim say about it, Dolly?' she said, ignoring everything else. 'Is he willing to marry you?'

She gave a bitter laugh. 'Jim ain't the marrying kind. And I ain't told him.'

'But you must! It's his responsibility.'

'If I tell him he'll run off like a scalded cat.'

'Bloody good thing too,' Gracie snapped. 'Can't you see what kind of a man he is, Dolly? But if it's his child — '

'Of course it's his. I ain't been playing fast and loose with every Tom, Dick and Harry, whatever you think!'

'What are you going to do then?'

'Get rid of it, of course. I don't have much choice, do I?'

Gracie gasped. Everybody knew the risk of trying to get rid of a baby. There were methods that rarely worked. Drinking gin until you were so drunk your head swam; sitting in a steaming hot bath until your skin was red and raw; taking endless rides on roller-coasters at the Empire Exhibition amusement park . . . she could see it all now.

'One of the girls at the factory knows this woman, see?' Dolly mumbled. 'She used to be a midwife, so she knows what she's doing. I've got her address but she'll want paying, and I ain't got that kind of money. I was thinking — oh God, I know I shouldn't ask, Gracie, but I don't know where else to turn.'

'You mean you want me to pay some back-street witch to help you get rid of a baby?' Gracie said sharply. 'That's as good as murder, Dolly.'

'No, it ain't. It's my body and I can do what I like with it. And I don't want this foreign thing inside it no more. That's all it is. A bloody growth that's invading me and making me puke every morning and night.'

She stood up jerkily. 'But if you ain't prepared to help me, I'm going, before the people downstairs wonder what we're doing up here all this time.'

'They won't do that. I've just paid them the first month's rent. This is my place now,' Gracie said, far more calmly than she felt.

Dolly's eyes were wild as she took in what Gracie had just said. She was feeling sick and shaky again, knowing she could hardly expect her friend to fork out money for an abortion now. Gracie had been her last hope, but Gracie had plans and a life of her own.

Then Gracie was gripping her cold hands. 'If this is what you really want, Dolly, then of course I'll help you. It's against all my principles, but I'll help you if you're really, positively, absolutely sure.'

She had no idea about the cost. She wasn't in the habit of helping friends have abortions. But what good was money in a post office savings account when it could be giving much-needed help to a friend? Nor could she overlook the fact that but for the grace of God and Mrs Jennings's intervention on the night Percy Hill tried to rape her, she might have ended up in the same position as Dolly. And there was no way she could have borne a child of his. It was that final ugly thought which decided her.

She was rewarded by being hugged nearly to death.

'I'll never forget this, Gracie. And I'll pay

you back every penny. Old Warby wants to get another girl to share with me, and I'll agree to it when all this is over. I won't have to pay so much if I'm sharing, and I'll put the difference aside for you every week, as well as some of my wages from Lawson's.'

'We can think about all that later. Let's get out of here now and decide what we have to do next.'

Gracie locked the outer door with the keys the Fosters had given her, together with the brand-new rent book, resisting the urge to show it to Dolly with a flourish of proprietorial pride. Now wasn't the time, with Dolly clinging to her arm so pathetically. And obviously the most urgent thing to do was to find this woman who used to be a midwife and now killed unborn babies for a price.

'You could promise me something else, Dolly, but I doubt that you will,' she said, when they were on the tram taking them south of the river to the address Dolly had been given.

'Anything!'

'You'd better wait until you hear what it is first.'

Dolly was quicker than she thought.

'I suppose you want me to stop seeing Jim. Don't worry, Gracie. He knocks me about sometimes, and he enjoys making me holler. He likes to feel he's controlling me, and if he does that now, what would he be like if we was to get married? He's always bragging that he ain't the marrying kind, and he can get any girl he wants without it, so there's not much chance of that happening, and in any case I wouldn't marry him now if he begged me!' she finished.

'Well, that's the best news I've heard all day,' Gracie said, wondering how long this resolve was going to last, and realizing that Dolly was talking fast to keep her mind off where they were going, and why. She must be scared to death inside.

'No it ain't. The best bit of news you've heard is finding your own place to live, and I'm sorry if I've spoiled all your pleasure in it.'

'You haven't. I've got the rest of my life to enjoy my new home. What's important now is getting you well again,' Gracie said delicately.

The next best bit of news, ironic and unsavoury as it was to Gracie, was that the woman who used to be a midwife could do the little bit of business there and then. Though she was cautious at first, asking so many questions, wanting to know who had given Dolly her name and so on. It was understandable, considering the grisly business she was in.

But they didn't have to make an appointment, thank goodness, because by the time the inquisition ended, Dolly was looking petrified, and Gracie doubted that she'd have come back. The woman looked like anybody's comfortable white-haired grandmother, which should reassure them, but certainly didn't, knowing what was about to happen.

'It won't take long,' she told Dolly cheerily. 'Your friend can wait down here while you and me go upstairs. You've got the payment, have you? I always ask for it in advance. Some girls have been known to take fright and run before they cough up.'

'It's here.' Gracie intervened, hating the woman and her outstretched hand. She counted out the amount she was asking, and although it was extortionate, it was a small enough price to pay for the life of a child. But she mustn't think of it like that. Dolly had called it a growth invading her body, which had to be got rid of, and to her it was as lethal as the cancer that had invaded Queenie Brown's lungs.

Dolly gave her a last despairing glance before following the woman, and for the next half-hour Gracie sat on the edge of a chair, tense and upset as she heard the various sounds from upstairs. The woman muttering, Dolly screaming, Dolly sobbing . . . then at last she came tottering back to the parlour, her face as white as parchment, her eyes huge with pain.

'Take her home and give her an aspirin or two,' the woman said callously to Gracie, as if Dolly no longer existed. 'It'll start quite soon, and it'll be no more than a heavy monthly. If it's very painful get her to bed with a hot-water bottle. Be sure that it all comes away — and then forget you've ever been here,' she added.

Gracie couldn't bear to answer. She was the most despicable woman she had ever encountered. She put her arm around Dolly, and the final humiliation was to hear her whisper 'Thank you' to the female butcher.

Several taxis were driving up and down the street and Gracie waved one down. She couldn't expect Dolly to walk to the tram stop, even if she was capable. Once inside the cab she gave the driver the address of the boarding-house and held Dolly's hand tightly.

'Was it awful?' Gracie asked quietly.

'Awful, and horrible, and I don't want to talk about it,' Dolly croaked, leaning back and closing her eyes as if to shut out the whole traumatic experience.

Thankfully, the boarding-house was empty when they returned. All Dolly wanted was to curl up in bed with a hot-water bottle. Nothing was happening yet, no stomach cramps or bleeding, but they might as well be prepared for when it did. Mrs Warburton would be told that Dolly had developed a nasty stomach bug.

'She's quite poorly,' Gracie told her when she came back from the market. 'She needs to stay in bed, but I'm quite willing to see to her to save you any bother, Mrs Warburton. I can stay a couple of days.'

It was surprisingly easy to lie when there was a real need for it. She could look completely artless when she tried, and anything was better than having old Warby suspecting what was really wrong with Dolly. In any case, lodgers weren't expected to be ill or to need waiting on.

'She ain't been looking too good lately, and I hope that girl appreciates what a good friend you are,' the woman said with a small sniff.

'I'm sure she does,' Gracie said. 'Do you have any aspirins, please? I'll pay for them, and for my room and board while I'm here. And it might be a good idea if I take up a pail, Mrs Warburton, in case Dolly wants to be sick.'

And to clean up what was to come . . .

It was even easier to say the right things to win the landlady over, tactfully assuring her that the routine of her boarding-house would run with its usual clockwork efficiency and that she wouldn't be required to handle anything messy.

'I think I should take up the acting profession,' she told Dolly cheerfully.

'How about doctoring?' Dolly said, wincing as the first pains began to bite. She sat up awkwardly, clutching the hot water bottle, and swallowed two aspirin tablets with shaking hands. Almost immediately she doubled over and let out a howl of pain.

'Do you want me to send for a doctor?' Gracie asked worriedly a while later, when the pains grew worse and Dolly got progressively whiter.

'You can't!' she gasped, clutching Gracie's hands. 'Just stay with me and shove a towel in my mouth if I start shouting out. We don't want old Warby to know what's going on.'

'Well, we're at the top of the house, so you just let rip if you have to.'

They had packed the bed with old cloths that could be disposed of, so as not to soil the sheets and arouse suspicion, but by now

Dolly was in a bath of sweat.

'You see what that bastard's done to me?' she moaned, and Gracie knew she wasn't talking about the abortionist. 'You needn't worry about me seeing him again, Gracie, because I'll see hell freeze before I let him touch me again.'

'I hope you mean it,' Gracie said, wondering how much longer this could go on before anything productive happened. It had been several hours now, and it was like having to go through the pangs of labour without giving birth at the end of it. Sterile and terrible.

And then Dolly let out a louder howl than before, and staggered off the bed to squat over the pail. The soiled cloths flew everywhere, but they both ignored them as Gracie held her hands tightly and let her sob her heart out as the abortionist's work came to its bloody conclusion.

It was some while before Dolly felt able to climb back into bed, completely exhausted. Gracie covered the pail and left it where it was, while she sponged her down with water from the jug on the marble washstand.

'Maybe I should have been a nurse after all,' she said with a thin smile.

'You'd make a bloody good one,' Dolly answered, her voice thready. 'But God

Almighty, Gracie, if that's a sample of what women have to go through to have a baby, I'm never having one.'

'You'd feel differently if you were married to someone you love and it was a baby you both wanted, Dolly.'

'Oh yeah? Remind me about it in ten years' time.'

Her face was still distorted with the aftermath of pain as she turned it into the pillow. But once the ordeal was over, Gracie knew she would bounce back again. She only prayed she would remember this day and who had caused it.

'Try to get some sleep, while I dispose of this,' she said now, turning to the covered pail.

It wasn't a job she relished, but it had to be done and the sooner the better before anyone wanted to use the bathroom. She wasn't squeamish, but the thought that what she carried along the passage would one day have turned into a living, breathing baby, was enough to make her weep. What had been done today was wicked and against nature, and she would never forget the terrified look on Dolly's face as the woman took her upstairs to butcher her.

In the bathroom, she emptied the pail quickly without looking, pulled the chain on it, feeling as though she committed murder by drowning. Almost sobbing, she washed out the pail and took it back to the bedroom. Dolly was sleeping fitfully now, looking younger and more vulnerable, and as though she had never lain with a man in her life — and spoiled herself for anyone else.

Gracie shuddered. That was what they said. Spoiling yourself. But it hadn't been Dolly doing the spoiling, it had been that bastard Jim.

But seeing how much pain Dolly had endured had shaken her too. Having babies always seemed so natural. Not that Dolly's ordeal was in any way natural, but presumably the pain was the same. Having babies was something you didn't have to think about, providing it was in the right order of things. You met someone, you fell in love, you married them, you had babies. Millions of women did it, so it couldn't be that bad . . .

She shuddered again, and sometime later, when Dolly was sleeping more steadily, she went down to the dining-room where she could smell the evening meal. Gracie realized that she was ravenously hungry; it wouldn't do for both of them to miss a meal.

Later, she found that a couple of hours' sleep had clearly worked wonders for Dolly. Despite the continuing discomfort in her belly, she sat up and wolfed down the dish of rabbit stew Gracie took upstairs for her.

'Well, that didn't touch the sides, did it?' Gracie said.

'I ain't felt like eating for days now, what with the worry and feeling sick all the time. I'm telling you, I ain't never going through that again for no bloody man,' she repeated feelingly.

'Tell me that again when you find your one and only.'

'Like you've found yours? Which one is it this month? Davey or Charlie?'

'The same as it ever was,' Gracie retorted. 'And I'm going back downstairs now, before Mrs W comes up to see for herself that you're all right.'

'She won't. She don't approve of her lodgers getting sick,' Dolly said. 'Don't wake me up when you come to bed. And Gracie,' she paused, her face flushing, 'if I ain't thanked you enough for all you've done for me today, you know I'd do anything for you, don't you?'

'All I ask is that you don't get involved with rotters,' Gracie replied. 'And that's all I'm going to say about it, so get some sleep.'

All the same, she was touched by Dolly's words. On the surface, she was so tough and worldly wise, but underneath she was as vulnerable and scared as a kitten when she got caught up in something she couldn't control.

But the worst was over now, and Gracie could no longer resist telling the landlady and the other lodgers of her good fortune in renting some rooms where she was going to start her own business.

'Good for you, gel,' came Mrs Warburton's response. 'I always knew you'd make something of yourself.'

'I haven't done it yet,' Gracie said with a laugh. 'But I've got some good references from the ladies I did some work for in Southampton.'

Her face clouded momentarily, for thinking of that last commission for children's frocks came the memory of how feverishly she had worked to finish them, with her darling mother lying cold in her coffin in the next room.

By the time she went to bed, she was beginning to realize how very tired she felt. Her own excitement was entangled with the trauma of today's events, and both had begun to take their toll. After checking that Dolly was sleeping soundly, she undressed and fell into bed, and didn't wake up until morning.

'Dolly, are you awake?' she hissed, gazing towards the other bed, where Dolly's hunched-up shape was buried beneath the bedclothes.

'No, I ain't!' came her usual muffled snarl.

Gracie grinned. Back to normal then. 'Yes you are, so how do you feel?'

'How do I know when I'm not awake yet! I still hurt if that's what you mean, and I ain't going downstairs to be gawked at.'

'Dolly, nobody can tell anything. You've just had a bug as far as they're concerned, and you can't stay up here for ever.'

Dolly unravelled herself from the bed-clothes then and turned a blotchy face towards Gracie.

'They could tell I'm upset, couldn't they? And I don't want nobody's pity, nor their questions.'

'I thought you'd be glad it's all over and done with.'

'Of course I'm *glad*, but it would have grown into — well, you know. If I'd been respectably married I wouldn't have had to kill it, would I? I ain't all bad, Gracie.'

Tears streamed down her face. She had obviously had time to reflect on what she had done, and Gracie leapt out of bed and put her arms around her friend, wishing she'd never been so thoughtless.

'Dolly, of course you're not all bad, and I'm sure this is a normal reaction,' she said.

'But you're right about one thing. It wouldn't have been big enough to have resembled anything at all, and the best thing you can do is to put it behind you — and just be glad that you didn't tie yourself to that awful man.'

She wondered if she had gone too far. Dolly had been mad about Jim, but now she nodded slowly.

'I know,' whispered Dolly. 'I think I'll stay in bed this morning, though, and I'll get up this afternoon.'

'All right. Breakfast in bed for you then. And if you feel like going out later on, how about if we take another look at my new flat, and laying one small ghost.'

It was an obscure way of reminding Dolly that she had told Gracie about the baby in the rooms above the shoe shop, but in Gracie's opinion the only way to get over something was to face it head on.

'And then we can forget the other thing ever happened.'

'What other thing?' Gracie said innocently, but with a definite catch in her throat. Wicked it might have been, but in her opinion Dolly had also been very brave to go through with it at all.

13

Gracie now had the keys to the flat and once they arrived there, she was just as thrilled with it as she had been yesterday. Dolly hadn't been able to summon up much interest then, but she was always resilient. It was hard to believe she was the same frightened girl who had made such a terrible confession, and even harder to imagine she had gone through such an ordeal at the hands of the abortionist.

'You'll have to advertise your new business, of course,' Dolly said. 'Didn't you say you did that in Southampton?'

'Well, I put a card in a newsagent's window.'

Dolly snorted. 'Not good enough, now that you're a woman of property, so to speak. You've got to start thinking big, to make yourself known to customers.'

'I don't have any customers yet. I'll be starting from scratch.'

'And when you're an international success,' Dolly went on airily, 'I shall be your valued assistant, and we'll both have our names up in lights.'

'Cripes, Dolly, I thought I was the one who was star-struck! All I'm doing is setting myself up as an adequate seamstress with a special interest in making children's clothes, not some Paris *couturière* or whatever they're called.'

Dolly was exasperated. 'You know your trouble, don't you, gel?'

'No, But I'm sure you're about to tell me.'

'You always sell yourself short. You ain't learned yet that you've got to fight for what you want, and you won't do that skulking behind net curtains.'

'Is that what you think I do? I could tell you a thing or two about fighting for what I want — or rather, what I *don't* want,' Gracie said, more viciously than she intended. But she should have known it would bring a glint to Dolly's eyes.

They had had the foresight to beg some biscuits, a packet of tea and a bottle of milk from Mrs Warburton, and by now they were sprawled out on the armchairs in the sitting-room, drinking tea and dunking biscuits.

'What's *really* decided you to move back to the Smoke, then? I reckon it's summat more than losing your ma and pa. Is there summat else you're not telling me? I know you practically see yourself as the Virgin Mary, so don't tell me sailor-boy Davey tried it on with you one dark night.'

She was laughing as she spoke, but Gracie was suddenly incensed. Good God Almighty, Dolly had just gone through hell because of some lout *trying it on*, yet she could joke about such things as if yesterday had never happened. It might be the only way for Dolly to deal with it, but right then, Gracie was enraged.

'You're an insensitive pig, aren't you, Dolly?' she said furiously. 'I know you don't love anybody but yourself, but I loved my mother dearly, and my dad too, despite everything, and unlike some people I can't brush off certain things in my life as if they were of no importance.'

'Blimey, I didn't mean to upset you, Gracie! And it's not true I don't love anybody but myself. You know I don't go in for all that soppy stuff, but I think of you as a sister, and I did love Jim — or thought I did.' She swallowed hard as she said the last words, her eyes filled with angry tears.

Gracie tried to calm down. Dolly could be brash and uncaring, but however she was behaving now, swinging from one mood to the next, the fact was that her body had gone through a horrible experience yesterday. There was no denying, either, that right from the start she had fallen for Jim, hook, line and sinker.

'You know you have to put it all behind you now, Dolly. Do you really think you could pick up with him again now and not tell him what's happened?'

'I suppose not,' Dolly mumbled. 'I ain't given it much thought.'

'Well, think about it now,' Gracie went on relentlessly. 'Is he the fathering kind? Would he get upset because you got rid of his child, or knock you about for what you did? If he was the marrying kind he'd have asked you before he did what he did. I'm not saying he didn't fancy you, but in the end he only wanted you for one thing, Dolly. He thought you were easy.'

'All *right*,' Dolly almost shouted. 'You really know how to put the boot in where it hurts most, don't you, Gracie?'

'It's worth it if it's getting through to you. *Is* it?'

Dolly let out a ragged breath. 'Yes. He's a rat and I'm a pig, and never the twain shall fornicate. Ain't that the posh word for it?'

'It's one word. It would be hard though, seeing the difference in size.'

Dolly looked at her in astonishment and then burst out laughing.

'Why, Gracie Brown, I do believe there's a

smutty sense of humour lurking beneath that saintly exterior. So are you going to tell me what *really* happened in Southampton to send you scuttling up here again when you had a whole house to yourself to set up in business?'

She sighed. 'If I don't, I don't suppose you'll ever let it go.'

'No,' Dolly said, folding her arms. 'So what's the gossip?'

When she had been told, her eyes widened.

'My *Gawd*, Gracie, how old is this landlord, and what's he like?'

'He's middle-aged, paunchy, slimy and horrible, and I wouldn't fancy him in a million years, so now that I've told you, can we please forget it?'

The memory of Percy Hill's pawing hands groping beneath her skirt could still make her shudder and feel physically sick.

'You've been through a hell of a lot in these past few months, ain't you, mate?' Dolly said quietly.

'We both have. But life can only get better from now on, can't it?'

'That's the spirit! So when are you moving in?'

★ ★ ★

227

On the train home on Monday morning, Gracie realized she had nothing to keep her there now, except to say goodbye to friends and neighbours, and check with the saleroom on the sale of her things. It might have been reckless to pay a month's rent in advance on the new flat, but she daren't risk losing it, and the Fosters obviously approved of her.

They would be good landlords, Gracie thought thankfully, and now she had to think about her future properly.

Dolly had decided to go back to work on Monday, rather than raise eyebrows at the boarding-house. She was a good worker for all her scatty ways. Apart from the dark shadows beneath her eyes it was as if nothing had happened.

Gracie wondered if anyone could really forget such a traumatic event. How would she feel if it had been her, knowing that what you allowed an abortionist to do resulted in the death of a child?

She shuddered, glad to her core that such a thing had never happened to her — and never would, she vowed. She might appear to be the Virgin Mary in Dolly's eyes, but when she gave herself to a man, it would be in love and marriage. She still couldn't forget the romantic dreams of a man she would probably never meet again, remembering that in one blissful evening, when she had danced in someone's arms, she had felt admired, if not loved . . .

The train rattled on its way, and she immersed herself until the journey's end in reading the magazines she had bought on a stall at Waterloo station. Once there, she went straight home from the station, opened all the windows in the house to air it, and then knocked on Mrs Jennings's door. Her neighbour wasn't in the least surprised at her news.

'Well, it had to come, my duck, and there's no point in prolonging the agony. It was what your mum wanted, so good luck to you. Do you want me to tell old fart-face?'

'No thank you,' Gracie said with a grin, not pretending she didn't know whom she meant. 'I'll have pleasure in telling him myself, but please keep it to yourself for now, Mrs Jennings.'

'You can rely on me, love.'

Which probably meant it would be all down the street in no time, Gracie thought ruefully, but what did it matter? She had told the Fosters to expect her to take up residence in a few days' time, and she meant it.

First though, she went to the saleroom to collect her dues from the sale of the furniture. She was reasonably satisfied with the amount.

It wasn't much for a lifetime of memories, but it would help to swell the coffers, and the salespeople promised to collect the few remaining things as soon as possible and send a postal order on to her new address in London.

She couldn't deny her thrill just to say it. It also gave her the courage to go to Percy Hill's house and knock on his door, despite the way her knees were knocking when she did so.

His eyes narrowed when he saw her, and if he intended asking her in, Gracie forestalled him by standing firmly beyond the doorstep.

'I've come to tell you I'll be moving out at the end of this week. Mrs Jennings will have the rent money up until then, and after that you can do what you like with the place. I'll be glad to be rid of it.'

He blustered, his face darkly red with anger.

'And I'll be glad to be rid of ungrateful tenants who don't know when they're well off, Miss high-and-mighty. But you know damn well you're supposed to give me notice.'

She looked at him coldly. 'I'm giving you all you're going to get from me. If you want to make a fuss, you'll have to find me first, but I'm sure the authorities would be interested in knowing how you tried to take advantage of a recently bereaved tenant, especially a young girl under the age of consent.'

As his colour deepened even more, she turned on her heel and stalked away with her head held high. Let him call it blackmail if he liked. She doubted that he would ever take it further, especially with Mrs Jennings to back her up — and with every other neighbour in the street knowing what he was like.

But now she was uncertain what to do next. She had done the necessary with Percy Hill and good riddance to him. She realized she was walking aimlessly, and that she had come to the dockside where her dad used to work.

The docks were alive with workmen, creating a pungent mixture of odours and sweat, the sea-water lapping greedily against the concrete walls. The smells were familiar and distasteful, reminding Gracie poignantly of the way her dad had met his end. Nobody deserved that, whatever their failings.

For all his hard-drinking ways, she knew her dad really had cared for her mum in his own clumsy way. It was a pity he hadn't been able to control himself enough to ease her passing, though, and her brief sympathy swiftly disappeared. But before she left Southampton she had to say goodbye to them both, because she doubted that once she left for London, she would ever come this way again.

She bought some flowers from a stall and set out purposefully for the churchyard where they were buried together, according to her mother's wishes. Gracie laid the flowers carefully on the mound of soil on the grave, which had only a wooden cross to mark it out. There was no money for anything more elaborate, and Queenie had insisted that she shouldn't waste any of it on fancy grave-stones. Gracie knew it hardly mattered. What mattered more, she thought with a shiver, was that they were together for all eternity now.

'I wanted to tell you what was happening, Mum,' she whispered, glancing around in case anyone thought her crazy to be talking to a wooden cross, but the churchyard was deserted except for herself.

'I'm doing what you wanted, Mum, and moving to London. I've found a place of my own, and first thing next week I'm going to buy a new sewing-machine and then I'll be all set. Dolly thinks I should advertise my skills, to let people know I'm a willing worker.'

She swallowed. 'In one way, it will be sad to leave the house, but I'll be taking my memories with me. I may not be talking to you here for a while, Mum — and Dad,' she added guiltily, 'but I reckon I can talk to you wherever I am, so this is goodbye for the present.'

She pressed a finger to her lips and then on to the wooden cross. A small, warm wind blew across the churchyard, ruffling the petals on the flowers, and she felt a small sense of comfort, as if it was her mum giving her silent blessing.

'Is that you, Gracie Brown?' she heard a woman's voice call out, and she jerked her head around, annoyed at the intrusion into her thoughts.

Davey Watkins's mother came bustling across the uneven ground of the churchyard, her face clearly disapproving. She paused beside her, red-faced and panting, her hand pressed to her chest. At this rate, thought Gracie uncharitably, she'd be the next one for a wooden overcoat.

'How are you, Mrs Watkins?' she said automatically. 'How's Davey?'

'I didn't think you cared how he was, but never mind about that. What's all this about you having a bit of fuss with that landlord of yours? If you take my advice, you'll get away from there. Young girls living alone like you are a temptation for the likes of him. Of course, if you was married, or engaged, it would be a different matter, because then he'd have a man to deal with, even if the husband wasn't around all the time.'

She paused for breath, and Gracie almost laughed out loud at her transparency.

'A husband who might be a sailor, I suppose?'

'You could do a lot worse,' the sailor's mother said tartly.

And a lot better, Gracie added silently.

The other's tone grew more spiteful. 'You should keep in mind that mud sticks, my girl. A landlord with a loud voice is just as likely to spread the word that you were easy and encouraged him.'

Gracie could hardly believe what she was hearing, and then rage took over.

'I certainly did not encourage him. The man should be arrested for what he tried to do to me . . . '

Too late she saw the gleam in the woman's eyes. Gossips like her . . . what they didn't know, they surmised or invented, and they didn't need the added ammunition that Gracie had just given her.

'Please excuse me, Mrs Watkins,' she said, turning away. 'I've really nothing more to say on the subject.'

'Well, *excuse me*, miss!' Mrs Watkins said, clearly miffed at this response.

As the woman marched angrily away,

Gracie knew she was about to get the reputation now of being hoity-toity and above herself. But to hell with Ma Watkins or anybody else, she thought angrily. She'd soon be well away from here, and the sooner the better. She gave one last look at the wooden cross above her parents' grave.

'You were so right, Mum. I do have to go, don't I?'

She straightened up and strode away from the churchyard with shoulders squared. She had already begun to realize it wasn't just the need to get away and start a new life any more. There was an awakening ambition inside her she never really knew she had until now. *Making something of yourself* was one of her old schoolteacher's favourite sayings, while never really expecting her class of uninterested students to have any idea of what it meant. Well, now Gracie knew exactly what she meant. And it wasn't settling for marriage with someone she had known all her life, thank you very much, just for the sake of holding up her head and being a respectable married woman to please the busybody conformists.

She found herself laughing, not even knowing where such a fancy word had come from or how it had popped into her head just then. Swallowing a bleedin' dictionary, as

Dolly would have said.

But that was the point. You never knew what you were capable of until you tried, and right now, with her spirits bubbling up, Gracie felt as if the whole wide world was opening its arms and beckoning her inside.

★ ★ ★

She didn't feel quite so euphoric on the day she finally left, when she went through every room in the house where she had been born, pressing her hand against the faded places where pictures had hung, the scullery sink where her mother had toiled for so many years, the bedroom where she had dreamed her childish dreams. She breathed in the atmosphere of all that had gone before, willing it all back, and knowing that she had to let it go. Such a mixture of memories and emotions: the love, the bitterness, the rows, the pain, the sadness . . . but above all, the love. She always knew she had been loved, and that love had existed here above all else.

She swallowed deeply, said a silent goodbye, then picked up her suitcase. She closed the door behind her for the last time and walked purposefully towards the railway station without ever looking back. Some wise person had written that.

Don't ever look back or try to change things that can never be changed — and nor would she.

★   ★   ★

The euphoria returned as soon as she stepped off the train at Waterloo station and hailed a taxi to take her to the new flat. This was the beginning of a new era, and fame and fortune awaited her. Well, perhaps not *quite*, she thought realistically, but with luck and a following wind, at least a comfortable living doing what she liked best. If all else failed, she could always return to Lawson's Shirt Factory . . . and that thought alone was enough to stiffen her resolve.

She hadn't expected it to feel so different, walking into the flat and knowing that this was now home. Even though she had been here several times before, she was now seeing it through different eyes. These were her chairs, her table, her bedroom. *Hers* — and she was accountable to no one but the kindly couple downstairs who were her landlords — and a world away from the rotten apple in Southampton. Gracie gave a shiver, remembering, and then put him out of her memory for good.

By the end of that first day she had

rearranged the furniture and made the place look her own, with photographs and pictures and her own little knick-knacks and mementoes of her mother. Tomorrow she would look for a sewing-machine, and then see about an advertisement to let people know she was here.

She had been so full of optimism, but for the first time, a tiny element of doubt crept in. What if no one ever answered her advertisement? What if they thought it presumptuous of a factory shirt-stitcher to set herself up as a skilled maker of children's clothes?

At the same instant, she felt angry at her mental dithering. Everyone had to start somewhere, and if she was going to fall apart at the first hurdle, she wasn't going to get anywhere.

She was still composing the words for the advertisement, and had discarded a dozen pieces of paper, when there was a knock on her door. Her first visitor! Common sense told her it would probably be Mr Foster from below, asking if she had everything she needed. She threw open the door, smiling.

'It ain't exactly New Year's Eve, but I thought I'd come first-footing. How're you settling in, gel?' said Dolly's cheerful voice.

'All the better for seeing you!' Gracie

exclaimed, meaning it. 'You can come and help me tell the world how wonderful I am without feeling a fraud, and knowing I should be a lot more modest about it.'

'My Gawd, Gracie, you are a bit of a dummy, aren't you? Of *course* you've got to tell people you're wonderful, or how the hell will they ever know it? Blow your own trumpet a bit — or even your own saxophone, which should be much more to your liking.'

'Have you seen him?' The words were out before she could stop herself.

Dolly shook her head pityingly.

'You know the best thing you can do, don't you? Find yourself another chap p.d.q. and get Charlie-boy out of your mind. What's happened to Davey the sailor, anyway?'

'Nothing, and I'm not thinking of any chaps right now. All I want is to get these words right, so are you going to help me or not?'

'All right, keep your hair on.' Dolly grinned. 'But you can't fool me, Gracie Brown. You're still carrying a torch for that saxophone player, and it's a waste of bleedin' time if you ask me.'

'I know, and I didn't.' But secretly, she knew damn well that Dolly was right. She simply couldn't forget Charlie Morrison. He was as much a part of her as breathing — which the logical side of her told her was plain daft since she hardly knew him. But who ever took any notice of logic when they were in love? And now that the events of the past months were fading and she had a breathing-space to think about him, she knew he was as unforgettable as ever.

But right now they had to concentrate, she told herself severely. And eventually they had worded the advert to Gracie's satisfaction, having discarded many of Dolly's glowing phrases that made her sound as if she had personally made dresses for royalty.

'You have to put the ad in the newspaper, and give yourself a business name for people to remember,' Dolly advised.

'I've already thought of that,' Gracie said, forestalling any more outrageous suggestions. 'I'm going to call it Gracie's Glad Rags.'

'Perfect! Sometimes I think you've got a cleverer head on your shoulders than you ever let on.'

Gracie laughed as they moved towards the kitchen. 'Flattery will get you anywhere, even a cup of cocoa and a biscuit.'

'Gosh, thanks,' Dolly said solemnly. 'So put the ad in the paper tomorrow.'

'Not until I've bought a new sewing-machine and all the cottons and other things

I shall need to get started. I let most things go, except my scissors and pins and tape measure. So it's first things first, Dolly. I can't have people calling on me with orders before I'm properly equipped.'

'See? You think first and act later, which is what I should have done, then I wouldn't have got myself in such a mess . . . '

As her voice trailed away, Gracie turned around and saw the sudden misery in Dolly's face. She might have been frantic to have the abortion, but it had still been a traumatic experience, and couldn't be forgotten in a few days. Nor could the feelings she'd had for Jim, however much Gracie despised him.

'Does it still hurt, love? Getting over Jim — and the other?'

'Of course it bloody well hurts! I can't stand the thought of Jim now, but I know what I did was wrong. It still feels like murder, even though I tried to pretend it wasn't, and I'm never going to get caught like that again.'

Gracie gave her a hug. 'Well then, some good came out of it, didn't it?'

'Yes, your angelship, and if you don't take that bleedin' saucepan off the gas, you'll stink the place out,' Dolly said tartly, back on form almost instantly.

14

Next morning Gracie awoke with a new resolve and a simmering feeling of optimism. She had made the final break with her old life, and it was all go-ahead from now on. She popped into the shop to ask the Fosters if they knew where she could buy her sewing-machine.

'Go to the arcade on Rose Street,' she was advised. 'Try Toby Dilkes, and say I sent you. He's an old pal, and he won't diddle you, Miss Brown.'

'Thank you — and please call me Gracie.'

'Gracie it is then. Let me know when you've made your purchase and I'll collect it for you in my car.'

'Oh, I couldn't put you to all that trouble!'

'How are you going to get it back here otherwise?'

She hadn't thought. 'I suppose I expected the shop to deliver.'

Richard Foster shook his head. 'Not in bargain-basement-land. But it's no trouble, and it will give me an excuse for a chinwag with my old pal.'

As she left, Gracie thought that he was a

world away from that other landlord, whose name she wouldn't even mention, even in her thoughts. He and his wife must both be nearing retirement age now. A fleeting thought entered her mind. Supposing, after they retired, they gave up the shop. And just *supposing* she made a wild success of her business and actually employed one or two girls to help her and had a showroom downstairs . . .

''Ere, look where you're going, miss,' she heard an irate voice shout as she stepped out into the road with her head still full of impossible dreams. She jumped back, apologizing swiftly as the baker's boy wobbled on his bicycle.

So much for dreaming . . . and such things only came true at the flicks, where the poor little Cinderella girl found her prince and lived happily ever after. She wasn't even looking for her prince, just a successful life . . . although if her prince *did* come along, nothing else would matter in the world.

Her thoughts were instantly transported back to that dance-floor at the burned-out Palais, and she was floating in Charlie Morrison's arms, her heart beating fast because the look in his eyes told her he had taken a real shine to her.

She ran across the road that led down to

the arcade before the motor car honking at her should run her down, and told herself that this was no time or place for dreaming. This was London, and the traffic didn't stop for one silly star-struck girl. Charlie was probably far away from here right now, and she doubted that he had ever given her another thought.

★ ★ ★

In the West End, rehearsals for the new show weren't going well. The leading lady had a cold and the understudy was hopeless. Charlie knew it was a bad time to get on the wrong side of the musical director, who was less than impressed when the new chap approached him.

Charlie knew he'd been lucky to join a new band as their saxophone player for this brand-new show, but Feinstein wasn't interested in keen, good-looking chaps who also thought they could write their own music and expected him to include it in his productions.

'If you'd just listen to it,' Charlie pleaded for the third time.

'Look, boy, I don't have time for this. Maybe when this show's over I'll give it a hearing, but I've got all the songs I want for this production. Stick to your saxophone playing and let the rest of us get on with the business.'

The drummer smiled sympathetically as Charlie took his place on the stage.

'You won't get anywhere with Feinstein. An agent would tell you if your song's any good or not.'

'I know it's good.'

'Yeah, but if you want the rest of the world to know it, you gotta get it played. What's it called?'

'Ode to Gracie.'

The drummer shook his head. 'Much too stuffy, kid. You need something catchy. Who's the girl, anyway?'

'Someone I once knew.'

'There you are then.'

'Where?' Charlie said, started to get irritated.

'There's your title. 'Someone I once knew' will go down much better than 'Ode to Gracie'. Take it from one who's been in the business longer than you. If you want to make it a winner, you gotta make the customers feel nostalgic. Were you romantic about this girl?'

Oh yes . . . 'More or less,' he said.

As the actors came on stage, the time for talking was over, and Feinstein began ranting as usual. But it had made Charlie think. He knew damn well that the music of his song was romantic enough, but he'd never thought of himself as a lyricist and the words he had put to it didn't convey the way he really felt. The music alone had been enough to stir his soul, and he'd expected it to stir the soul of anyone who heard it. But it wasn't enough, and in his heart he knew it.

All the same, he revised his initial thoughts of getting someone else to put the words to his music. That wasn't the way to go about it, when the song was dedicated to the beautiful girl he had met on that one magical night that had ended so terribly, because the feelings she had awoken in him were his feelings alone, and not some stranger's.

'Mr Morrison, if we *could* have your full attention this morning,' Feinstein suddenly roared at him, and Charlie pushed his private thoughts to the back of his mind.

★   ★   ★

Toby Dilkes turned out to be a whiskered, dapper old boy in a fancy waistcoat. His shop in the arcade was an Aladdin's cave of sewing-equipment, from brand-new machines to second-hand ones, to all the silks and cottons anyone could need, swatches of fabric, needles, pins and measuring-tapes.

Gracie could happily have stayed here all morning, and since Toby welcomed the company on a slack Monday she spent a long time browsing. Once she mentioned her landlord's name, Toby gave a delighted chuckle.

'Me and Dick Foster go back a long way. Served in the war together, and shared some high old jinks. I don't mean this last lot with the Jerries, but the one before that, before you were born. So if Dick sent you to me, I'd say you deserve a bargain for old time's sake. Fond of sewing, are you, duck?'

'I've made my living at it. I used to work in a factory, but now I'm branching out on my own.'

'That so? I often get ladies coming in here for bits of material and needles and such like. If you want to put a card in the window, it might bring you in a bit of trade. This is the right place for it, see?'

Gracie beamed. 'I'm going to put an advert in the newspaper, but I suppose I could put a card here as well.'

'Blimey, flying high, aren't we? But it may bring you in work quicker than a newspaper advert.'

'I never thought of that, and you're sure I can leave the sewing-machine here for Mr Foster to collect?' she said, when they had finished their negotiations.

''Course you can, love, and you can tell that old rogue that I'll look forward to seeing him again to chew over old times.'

She was still smiling when she left the arcade, with the thought of the precious new sewing-machine which would be delivered soon. She had copied the wording of her advert on to a card, emphasizing that home visits could be arranged. She wouldn't want hordes of unknown people tramping up to her flat.

Now all she had to do was to find her way to the newspaper office. It was a couple of tram-rides away, and she decided she might as well enjoy her days of freedom while she had them. Soon enough, God willing, she would be too busy for days like these, when she could ride on the top deck of the tram and watch the streets of London go by.

She gave a sudden gasp, loud enough for the woman in the seat alongside her to glance sideways at her.

'Are you all right, miss?'

She answered clumsily, caught off balance.

'Yes, thank you. I just thought I saw someone I knew.'

But why on earth should it be him, when she didn't even know if he was in London, and when he could be anywhere else in the world! It had only been a fleeting glance . . . and it probably hadn't been Charlie at all. She must have been mistaken, and it was all a case of wanting to see him so much . . . And then she could see that the woman was showing interest and wanted to talk.

'Excuse me, this is my stop,' she gasped, having no idea where she was.

Her heart was beating erratically enough without entering into conversation with strangers. And she knew how stupid she was being. She was only half-sure it really had been Charlie she had glimpsed . . .

Or had she just conjured him up out of her own imagination? It wouldn't be the first time — or the last, probably.

This Is No Good, she scolded herself, when her heart eventually slowed down to its regular rhythm. Not every dark-haired young man with a particular sway to his hips as he walked — nothing like Davey's sailor's gait, but more to do with the music in his soul — could be Charlie Morrison. There must be hundreds of young men in London who fitted such a description.

But there was only one Charlie, her treacherous thoughts meandered on. Only one who had filled her dreams all this time . . . whether consciously or unconsciously.

Without being fully aware of where she had

been walking, she realized she had inadvertently arrived at the very place she was seeking. The gilt wording above the portals of this ancient building told her she was at the newspaper office.

She walked through the swing-doors as boldly as she could, hoping no one would realize the way her heart was thumping again — but for a very different reason now. She was just plain scared, and the snooty-looking young woman behind the reception desk with the rigid waves in her immaculate hair, did nothing to calm her nerves. She took a deep breath.

'I want to place an advertisement. Can you tell me the cost please?'

The girl looked up boredly, then recited her answer in a voice that was definitely more cockney than classy.

'Depends if you want it for a week or a month. Rates vary, but it's cheaper if you go long term.'

'Oh. Long term, I should think.'

'Doncha know? What's it about, anyway?'

Gracie handed over the piece of paper. The girl wasn't so intimidating now she had heard her speak, and she whistled when she read Gracie's words. It made her seem more human, and the grin that followed did the same.

'Sounds real flash. I'll give you a list of our rates, then you can decide. I'd say you'd want to keep it in the paper a few weeks, prob'ly longer. Give people a chance to find it, see?'

She knew far more about such things than a mere amateur, Gracie thought humbly, and although the cost of placing an ad for a period of time seemed horrendously expensive, she knew it made sense. Once people had read their newspapers they often took them to the fish-and-chip shop for wrapping up their suppers. Some tore them into squares to make a pad, pushed a length of string through the holes in one corner, and hung it on a wall in the lavvy. Some people never bothered looking at the adverts at all.

'I'll pay for a month and see how it goes,' she said quickly. This was her future now, and she had to think big. She had to see it as the difference between being her own boss and begging for her old job back at Lawson's.

'No — make that three months,' she went on. 'Might as well make a splash while we're about it.'

'Attagirl,' said her admirer behind the reception desk.

They smiled at one another almost conspiratorially once she had filled in the necessary form. Gracie parted with the money and got her receipt, and her new friend-of-sorts wished her luck.

By the time she went out into the sunshine again, she realized she had spent more money in one morning than she normally spent in a couple of months. But she now had a brand-new sewing-machine of the latest kind, instead of the second-hand one she had been tempted to buy, since Toby had been a pretty good salesman for all his banter. And she had blown all that money on advertising . . . but it was the only way to go about letting people know she existed. It was the way all businesses were run, and she couldn't deny the thrill of seeing her name in print when it appeared in a few days' time.

Gracie's Glad Rags was going to be put on the map, she thought optimistically, and the orders would come pouring in. She hoped.

Once back at the flat she set about turning the boxroom into a proper workroom. It was good to have a separate workplace so that she could keep all her things together — and if clients did turn up with their children to be measured or to collect the finished garments, she had the nice little sitting-room in which to show them. In Southampton she had always delivered her work to her clients' homes and she would really prefer to do the same here. You could spend too many hours bent over a sewing-machine, straining your eyes and your back . . .

'Good Lord, stop being such a softie. Any minute now, you'll be regretting taking this on!'

She had spoken out loud before she realized it, which was what people did when they lived alone or they were slowly going mad, but she didn't think she was in any danger of that. The old saying was true, though. All work and no play did nobody any good . . . which was why she found herself lurking outside Lawson's that evening, waiting for Dolly.

As her old workmates spilled out of the factory, they crowded round her, asking when she was coming back.

'Never, I hope,' she said, laughing. 'Hasn't Dolly told you I'm a woman of property now? Well, renting a flat, more like, and branching out on my own.'

'Good for you, duck,' one of the older women said. 'You were always the best stitcher among us. We always said you could do better.'

Dolly overheard and her smile was tinged with irritation.

'Gawd, don't tell her that or she'll get more swollen-headed than ever. It's good to see you though, gel. Were you waiting for me?'

'Of course.' Gracie linked her arm through her friend's. 'Now I've moved in properly I want you to celebrate with me tonight after you've had your dinner at old Warby's.'

'You ain't treating me, then?'

'Uh — well, I hadn't thought about that, but why not?'

'Oh Gracie, don't be daft. I was only kidding!'

'I'm not. Yes, let's go and tell Warby you're dining out tonight,' Gracie said, putting on a posh accent. 'I've spent so much money today a few bob more won't hurt — providing we can find a caff that don't overcharge us.'

'Going up in the world, ain't you? A nice bit of cod and chips would suit me down to the ground, and old Ma Warby hardly ever gives us any.'

'That's because she thinks we need our greens for roughage,' Gracie said.

'For farting, more like,' Dolly said, which started them laughing in the street until Dolly clutched at Gracie's arm in desperation.

'For Gawd's sake let's get going, or I'll be blowing like the wind already and frightening the horses.'

'What horses?'

★   ★   ★

Late that night, lying in the unfamiliar bed in the flat which was now home, and having looked at the brand-new sewing-machine, which was now safely installed in the boxroom, a hundred times, Gracie felt a glow of contentment. They'd had a hilarious evening, and there promised to be plenty more. She hadn't felt so good since before the fateful phone call from her father telling her of her mum's illness.

As always, the memory tempered her happiness, but Gracie knew that Queenie would never have wanted her daughter to mourn for ever. You didn't forget, but it didn't control your thinking, either. Queenie had always said that life was for living and you had to make the most of the life you were given, because you never got a second chance. Her mother was a wise old bird, Gracie thought.

She had decided by now that she should make the most of enjoying the lovely summer weather and the pleasures of the London parks before the work came in. Once it did — she mentally crossed her fingers — there would be little time for gadding about. For one thing, she loved her work, especially the smell of brand-new fabric, and she always got engrossed in creating something out of nothing, so she would probably have to force herself to take time off!

Besides which, although she had lived in London for a while before, she'd never indulged herself as a proper tourist. So during the next few days she took tram rides around the city, admiring the ancient buildings and museums; she watched the Changing of the Guard at Buckingham Palace; and spent time watching people go by in Hyde Park and feeding the ducks. She actually started to believe that she was Miss Gracie Brown of Gracie's Glad Rags now, and not beholden to anyone. It was a heady feeling.

On Saturday morning there was a band playing in the band-stand in the park. She knew in her heart that Charlie wouldn't be there, but it was no good. No matter how she tried to resist it, Gracie had to follow the sound of the music. People were sitting on deckchairs in front of the bandstand, and some of them were singing the ditties that were being played. The grass smelled sweet, and it was such a cosy scene, but of course, there was no familiar figure in the band.

'Well, well, look what the cat's dragged out of the woodwork,' she heard a man's disagreeable voice say. 'So you're back in town.'

Coalman Jim looked her up and down

coldly. He was done up a bit tidier than his normal working clothes, and she just managed not to give his fingernails a quick once-over. Draped over his arm was what she and Dolly would call a flashy piece of goods, all dyed blonde hair, scarlet lipstick, and glittery beads sitting on an unnaturally large bosom.

'Who's your friend, Jimbo?' the flashy piece said, oozing jealousy.

'Nobody in particular,' Jim said insultingly.

'How's Billy?' Gracie asked, as graciously as possible.

'How the hell should I know? I ain't his keeper, am I? Any more than you're a certain somebody else's, if you get my meaning, and you'd do better to keep your nose out of other people's business.'

There was no doubting the venom in his voice now, nor his meaning. He wasn't going to spell it out loud in front of his new lady-friend, but he was definitely letting her know he was aware of why Dolly had turned against him. Which probably meant that Dolly had been unable to resist yelling out all her pain and frustration on him after all instead of keeping her mouth firmly shut.

'I hope you're not threatening me — '

''Ere, what's going on?' Miss flashy-piece

said suspiciously. 'I thought you said she weren't nobody.'

'She ain't, babe. Nobody worth talking to, anyway.'

He pushed past Gracie, almost knocking her off balance. She didn't think she scared easily, but there had been real hatred in his eyes then, and the flashy piece was welcome to him. For a second or two she wondered what his reaction had been when Dolly confronted him, and if he really would have married her if she'd kept the baby. But the moment of doubt quickly passed as she heard his crude, honking laughter, and she knew he wouldn't have.

She was tiring of the great outdoors by now, though. The sun was hot overhead and her feet ached. It was time to go home.

★ ★ ★

As she approached she saw Mr Foster wiping down the windows of his shop-front with damp newspaper and making them squeaky-clean.

'Been taking the air, have you, Gracie? You had a lady visitor while you were out, and she said she'd like you to call after the weekend.'

'A lady?' She didn't know any ladies, unless it was one of the girls from Lawson's, but none of them could be exactly termed 'ladies'. She took the card Mr Foster gave her, and her heart gave a jolt.

On one side of it was printed the name 'Mrs Jemima Barnes-Gilbert' and a Chelsea address; and on the other there was a neat, handwritten message.

'Please call at your convenience with a view to some commissioned work. Please bring your references.'

She gasped. How could word have got around so soon? The advert wouldn't appear in the paper until Monday — but it had gone up in Toby Dilkes's window almost as soon as she left his shop. That had to be it. God bless Toby Dilkes!

'Good news?' Mr Foster said.

'I really think it is. It looks as if I'm going to get some work pretty soon. Isn't it wonderful?'

She felt like dancing on the pavement, but you didn't do that in broad daylight, so she went upstairs to her flat instead and danced around the rooms, as elated as if she had lost a penny and found sixpence.

It was beginning, just as she had known it would. And no encounters with all the hateful Jims in the world could dampen her spirits now. There was nothing like a feeling of success to send them soaring.

Her feet had miraculously stopped aching, and she was going to suggest to Dolly that tonight they went dancing, her treat. She felt reckless. This week she had already spent more money than she would normally have dreamed of spending, but it had felt good to be a woman of means, however modest. Knowing Dolly's notions of a night out, it would probably mean they'd be on the lookout for some fellows as well, and she wasn't arguing with that, either. There was no point in looking back at things that might have been. This was the start of a new life, and it was time to put the past behind her.

15

Mrs Jemima Barnes-Gilbert lived in an expensive area of Chelsea. One look at the imposing house on Monday morning, and Gracie felt ready to turn tail and run. It was practically a palace, with its white columns and steps leading up to the front door, and two stone lions guarding the gates.

She'd never been in such a house before, and she must tell every single thing about it to Dolly later. Though by now, Dolly's head was full of the bloke she had met on Saturday night, who had quickly put an end to any lingering feelings she had for coalman Jim.

Gracie's next thought was why would a lady who lived in such a house, ask for her services? She could surely have professional people doing her sewing. And what would she have been doing in the arcade in Rose Street, which was a noisy and cheerful trading place, only just a cut above market trading, and surely not the kind of place such ladies visited?

For one crazy moment, Gracie wondered if there was some sinister plot going on, and that behind those lovely long french windows there was a flourishing white-slave trade, and she was about to be drawn into it . . .

That perishin' imagination of yours will get you into trouble one of these days, Dolly used to say. And she was being perfectly stupid, standing here like a ninny. She had been invited here, hadn't she? With a view to doing some *commissioned* work.

Her chin lifted, but as she walked up the steps and rang the bell firmly, her hands were damp inside her gloves. A uniformed maid opened the door.

'I'm here to see Mrs Barnes-Gilbert. Please tell her it's Miss Gracie Brown.'

She felt almost ashamed to say it to this snooty-looking young woman, knowing that her name sounded so ordinary. Why couldn't she have been called something exotic, like Penelope or Pandora . . . and *Brown* too . . . plain old Gracie Brown, that's what she was, and what the blue blazes did she think she was doing at the door of this grand place?

The maid suddenly smiled, and she spoke in a perfectly ordinary voice, not unlike Dolly's, but smartened up a bit for proper visitors, Gracie guessed.

'Oh, good. We was hoping you'd call soon.'

'Were you?' Gracie said, taken aback as she was ushered inside. The parquet floor of the entrance hall was polished to such a shine it

262

was more like a skating rink, and there were elegant little tables with great bowls of flowers everywhere. And this was just the entrance hall . . .

'It was me that saw your card in old Toby's window, see, when I was buying some cottons, and I mentioned you to Mrs B-G straight away. Follow me, miss.'

So that answered one little question. Gracie had hardly expected a person of quality to visit Toby Dilkes's little establishment, even though it had seemed like an Aladdin's cave to her.

She followed the maid to the drawing-room, where Mrs Barnes-Gilbert was reading some letters. The girl gave a small bob and introduced Gracie to the fashionably dressed lady before leaving the room.

'Thank you, Hester,' the lady said. 'Bring us some tea, if you please. Now then, Miss Brown, before we get down to business, you have some references to show me, I believe.'

⋆　⋆　⋆

'Thank God for my ladies in Southampton who gave me the references,' Gracie said excitedly to Dolly that evening. 'You could have knocked me down with a feather when I saw the house, and I was almost ready to turn turtle. But Mrs Barnes-Gilbert was a really nice lady, and even though it's not exactly making frocks for royalty, it'll do for a start.'

'What is it then? You ain't told me anything yet, except how posh the house was,' Dolly said, sprawled out in one of Gracie's armchairs.

Gracie pulled a small face. 'Now, don't start scoffing, but her maid told me afterwards that she runs some charities — '

'Blimey, are you a charity case then?'

'Of course not. Well, not exactly. It's just that she likes to give work to small businesses where she can. And at the moment, that's me.'

'It still sounds like charity to me.'

'You would think that, wouldn't you? But if I do a good job, I'll probably get more references from her, and more work too.'

'All right, hold your hair on, I'm not running you down — '

'Well, that's what it sounds like.'

They glared at one another, and Gracie felt all her elation at the new job slipping away. And then Dolly grinned.

'You know I'm only jealous, doncha, Gracie? I think you're a bloomin' marvel, if you must know, only I don't want to keep on saying it or you'll never get your head through the door.'

Gracie laughed back, her good humour restored. 'I'm not a perishing marvel, just anxious to make a go of things.'

'You will too,' Dolly assured her. 'I can feel it in me water. So what's the job for this Mrs double-barrelled?'

'Bridesmaid dresses for her two nieces. Her daughter's getting married, and the bride's dress is a posh affair, of course, being made at some high-falutin fashion house, but Mrs B-G wanted something simple for the little girls. And she says they'd be too nervous to go to some posh place for fittings.'

'See? It's like I said. You're one of her charity cases.'

'As long as it gives me a start, I don't care. They always say oak trees grow from little acorns, don't they?'

As Dolly looked blank, she added:

'Oh, never mind. I'm just glad to have got the work so quickly, even before my advert goes into the paper, and you never know where it will lead, do you?'

'So you probably *will* be making frocks for royalty next, I don't think!'

'Or debs,' Gracie said, refusing to be down-hearted, when she had absolutely no cause to be. 'Anyway, we're not going to sit around here all evening, are we? Come on, let's go out on the town, my treat.'

'Yes, Miss money-bags!'

She didn't argue though. It was easy to dream, and Gracie had always been far more of a dreamer than Dolly. And she would be returning to that lovely house tomorrow with some swatches of material from Toby's shop, and some patterns for Mrs B-G to approve, and then she would be all set to start work. Her fingers itched at the thought. She loved making children's clothes, and she could have said on her advert that they were a speciality. But it might have prevented her from getting other work as well, and right now she needed to spread her wings as widely as possible. She tried to concentrate on what Dolly was saying, but it wasn't always easy when dreams filled your head . . .

'There's a new musical show at the Roxy,' Dolly announced. 'Why don't we see if we can get last-minute tickets? It won't matter if we're up in the gods.'

'Suits me,' Gracie said.

★   ★   ★

Much later, when she was back in the flat and Dolly had caught the tram to Ma Warburton's, Gracie decided that there was a God after all — not that she had ever doubted it really, she added hastily, in case He thought

266

she was blaspheming. Oh yes, there was definitely a God and he must have sent her guardian angel to watch over her that very night.

Why else would she have had a glimpse of someone she had never thought she would see again? It was *only* a glimpse, when the band had entered the Roxy to take their places in the orchestra pit at the front of the hall, and a tall, handsome dark-haired man with a saxophone had walked in to take his place.

'Did you see him, Dolly?' she almost croaked.

'Who?' Dolly was too busy scanning the gods to see if there were any unattached young men in the cheaper seats, and scowling at the numbers of family groups there instead.

'It was Charlie!'

'Charlie who?' Dolly asked, still minding her own business.

Gracie felt like hitting her. Couldn't she see that this was a most important moment in her life, when fate had sent her to this very place tonight, where Charlie Morrison happened to be in the band?

Dolly finally registered what Gracie had said.

'You don't mean your saxophone player?

You're going daft, you are, imagining you see him everywhere you go. I'm sure a head-doctor could put a fancy name on what's ailing you!'

She was giggling now, as a young man in a brown pin-striped suit turned and smiled at her. Then she quickly stopped giggling, as the young woman beside him pulled at his arm and glared at Dolly.

'I didn't imagine it. It *was* him,' Gracie went on.

'Well, what you going to do about it?' Dolly said sarcastically. 'Hang around the stage door until he comes out and tell him you've got a pash on him?'

'Of course not. He'd think I was crazy.'

'Ain't that what I just said?'

They were shushed by the people all around them then, as the house lights were dimmed and the band struck up the overture to the show. Gracie saw hardly any of it, even though she registered that the songs were catchy and the dancers were energetic, and there was a story of sorts. It was the music she enjoyed the most, and through it all, she was totally in tune with the mellow, seductive sound of the saxophone, and to her ears it could only be Charlie playing. His style, his rythym. She knew it was foolish to think she could distinguish it, and that Dolly would

268

probably pooh-pooh her for being so daft, saying that all saxophone players sounded the same. But in her heart and soul she knew it was him.

She was enjoying the show, though she couldn't have told anyone what the story was about. They were always flimsy stories anyway, and what really caught the eye was the singing and dancing and the beautiful costumes worn by the artistes, made of silks and satins and beautiful gossamer fabrics that Gracie would give the earth to sew.

Her creative fingers twitched at the very thought, and without warning she caught her breath as an idea hit her straight between the eyes. A wild, crazy, impossible idea, but one that she simply had to tell Dolly about or she would burst. She hissed in Dolly's ear, her voice hoarse with barely suppressed excitement.

'Somebody's got to make those show costumes, Dolly. We could do it! If I could get us a good commission, we could go into business together and make our fortunes!'

Her stage whisper was followed immediately by Dolly's guffawing laugh, resulting in everyone around them shushing them angrily.

'You're bleedin' mad, gel,' Dolly whispered back. 'I always said you were, and now I know it!'

But it was going to take more than Dolly's reaction to put her off, even if she didn't have the faintest idea how to go about getting such a commission. She didn't know anybody connected with the glamorous world of show business, and the costumes were almost certainly made by professional costumiers. The idea of two amateurs doing it was fizzling out almost before it had taken root . . .

But then she realized she *did* know somebody in show business. She knew Charlie Morrison.

⋆   ⋆   ⋆

'You're not really going to stand outside the stage door like all these idiots, are you, Gracie? I was joking earlier,' Dolly said in exasperation, after they had fought their way out of the theatre and had their toes trodden on a hundred times.

'Yes I am, but you needn't wait.'

'I'm not going to, but don't blame me if you get more than you bargained for. Some of these show-business people lead very dodgy lives, but if you're determined to make a fool of yourself, catch up to me at the tram stop.'

She flounced off, head in the air, and Gracie turned away without a minute's hesitation. Sometimes you had to do what

270

your head and your heart dictated, and right now, they were both shrieking at her that there was never a better chance of waiting for Charlie to come out of the stage door, and to talk to him on a business matter. It wasn't being star-struck, and it wasn't a crafty move just to be close to him. Not really. Not entirely.

She wouldn't let herself think that Charlie might think so, and remembered instead the way they had danced together, the feeling of being held in his arms, and the way he had looked into her eyes. There had been a definite spark between them then, and there was nothing wrong in waiting to speak to an old friend . . .

She was almost squashed in the rush of other theatre-goers eager to see anyone glamorous at the stage door, but most of them were waiting to see the stars of the show, hoping to get their autographs. It was doubtful that any of these people would be waiting for the band members. In fact, it was a very long while before any men carrying instrument cases began to appear, and by then most of the crowd had drifted away.

Gracie began to feel foolish. It had been a spur-of-the-moment thought about creating theatre costumes, and when she thought about it more sanely, common sense told her that such productions, even relatively minor ones like this one, would need a professional team of workers to create the costumes.

Such a commission would never be given to an unknown seamstress and her friend, working on their own, in a rented flat above a shoe shop.

She was almost ready to slink away into the shadows, overcome with embarrassment at her own temerity, and acknowledging that Dolly Neath had far more sense than she did in certain matters. Dolly had her feet on the ground, while Gracie was still looking at the stars. And ordinary people who did that usually fell flat on their faces.

She was pushed aside as a crowd of chattering extras came out of the stage door, followed by more band members. And there he was. Her heart beat louder than any drum, as for one, dazzling, glorious moment, she saw Charlie, illuminated in the light of the doorway before he stepped out into the night. She made an involuntary move to step forward, and then resisted it when a musical voice called out to him.

The girl was beautiful, tall and willowy with a dancer's grace, and she clung laughingly to Charlie's arm as they came outside. Gracie tried to flatten herself against the wall, but in any case, they weren't going to notice her. They were far too intent on themselves.

So much for dreams, she thought, with an unexpected sob in her throat. The sound was obviously louder than she thought, because Charlie turned and glanced her way. She was mostly in shadow, but she could see his frown, and virtually trapped as she was, she knew she would lose all her dignity if she upped and ran, even though she felt like doing just that.

But, oh God, he was moving forward, loosening the other girl's grip on his arm . . . coming towards her . . .

'Is something wrong, miss? Are you hurt?'

The next moment it was as if a small tornado was hurtling towards her as Dolly came rushing back, yelling that they were going to miss the last tram if they didn't hurry, and she wasn't going to leave her to get trampled by all these toffs. She effectively blocked her from Charlie, and to Gracie's despair she heard the glamorous girl calling him and pulling him away.

'Do come on, darling. We don't want to get caught up with these people, and we'll be late at the supper club if we don't hurry.'

'All right, Joyce, I'm coming,' he said, his voice becoming fainter as he moved out of

Gracie's sight. 'I thought I saw someone I once knew . . . '

Gracie could have felled Dolly as soon as look at her. Eyes blinded by tears, she lashed out at her with words instead, as she shook off her arm.

'Do you know what you've done?' she raged. 'Charlie was on the point of recognizing me, and you've gone and spoiled everything.'

'Oh really?' Dolly said sarcastically. 'I suppose you didn't hear that glamour puss call him darling? He's already spoken for, and you're wasting your time.'

'You don't know *anything*, do you?' Gracie said furiously. 'People in the theatre call each other darling all the time. It doesn't mean anything.'

'Oh, come on, stop going on about the bloke. We'll get arrested for hanging around on street corners if we're not careful. You and your crazy ideas! We'll have to run for the tram now, and I want to get home sometime tonight.'

It had all gone sour for Gracie now. One minute her hopes had been as high as the sky, with her wonderful, unrealistic idea of creating spectacular stage costumes, and having an excuse to speak to Charlie.

She had already imagined his eyes gazing at

her wonderingly, joyfully . . . and then Dolly had come blazing along to spoil it all. As they jogged along on the rattling tram towards home, she was plunged into misery and fury. But as the usual late-night revellers catcalled to them, and Dolly answered back in kind, she began to think how pointless it had all been.

'Sometimes I think I need you to keep my feet on the ground,' she muttered by way of an apology for her temper.

'Didn't I always tell you so, gel?' Dolly said cheekily, half her mind on one of the lads winking at her from the back of the tram. 'Forget him, and I'll see you in the park on Sunday afternoon.'

As she climbed the stairs to her flat, Gracie thought that Dolly was right about a lot of things, but not everything. She was fast realizing that making theatrical costumes wasn't for the likes of them. And not *all* stage artistes called one another darling without meaning something more, but as for forgetting Charlie Morrison . . . well, she agreed that that was sensible advice, but who ever thought sensible thoughts when you were in love?

All the same, it was the closest she had been to Charlie ever since the night of the fire, and she might be able to block out those wayward thoughts while she was awake, but dreams were out of her control, when the wildest, most romantic things could happen, and often did.

★ ★ ★

Gracie knew that the best thing to do when the heart was involved was to plunge straight into work matters. She got the swatches of material from Toby's shop and presented them and the patterns to Mrs B-G to their mutual satisfaction. Later she was introduced to the small bridesmaids.

The seven-year-olds weren't intimidated by this very pretty girl with a mass of red curly hair and laughing blue eyes who told them funny stories while she measured them, especially when she had a mouthful of pins that fascinated them both, as they wondered, half-hopefully, if she was about to swallow them every time she spoke.

But by now Gracie was impatient to see her advert in the newspaper, and when at last it appeared, it looked gloriously professional. Even Dolly was impressed, as were the elderly couple in the shoe shop downstairs.

'Old Lawson saw it as well,' Dolly informed her in the park that Sunday afternoon. 'He was even bragging about it to the girls, just as if he'd taught you everything you know, and he said he always knew you'd make good.'

'Pity he never said it while I worked for him, then!'

'You were always his star machinist, Gracie.' She sat up and looked at Gracie quizzically. 'What's up? I thought you'd be over the moon now you're so famous, but you look as if you've just lost a tanner.'

'I'm not famous just because I've got my name in the paper,' Gracie said crossly. 'You can be so daft sometimes, Dolly.'

'Well, pardon me for breathing, I'm sure. What is it then? You're not still mooning over that Charlie bloke, are you?'

'No. If you want to know, I've given up thinking about him.'

She didn't add that she could hardly stop dreaming about him, but that was something Dolly didn't need to know.

'Thank God. Now perhaps we can find a couple of blokes to suit us both.'

'I'm not looking for a bloke at all.'

Dolly stared at her as if she had grown two heads. 'Are you planning to be a nun or something?'

'Of course not. I just want to earn my living at what I do best, that's all.'

Dolly relaxed. 'Yeah, well, I aim to find me a bloke with enough money so I don't ever have to work again. That's my ambition.'

'Why doesn't that surprise me?' Gracie asked with a grin.

'There's nothing wrong in it. Wouldn't you like to be a lady of leisure like your Mrs double-barrelled, sitting around all day putting flowers in vases and having a maid to see to the children and all that stuff until your adoring husband comes home from work and makes mad, passionate love to you?'

Gracie laughed as Dolly got more and more enthusiastic, and several passers-by tut-tutted as they overheard Dolly's last words.

'For goodness' sake, Dolly, put a sock in it. People will think we're a couple of tarts.'

'You can't tell me it don't appeal to you! The truth now, Gracie.'

'Oh, all right, of course it does. But I'd soon get tired of being so idle, and I'd still be making clothes for the children, even if I had a dozen of them.'

'Blimey, gel,' Dolly said with a grin. 'You and your old man are going to be kept busy in the bedroom department then, aren't you!'

★ ★ ★

A couple of weeks later, Charlie Morrison unwrapped his fish-and-chip supper from the newspaper without much interest, his mind on other things.

Or rather, on some*one*. The minute he'd said those words to Joyce after the show at the Roxy that night, he knew why the girl outside the stage door had seemed vaguely familiar.

I thought I saw someone I once knew.

The words echoed the title of his song that he was now toting around the music publishers . . . 'Someone I once knew' . . . and he was sure that the girl outside the stage door had been that someone. She had been Gracie Brown, and she was as elusive as trying to get his song published. In a way the two seemed to go together. If fate dealt his cards successfully, then once he found someone to publish his song, he would find his true love, because in his heart they were one and the same. The 'someone' in his song was the elusive Gracie Brown.

As if to taunt him, his eyes were drawn briefly to an advertisement in the discarded newspaper. Or perhaps it was simply because her name was so dear to his heart that he expected every Gracie in the world to be her.

He put his fish and chips on a plate and screwed up the paper quickly, disgusted at himself for being a sentimental fool. She would have forgotten him long ago. A beautiful girl like her would have a dozen young men wanting to marry her, and he was wasting time in dreams instead of putting all his energies into his work. He was tiring of being constantly on the move with the band, and he just wanted to be a songwriter.

Besides, if he really had marriage in mind, he knew Joyce was ready and willing. The band-members always said she sang her soulful songs just for him and he could do a lot worse. They were in the same business, and they were fond of one another . . . but he didn't love her as a man should love his wife, and Joyce was too fine to settle for being second best.

The stray cat who had lately acquired him as its owner came swathing around his legs, purring seductively, and he laughed at her antics.

'All right, Cat, you want to share my supper, do you?'

He picked up the newspaper again, smoothing it out and putting it on the floor ready to break up a piece of his fish for the cat. And just as quickly, he picked up the paper again, his heart jumping. The cat would have to wait.

It was sheer coincidence that he had spread out the paper so that Gracie's name leapt up at him again. But Charlie didn't believe in coincidences unless they were there for a purpose. He had seen the girl the other night, or thought he had, unless she was a ghost who was haunting him. And now this name was in bold letters, leaping up as if inviting him to find her.

'And what would I be doing, visiting a strange woman at this Gracie's Glad Rags and asking for alterations instead of going to a tailor? She'd probably think I was turning the other way!' he said aloud, mocking himself.

The cat purred more loudly, clawing at Charlie's trousers, and clearly seeing its chance of a choice bit of haddock slipping away. At the intrusion, Charlie chopped up the fish almost savagely, before sliding the cat's portion on to the paper and blotting out the advert altogether.

But the night was hot, and later, with thoughts that should have been long forgotten still vivid in his mind, he rescued the greasy paper from the waste bin and copied out the name and address. It would probably be some old girl, trying to make ends meet by taking in sewing, but when he had the time and inclination, he intended to find out, and to exorcise the ghost of another woman called Gracie, once and for all.

16

During the next weeks there were too many fractious rehearsals and last-minute changes to the show at the Roxy theatre for Charlie to think about putting any such thoughts into action.

On a day when tempers were particularly stretched to near boiling-point, the leading lady threatened to walk out half a dozen times, one of the dancers broke an ankle and was carted off to hospital, and a piece of the scenery came crashing down, Charlie was summoned to the musical director's office.

Feinstein continually prowled around the room, wreathed in a haze of cigar smoke, the half-empty bottle of whisky on his desk attesting to the fact that he had marginally calmed down from the day's rantings.

'You wanted to see me, sir?' Charlie said, wondering what he'd done to blot his copybook. Feinstein rarely summoned anybody to his sanctuary without good cause, and even more rarely to the artiste's benefit.

'Sit down, boy, you're making the place look untidy,' the man said, waving him irritably to a chair. 'I've been thinking about you.'

Charlie felt his heart sink. This was definitely not good news. Then Feinstein retreated behind his desk and smiled, flashing his gold fillings.

'It's about that song of yours. I'm not saying we're going to use it, mind, but before this entire show goes up in smoke, we need something new to pep up the second act. The tune sounded catchy enough the one time I heard it, but unless you have lyrics as well, it's no good to me.'

Charlie was stunned for all of five seconds. It was the last thing he expected to hear, but he recovered quickly. Feinsten had to time for ditherers.

'Yes, there are lyrics,' he said swiftly. 'I've been trying to find a music publisher to produce it, as a matter of fact, but if it got a hearing in the show . . . '

He didn't need to go on. *Couldn't* go on, because there was a such a lump in his throat. If it got a hearing in the show and people liked it, he'd be made. Music publishers would be seeking him out, instead of the other way around.

'Do you have it here?' Feinstein went on. As Charlie nodded, he stood up and went on testily: 'Then let's hear it. Get that young

Joyce Wilkinson to sing it. She can hold a tune better than most around here. Chop-chop now.'

Charlie shot out of the office. Joyce didn't always come in for rehearsals that didn't involve her, but these days, with Feinstein in his present mood, it didn't pay to be absent. Much to his relief, he found her and grabbed her around the waist.

'Feinstein wants to hear my song, and he wants you to sing it. You've heard it and you've seen the lyrics, so are you game?'

'Of course. Oh Charlie . . . '

She didn't need to be told what this might mean. She gave him a quick hug and then he was off to find the pianist. The song would work best with the whole band, especially with Charlie's plaintive saxophone accentuating the music, but for clarity of sound, the pianist and Joyce's husky voice would do.

Ten minutes later, after listening intently, Feinstein sat thoughtfully stroking his chin. The kid had something, that was for sure, but there was something not quite right.

'Who's this Gracie in the lyrics? There's no Gracie in the show. You'll have to change that if we're going to use it.'

'No,' Charlie said flatly. 'The song is dedicated to Gracie, to someone I once knew, and it stays the same, or I don't let you have it.'

There was a shocked silence. Nobody dared to defy Feinstein unless they risked being thrown out.

'And you can't have a girl singing about another girl,' the pianist put in.

Charlie began to feel reckless. It was clear now that Feinstein wanted to use his song. It was good, as he had always known.

'I know. The male lead should sing it, especially with an extra scene — '

Feinstein was screaming now, his nervous temperament erupting. 'You damn pipsqueak, telling me what I have to do.'

The leading lady hovered nearby; she put a restraining hand on his arm. 'It wouldn't take much of a rewrite, sweetie, and Charlie's right. Ralph can sing the song, and we could have a sort of ghostly scene going on in the background with this unknown Gracie. Maybe she's died, and he has to move on to someone new — meaning me. Whadda you say, Feiny? Let's face it, at the moment the show's too static, and this will put some romance back into it.'

Charlie held his breath. The leading lady was forty if she was a day, but once she was on stage she was transformed into a stunning beauty, like a butterfly emerging from a chrysalis, and she could twist Feinstein around her little finger.

'Get Ralph,' he barked out. 'Let's see what he makes of the lyrics first.'

★ ★ ★

Charlie phoned his parents that night.

'I still can't believe my luck. One minute I thought I was going to be slung out of the show, and the next, they're using my song, and Feinstein reckons that once the critics hear it the music publishers will come running, and there'll be thousands of sheet-music copies of it before you can say Open Sesame.'

His father was congratulating him and he was sure his mother was crying in the background. It wasn't so far from his own feelings. If this song worked and he made enough money from it, he would be able to give up touring and set himself up as a proper composer and lyricist.

'It's wonderful news, Charlie, and it's time you came home to celebrate your success with your family as well as your theatre friends. Your mother misses you,' his father added meaningly.

Charlie was too wrapped up in the thrill of what was happening to do other than agree.

He hadn't been home for several months, and he promised to do so as soon as he could. No doubt his mother thought that now that success was beckoning so fast, Charlie would be thinking of settling down, getting married and producing the grandchildren she craved. Well, so he might, in time, but not unless it was with the right person.

★ ★ ★

Feinstein was a fair businessman, and he advised Charlie to register the song in his own name. He paid him handsomely for the use of it in the show, and the arrangement would continue for as long as the show ran. But now Charlie needed an agent to deal with the business side of things, and from then on, everything proceeded so fast he didn't know if he was on his head or his heels.

The agent knew a music critic who would be in the audience on the night the new scene was included. He introduced him to Charlie after the show, and the next day Charlie Morrison's name was blazoned all over the theatre pages of the newspapers as the new songwriting discovery of the year, together with several photographs of the cast, including one of him and Joyce looking very cosy together, and clearly speculating on their relationship.

'My mother will enjoy seeing that,' Charlie said. 'She'll probably think wedding bells are in the air now I'm about to become rich and famous.'

Joyce laughed. 'Oh well, you know how the gossip rags love to make something out of nothing, but we both know it's not going to happen, don't we, darling?' she teased.

She kissed him lightly on the cheek before he could say anything to embarrass them both, and thought that whoever his Gracie was, she didn't know what she was missing.

*   *   *

On Sunday Gracie was up early, putting the finishing touches to the bridesmaid dresses. They weren't needed for another month, but she had always been a quick worker, which always produced satisfied customers. Her mum would be proud of her. She had been thinking about Queenie a lot lately, and wishing she could see how well she had got on.

She could never quite resist dreaming of the day when she might be creating such pretty garments as these for the attendants at her own wedding, but the other, more

288

practical part of her head was considering using her skills to make a stock of children's clothes and set up a market stall. It was only a vague idea at present, and she wasn't really sure if it was right for her. She couldn't see herself yelling out her wares like some of the cheerful market traders did.

The clothes would be exclusive, made to her own designs, and she could easily make them in between the orders that kept the money coming in. It might be a small step on the ladder of success, but it wouldn't exactly compare with getting commissions from the likes of Mrs Jemima Barnes-Gilbert!

By now she had given up the wild idea of being a theatre costumier, knowing instinctively that such work took years of professional training. She was also pretty sure Dolly didn't really want to be her working partner, and she certainly wouldn't agree to being just her assistant. Working together at Lawson's Shirt Factory was one thing. But fond as they were of one another, they would probably squabble far too much if they were together constantly without other people to act as buffers.

She was brought quickly down to earth as she stabbed a pin into her finger. She winced at the sudden sting, though she was more concerned that there should be no blood on the delicate fabric she was working on. She smiled wryly at her own fantasies, but there was nothing wrong with dreams, and for some people they even came true.

A sudden clatter of someone coming up her stairs two at a time made her jump. The footsteps were followed by a loud thumping on the door, and then Dolly came bursting in, waving a newspaper in her hand.

'Well, come in, why don't you?' Gracie exclaimed, half-annoyed that for a moment she had been scared. 'I thought I wasn't seeing you until this afternoon. And what the heck are you doing up so early of a Sunday morning?'

'I ain't even had breakfast, but never mind all that,' Dolly gasped, holding her side from the stitch she was getting in all her agitation. 'Have you seen this? One of the early birds at Ma Warburton's was reading it out loud this morning. It's last week's rag, but he ain't too quick with his reading matter. Anyway, of course you ain't seen it, or you wouldn't be looking so bloomin' cheerful, but I s'pose you'd have to know sometime, so I thought I might as well show it to you.'

She paused for breath, breathing heavily. Gracie knew she wouldn't get any more work done until she knew what was up, so she abandoned her sewing, covering the bridesmaid dresses in tissue paper to protect them.

'Well? Is it my advert? Were they so surprised to see it at Ma Warburton's? I suppose they didn't think I'd be so bold as to put it in the paper,' she added, feeling miffed if that had really been their reaction.

'For God's sake, Gracie, stop going on about your bleedin' advert,' Dolly screamed. 'It's nothing to do with that. It's your chap, the one you took such a fancy to. The saxophone player.'

Gracie's heart lurched, and for a moment the room spun.

'What's happened to him?' she whispered.

Her imagination soared crazily. Because she had been thinking about her mother so much lately, her thoughts immediately went to her father and his grisly fate. Not that Charlie could have drowned — well, of course he could, if he'd gone over one of the bridges into the Thames, either by accident or worse — but he wouldn't have been out of his mind with drink like her Dad — or maybe he would. How well did she know him after all? She didn't know him at all . . .

'Are you all right, Gracie? You've gone the colour of that tissue paper. Shall I get you some water, or should I fetch somebody?'

She heard Dolly's anxious voice as if

through a fog. Then she registered the ludicrous thought that Dolly couldn't be doing with illness, so she had better pull herself together, or she'd be the one fetching somebody to see to Dolly.

'I'm not going to faint,' she managed to snap. 'You gave me a shock, that's all. Show me the ruddy paper then, can't you?'

She had been so stupid to think the worst. Why should it be?

Dolly handed her the paper silently. It was open at the theatre reviews, but she barely scanned the enthusiastic piece about the show at the Roxy, and how it had been revived by the inclusion of a brand-new scene that was totally transformed by a song by a new and exciting young songwriter.

All she saw was the photo of Charlie Morrison with his arm around the sophisticated girl she had seen coming out of the stage door with him. The same girl who had called him 'darling', and who was now looking up at him so adoringly and possessively in the photo. The gushing text beneath the photo implied that these two were more than cosy.

'I'm real sorry, Gracie,' she heard Dolly say more falteringly. 'It looks as though there'll be wedding bells for them two soon, don't it?'

Gracie crunched up the newspaper and

flung it away from her.

'Sometimes I *hate* you, Dolly Neath!'

'Well, if that's all the thanks I get, I wish I'd never bothered gettin' out of bed this morning,' Dolly yelled, scrambling to her feet at once. 'I was only doing what I thought was best.'

'Oh Dolly, I didn't mean it. I don't even know what made me say it. It's just that I feel so — so . . .'

She shook her head wildly, not knowing what she was trying to say, nor if she could ever put it into words. How could you describe a broken heart? Poets could do it, but she was no poet. She was just an ordinary girl, and you had to feel the pain of heartbreak to know what it really meant . . .

Such feelings were far too private to be talked about; you didn't want to howl out loud that your stomach felt as if it was turning to water, that your legs had no substance in them, no bones to hold you up, and your eyes felt as if they held an ocean of tears just waiting to brim over; you couldn't say any of that, you could only feel it. She drew in a shuddering breath.

Dolly was still watching her uneasily.

'It probably ain't true, anyway,' she said at last. 'You know what these rags are like. They'll say anything.'

''Course it's true,' Gracie said angrily. 'You heard her call him darling, same as I did.'

'You said all show business people did that. You said it meant nothing.'

'I know what I *said*. And I know what I think. And I don't want to talk about it any more. I don't want to hear his name mentioned again, either.'

Dolly was really alarmed now, wondering what this unusually aggressive Gracie was about to do. As her stomach rumbled, she snapped at her.

'You're being a bit daft over this bloke, I reckon. What are you going to do then? Shall I go away and come back this afternoon like we agreed?'

She didn't really think she should leave Gracie alone. She could tell by her clenched hands that in this mood, she was more likely to hack at the delicate fabric she'd been working on, than make her usual perfect job of it.

As if in silent agreement, Gracie looked at the pile of work beneath the tissue paper, which she had taken such a pride in, and now felt like hurling the lot out of the window. In her heart she knew this was only a temporary thing, and that in work lay her salvation. But she wasn't thinking sensibly now, and she didn't want to slave over the bridesmaid dresses. She would rather be working on one of Lawson's ruddy shirts than suffer the irony of helping prepare for another bride's beautiful day.

'I'm not working any more today, nor staying indoors. Let's go out for the day, somewhere different — to the seaside if you like.'

'Blimey, you don't do things by halves, do you?' Dolly said, but she was more relieved than she let on.

That wild look in Gracie's eyes just now had been really scary, and it wasn't until that moment that she knew how much Gracie had wanted the saxophone player. She'd have given anything not to have burst in with that perishin' newspaper, but you couldn't change what was already done. But thankfully Gracie's colour was returning to her cheeks now.

'Are you game then? I could make us a few sandwiches to eat on the beach, but whatever we do, I'm not staying indoors all day.' Gracie was sharper than usual, and she couldn't stand much more of Dolly's scrutiny.

''Course I'm game. When did you ever know me to miss the chance of a day out, 'specially by the sea. You never know, we might meet the men of our dreams,' she said recklessly, before she stopped to think. 'Oh Gawd, I'm sorry.'

'Well, don't be. I told you, I don't want to hear *that* name, nor to even think about *that* person any more, but I'm not turning myself into a nun on his account, neither,' she added for good measure.

'Attagirl. Chaps ain't worth it, and there's plenty more pebbles in the sea.'

She hooted, realizing what she had just said. 'Did you hear that? There's plenty more pebbles in the sea, and we're off to the seaside.'

'I heard,' Gracie said, forcing a smile. 'You're a real brain-box today, aren't you, Dolly?'

To her surprise she was given a quick and embarrassed hug.

'That'll be the day. I just want to be the best friend you ever had, gel. I don't forget what you did for me over my bit of trouble, so I mean to make sure you're feeling cheered up by the time we get back.'

Gracie was touched and embarrassed, and mumbled that she was already the best friend she'd ever had, just by keeping her sane. And that if she didn't hurry up and cut these bloomin' sandwiches, there'd be no point in catching a train to take them to the seaside.

Dolly could see she was already on the up.

She wanted to tell her how much she admired her guts, but if she did, she was sure there'd be tears or fury, so for once she let things be — providing Gracie let her eat one of the sandwiches right now, before she faded away completely.

★ ★ ★

An hour or so later they were being jostled and squashed on one of the rattling excursion trains to the seaside, which they had caught by the skin of their teeth.

'Margate, here we come,' Dolly said gleefully, giving a wink to a couple of fellows in their compartment.

'You girls meeting anybody?' one of them said.

They were about their age and both wore open-necked shirts and jackets over loose-fitting trousers, like most of the young chaps off on a day's outing. Dolly was still deciding how to handle this one without riling Gracie too much, when she realized her friend was forcing a smile at them.

'Not until now,' Gracie said, with what was undoubtedly a flirtatious note in her voice. 'Must be our lucky day, eh Dolly?'

An older couple in the compartment glanced at one another, clearly thinking they were girls out for a lark, and probably up to no good.

The chaps grinned.

'Ours too, eh, Norm? This is Norm, by the way, and I'm Roger. Roger the lodger, or as some say, the artful dodger.'

He winked at Gracie, and she tried not to cringe. Norm did the same to Dolly, who was giggling under her breath by now as they neatly paired them off.

'Don't take no notice,' Norm spoke up. 'He's as straight as a die, really.'

'So what do you girls do, then?' Roger continued as if he hadn't spoken.

Dolly had recovered by then.

'I'm a machinist, and my friend here is a professional seamstress. She makes clothes for all the nobs.'

'Is that so?' Roger said. 'I could do with a new shirt, couldn't you, Norm?'

Dolly dug Gracie in the ribs, thinking that this comment was too close for comfort when she was trying to give themselves airs. These two didn't look too bad, and at least they were scrubbed up for the day, with clean hair and nails, no sign of whiskers on their chins, and their hair cut short and neat.

Anyway, as long as they cheered Gracie up and got her mind off that blooming saxophone bloke, she'd be well happy.

'Fancy dipping your toes in the sea then, girls? If you want to team up with us for the day, we'll treat you to a bag of whelks for your dinner.'

Gracie spoke quickly, since the very thought of it could make her stomach curdle.

'Ta very much, but we've got our own sandwiches — '

Dolly dug her again. 'I daresay we could share them with you in exchange for a bag of whelks, couldn't we, Gracie?'

Gracie glowered at Dolly. This was going too far, but she'd reckoned without the way Roger had sensed her reaction.

'Nah. We wouldn't want to deprive you. So you're Gracie with the ginger curls, and you're Dolly, is that right?'

'Right,' said Dolly. 'So what do you both do?'

'We're home on leave from His Majesty's good ship *Bountiful*,' Norm said. 'You'd think we'd have had enough of the sea, but at least we'll have sand beneath our feet and not the jolly old rolling decks.'

Gracie stared at them as the train rocked along at breakneck speed.

'You're sailors!' she exclaimed.

'Full marks, Gracie.' Dolly sniggered.

'No, what I mean is, I knew another chap who was a sailor.'

'She was practically engaged to him!' Dolly put in.

'His name's Davey Watkins, and he lives in Southampton. I don't suppose you know him?'

Roger grinned. ''Fraid not. It's a big Navy, love. Still, it's our good luck that you're not engaged to him any more, or you wouldn't be on this train with us now, would you?'

'We're not exactly *with* you,' Gracie said, already realizing she had gone a bit far, and annoyed with Dolly for making her relationship with Davey seem more important than it was. On the other hand, it might not do any harm to let these chaps think there was still something between them both.

'I'm still very fond of Davey, though, and we still write to one another often,' she fibbed.

'What ship's he on, then?'

At Roger's question, Gracie knew she had backed herself into a corner, because she couldn't even remember the name of Davey's ship, and it wasn't something you could invent on the spur of the moment.

Before she could gather her wits and think of something intelligent to say, the train lurched around a bend in the tracks.

'Whoops, hold on to your hats, girls, the driver's been on the beer already.' Norm laughed, and then came a second lurch, and the bag of sandwiches on the overhead rack came hurtling down on Dolly's lap and split open on the floor.

'Well, I know I was hungry, but I wasn't ready for my dinner yet,' she said with a little screech of laughter, and then the older lady in the compartment clutched her husband's arm.

It was hard for any of them to say exactly what happened next. One minute Norm and Roger were scrambling about, trying to scoop up the ruins of Gracie's sandwiches, and saying they'd have to settle for a bag of whelks after all.

In the next, everyone in the compartment was thrown together in a heap. Somewhere outside they could hear the sound of screeching metal and a horrific sound of something splintering. For a second their compartment seemed to waver on the track, and then nothing could stop it following in the chaotic wake of the ones nearer the front of the train. It toppled over on to its side, the windows caved in, and shattered bits of glass and twisted metal shot everywhere.

The warm summer days had merged into a lingering mellow autumn. The ground was baked, grass and farmland was tinder-dry, and clouds of choking dust immediately enveloped the derailed train to add to the confusion. There was so much shouting and screaming that it was impossible at first to tell who was hurt and who wasn't.

'Are you all right, girls?' they heard Norm shout.

'I don't know. I think so,' a voice came faintly from where Gracie and Dolly had been sitting. And then the man travelling with his wife screamed frantically.

'Somebody help me. My wife's not breathing. She's bleeding.'

The couple had been sitting by the window, and because of the sharp angle at which the compartment had crashed, the other carriages had been in danger of crushing them. It was only the tough training of the sailors which made them hang on tight and prevent a worse accident.

Ignoring their own cuts and bruises, they scrambled to where the man was clinging on to his wife in the middle of a chaotic mess of tangled metal and debris. They could see at once that the woman was dead. A huge shard of glass was sticking out of her neck, and the scarlet artery-blood was bubbling out profusely.

'Should I pull the glass out?' the man said pathetically.

'I should leave it where it is, mate,' Roger

said quickly. 'It won't make any difference to her now.'

The man howled like an animal as he realized what Roger meant, but by then the two sailors had turned back to see what was happening with Gracie and Dolly. It was still difficult to see properly, but as dust stung their eyes and dried their throats they could make out the two girls huddled together.

'Are you all right?' Norm said hoarsely, trying not to gag.

'One of us is,' came a terrified voice. 'I'm not sure about her though.'

17

Dolly awoke with a blinding headache. She had no idea where she was, and it felt as if her brain had been scrambled. It hurt like stink to look at the light, so she decided it was far better to keep her eyes tightly closed.

She was surrounded by horrible antiseptic smells, but there were even worse ones that she didn't care to identify. It made her want to puke, momentarily taking her mind off the feeling that her arm was being stabbed by red-hot needles.

She realized that she *was* being stabbed by red-hot needles, or at least, by one very sharp and very long needle, and she risked opening one eye to look at the vampire in nurse's uniform bending over her.

'What are you doing?' she croaked. 'And where the hell am I?'

'You're in hospital, my dear,' the nurse said briskly, not pausing in her efficient stabbing with the needle that made Dolly's senses swim. 'Do you remember your name?'

''Course I do. I'm not bleedin' stupid,' Dolly said crossly, and then paused, her stomach turning cartwheels. What the hell was her name?

'Never mind,' the vampire continued. 'It'll come back to you soon.'

'Oh really?' Dolly said, trying hard to be her usual sarcastic self, and failing miserably as the stuff in the needle was already doing its job.

She made one last effort.

'All right, Nursie, have I been in an accident, or is this a fancy dress party and you're the chief ghoul?'

The nurse laughed, but the bravado was slipping away from Dolly by the second. She was starting to feel stupid and close to tears, and whatever she was told after that was lost on her as she lapsed into dreamland again.

The nurse reported to the ward sister that the one the young men had called Dolly was still very vague, and as for the other one . . .

'It's a bad business altogether,' the older woman said. 'Were they travelling together on the train?'

'It looks like it, though the young men discharged themselves smartly to return to their ship in Portsmouth.'

Sister made a few choice comments about flighty young men who couldn't be bothered to stay at the hospital long enough to see how their girlfriends fared after an accident in which four people were killed, including an elderly lady in the same compartment.

'Don't speak to any newspaper reporters,' the sister warned the nurse. 'Doctor Grayson will give an official statement in due course, but we don't want those scandalmongers cluttering up the wards.'

★ ★ ★

The news about the derailment of the excursion train half-way to Margate made headline news for a day and was then relegated to the inside pages with the usual news that an investigation was in progress. Considering that the train had been packed with day-trippers, fatalities were few, and those who had been taken to a local cottage hospital were said to be recovering quickly from their ordeal.

Mrs Warburton assumed that Dolly was staying with Gracie, and when she didn't turn up for work on Monday, her boss decided she'd taken the huff at being rebuked lately, and if she wasn't such a good worker, he'd be bloody well tempted to give her her cards.

Since Gracie was completely self-contained in her flat and worked alone, nobody realized she wasn't there. The Fosters, in the shop and flat below, kept themselves to themselves, and were more than happy with their quiet new tenant.

A week later a young man came looking for Gracie's Glad Rags. Confronted with a shop window full of shoes, he checked the newspaper advert, wondering if he'd got it wrong. He stood outside for so long that he attracted attention, and the proprietor came out to ask if he needed any help.

'I'm not sure,' Charlie said. 'I was looking for a young lady called Gracie. I think her name may be Gracie Brown.'

He realized he was being studied carefully, and knew that he didn't look the type of person to be looking for a seamstress in an out of the way location. He was smartly dressed, his dark hair shining as usual, both with health and the required brilliantine for musicians.

'Perhaps I've made a mistake, but the advert in the paper gave this address.' He held out the piece of paper to show the man, embarrassed at the greasy state of it. But Mr Foster concluded that the chap looked too sincere to be a gigolo, despite that glossy black hair that was a shade too long, in his opinion, but he had also noticed that his shoes were polished to perfection, and that meant a lot to a man who had spent his life in shoes, so to speak.

'You've come to the right place, young man, and it's up the stairs to the flat above. I'm not sure if the lady is at home though, as I haven't heard her moving about recently. But you try ringing her bell.'

And I'll stand at the foot of the stairs to see there's no funny business going on when she answers, he said to himself.

Charlie resisted the urge to bound up the stairs two at a time. As he rang the doorbell, the delicious thought spun through his mind that there was now only a thin piece of wood between him and the girl whose image had been haunting him all these months. He knew he had been tardy in trying to find her, but something always seemed to get in the way; a tour with the band; the excitement of the show; the need to make some money; the urge to write his song and prove himself . . . and besides all that, why should she even remember him?

He knew her name, because it had been given in the newspaper after the fire at the Palais, together with her photo. He wished he had kept the photo, but the band had been on the move, and it had simply disappeared, just like her. Sometimes the Gracie of his dreams seemed little more than a beautiful mirage that he had danced with and held in his arms, her fragrance filling his head and his heart.

But now she was almost a reality.

Like a lovesick calf, he was aware that his heart was pounding, but it slowly dawned on him that nobody was answering. The pounding quickly turned to sick disappointment when he heard the old boy's voice calling to him from the foot of the stairs. Keeping a check on him, he thought without humour.

'I don't reckon she's there, young fellow. She often goes off to visit clients, and she goes out a lot with that friend of hers.'

'Friend?' Charlie said, fearing the worst. But why wouldn't she have a friend, a gentleman caller, a good-looker like her . . . ?

'A young lady. But if you want to leave a message, I'll see that she gets it.'

His mind flooding with relief, Charlie knew he couldn't stand here for ever, like a spare part at a wedding, so he went down to the shoe shop again.

'I need to be sure I've got the right person first. Would you mind describing her to me — Mr Foster?' he added, remembering the name above the shop door.

'Why don't you describe the person you're wanting?' the reply came keenly. He wasn't born yesterday.

Charlie gave a slight smile, seeing right through him, but appreciative of the man's caution. He imagined that the Gracie he remembered would attract that kind of fatherly concern. He wished again that he hadn't lost the photo of her and her friend in the newspaper, so he could have proved his credentials, but she might not have cared for her landlord to know she was involved in the fire at the Palais.

'Well, the Gracie Brown I'm looking for is quite small and she's very pretty and softly spoken. She has curly auburn hair and blue eyes.'

He could have added that she danced like an angel, and that she had fitted under his heart as if they were two halves of the same person, but he didn't think that was something the man needed to hear either.

'There was another girl with her the last time I saw her,' he went on hastily. 'I think she had fair hair with stiff waves in it. She might be the friend you're talking about, but it's Gracie I remember the most.'

'I can see that,' Mr Foster said, 'and it certainly sounds as if it's our Miss Brown, so if you want to leave a note for her, I'll see that she gets it when she comes back. I can give you some writing-paper and an envelope.'

If Charlie had his way, he'd have waited around all day, knowing he was so near to finding her again, but he couldn't do it. He had an appointment that very day with his agent and a music publisher, and although he had hoped to achieve the two things he wanted most in the world on the same day, it wasn't to be.

So he did the next best thing and wrote her a note as the man had suggested. He merely said he thought she was the girl he remembered from that night at the Palais in the spring, and that he'd like to see her again and to know that she was well. It sounded trite and stilted, but he could hardly vow undying love to her and frighten her off for good.

He tucked a front row ticket for the show at the Roxy inside the envelope, adding that any time she could use it, she should present it at the box office with his compliments, and be sure to come backstage afterwards.

And that was that. It was probably best to keep things as informal as possible. He couldn't overlook the fact that Gracie Brown might well have a young man by now, who would be irate that a musician was contacting her. Some people had the weirdest idea of what musicians did and how they behaved, but he had lived and worked among them for so long, and he knew very well they were ordinary people earning their living, just like everybody else.

The music publisher, Barnaby Jordan, was as round as he was tall in his expensive silk suit. He immediately made Charlie revise such mundane thoughts as he pumped his hand up and down, his own hands bristling with gold rings.

A little bemused, Charlie thought it was a very different reaction from the way nobody had wanted to look at his song before Feinstein had finally decided to use it in the show.

'You have real talent, my boy, and *Someone I once knew* is going to make you rich. I've spoken with your agent, and there's a light-music programme on the wireless that's willing to give it airtime, and several popular singers interested in giving it a hearing. We should also get a gramophone recording deal out of this, Charlie boy. But you can't afford to rest on your laurels, so what else do you have up your sleeve? We need to cash in on it quickly. Being a musicman yourself, I don't need to tell you that the public is very fickle, so we need a follow-up song in the same style. More, if you have them.'

Charlie's brain was starting to reel as the man went on talking so enthusiastically. In his wildest dreams, this was exactly the way it went. But he had never expected his dream to become such a thrilling possibility — and he had never got as far as considering a gramophone recording, which would definitely put his song on the map. It was logical though. If one of the popular crooners of the day was willing to sing it on the wireless with one of the big bands, he would also be keen to have it made into a gramophone record.

It wouldn't be Charlie's band, and it would be the singer's name that sold the record. The singer's picture would be on the record sleeve, because that was the way these things were done, but Charlie could live with that, knowing that without him, there wouldn't be a song at all.

Barnaby Jordan was still rabbiting on about royalties and airtime, and half of it was going completely over Charlie's head, until at last the man gave a large grin. 'I can see you're a bit overcome, my boy, so I'll be in touch with your agent about contracts, and things will start moving from there. Congratulations, Charlie — and you be sure to let me have that next song just as fast as you can.'

The interview was finished on a handshake, and Charlie still couldn't quite believe it. His stomach was turning somersaults with all that he was hearing. The man didn't just want one song, he wanted more. It was better than he had ever dreamed of — and once he could get his brain thinking normally again, he knew that pretty damn quickly he had better dig out all those pieces of paper on which he'd scribbled abortive lyrics and written scraps of music!

★ ★ ★

Dolly couldn't make sense of the image hovering over her. It was indistinct, with no clear outlines, like something in a watercolour painting. She couldn't really be bothered to decide what it was. Her head still hurt, and her brain was fogged up from the stinging injections the vampire nurse kept giving her. She'd much rather keep her eyes closed, and hope that the hazy image would disappear. Unless she was dead, of course, and it was a blooming angel come to spirit her away . . .

The thought was so unnerving that her eyes flew open at once.

'Thank goodness,' Gracie said. 'I thought you were going to sleep for ever.'

'It's you!' croaked Dolly, unwilling to admit, even to herself, how the thought that she could be dead had petrified her.

She'd also started to think Gracie was dead. Nobody would tell her anything, no

314

matter how often she asked them. Or maybe they had told her, and she had just drifted off again, blocking the awful news she couldn't bear to hear.

'Of course it's me, and doing a bit better than you, by the looks of things.'

Dolly registered now that Gracie was sitting in a wheelchair. Her leg stuck out in front of her, swathed in a heavy bandage and supported by some sort of splint. The toes that peeped out from the bottom of the bandage were swollen and black. Another bandage was held on by sticking-plaster at the side of her face, and there was a lot of ugly bruising around her eyes and cheek.

'Blimey, gel, what happened to you?' Dolly said hoarsely.

Gracie shuddered. The horrors of that day hadn't left her yet. She wished she could have blacked out quickly, the way Dolly had. She probably didn't even remember it clearly, but the noise and the screams and the smells would remain with Gracie for ever.

'Facial injuries, and my leg was crushed,' she said briefly. 'At one time they thought they were going to have to chop it off, but they decided against it. Good thing too. How would I ever have gone dancing again with only one leg?'

She tried to make a joke of it, but her last

315

words were lost in an enormous, choking swallow. Dolly couldn't speak, as all that she was hearing sank in. She wasn't much for what she called slushy stuff, but right now she knew that if she had the strength — and if Gracie could get flipping well near enough with that bandage on her leg — she'd hug her and hug her, just to show how thankful she was that they were both alive.

'Well, we're both still here. We may be battered and bruised, but I reckon Somebody Up There was looking down on us,' she managed eventually.

And saying 'Thank God' — and meaning it — didn't seem quite so against her principles now, either. In fact, when she came to think of it, she had quite a lot to thank God for, especially having a friend like Gracie Brown.

'They're keeping me here for a couple more weeks to make sure my leg heals properly,' Gracie went on, 'and I don't suppose you'll be going home yet either. Not much of a way to end a day's outing, is it? I wish I'd never suggested it now. I should have stayed home and finished those bridesmaid dresses.'

'Don't be daft,' Dolly answered, alarmed at her dispirited voice. Gracie was always so strong, coping with her mum's illness and then her dad's drowning, but she looked anything but strong now. 'You need a day off now and then, and you couldn't have guessed the train was going to go off the rails, could you? You ain't a clairvoyant.'

But Gracie's thoughts were already going off at a tangent.

'They've been giving me stuff to deaden the pain, and I reckon it deadened my brain as well. But now that I feel a bit more sensible, I'll have to let Mrs Barnes-Gilbert know what's happened, so I'm going to write to her and explain. Thank goodness there's still some weeks before the wedding, but I don't want her to think I'm a lazy worker.'

'For heaven's sake, Gracie,' Dolly said, but her voice was becoming slurred as the drugs took over again. 'Everybody knows you're the best there is, so stop worrying about other people and think about yourself. At least when it comes to *your* wedding, you'll be walking up the aisle instead of hopping on one leg!'

Gracie laughed, but there was little mirth in the sound. 'I've got to find somebody to marry me first.'

Involuntarily, she touched her fingers to the bandage on her cheek, and without being told, Dolly knew she was dreading the time when it came off and she saw just how scarred she really was.

★   ★   ★

Two weeks later a small bouquet of flowers arrived at the hospital, addressed to Miss Gracie Brown, together with several letters. The one accompanying the flowers was from Mrs Barnes-Gilbert, who assured Gracie that there was still plenty of time for the bridesmaid dresses to be finished, and that she wasn't to worry about them until she was fully recovered.

'What she means,' Dolly said cynically, on the Saturday afternoon she came back to visit, bringing good wishes from all at Ma Warburton's and Lawson's Shirt Factory, 'is that she can always get some more dresses run up if you ain't capable of finishing them.'

'Well, thank you for that vote of confidence! What are you doing here, anyway? You should be out enjoying yourself, not visiting the sick.'

'And ain't you the touchy one, now you're getting better!'

'I'm sorry,' Gracie said. 'But my leg is itching fit to burst. It's healing better than they thought, though, and I'll be thankful when this blessed bandage comes off next week.'

And even though there would be scars, she was assured that they would fade in time, and

318

meanwhile they would be hidden underneath her stockings. She refused to look in the mirror except when absolutely necessary, though the nurses had assured her that the angry scar at the side of her cheek would also fade, and that she could easily dress her hair to cover it.

'So who's the other letter from?' Dolly said.

Gracie felt her face flood with colour.

'I wrote to my landlord to let him know what had happened, and he sent a note back and his wife sent me a card, which was very sweet of her.'

'*And*? It's not a card from an old dear that's put that look on your face!'

Gracie just managed not to snap that no, it was flying glass from a train window that had done that. Instead, she put her hand in her pocket, and pulled out the letter that she had read and reread a hundred times already.

'You'd better see for yourself,' she said, handing her Charlie's letter.

Dolly read it quickly, her eyes widening.

'It's your bloke,' she exclaimed. 'Your saxophone player!'

Gracie couldn't be bothered to repeat that he wasn't *her* saxophone player. She was still too bemused and excited and stunned and overwhelmed that Charlie had tracked her down at all. And that he wanted to see her again. He wanted her to go to his show and go backstage afterwards. She swallowed, feeling the familiar tingling in her veins and the quickening of her heartbeat.

And just as quickly came the downbeat of it all.

'The trouble is,' she said flatly, 'it's been more than two weeks since he left the letter with Mr Foster, and now he'll think I'm not interested in going to see his show, and even more, that I'm not interested in seeing *him*, won't he? And besides, there was that picture of him with that singer in the paper, wasn't there?'

'Oh, that was just *newspaper* stuff, and you're never going to find out if you sit and twiddle your thumbs. Write and tell him why you haven't done as he asked. Send a letter to Charlie Morrison, care of the Roxy, and explain that you've been otherwise engaged all this time,' she added, trying to coax a smile out of Gracie. 'He could hardly have expected you to hop to the theatre, could he?'

'I don't know what to do. Even if the picture didn't mean anything, he'll probably have lost interest in me by now.'

It was so important, such a milestone in her life, that she couldn't simply bear it if Charlie had gone all arty-farty and thumbed his nose at a girl who couldn't even be bothered to take up his invitation. It was irrational and she knew it, but the feeling wouldn't go away. It was almost better not to know.

She saw Dolly purse her lips.

'Well, I never thought you'd be so spineless, Gracie Brown.'

'I'm not spineless, just realistic.' She touched the side of her face. 'This isn't going to help either. I'm not the girl he remembers. I never thought I was vain, but every time they change the dressing and I catch sight of myself in the mirror I . . . '

Without warning, angry, self-pitying tears filled her eyes, and it was shameful, because she knew there were people far worse off than she was. She saw them every day, here in this hospital. She heard their anguished cries, and knew the helpless pain of their relatives.

She knew what it meant when the curtains were pulled around a bed amid a flurry of activity, before all the bedding was whisked away and disinfected for the next patient. Oh yes, there were people far worse off than she was.

'If he thinks anything of you, he won't worry about a little scar,' Dolly went on roughly. 'And he obviously *does* think something of you. He took the trouble to find you, didn't he? No bloke ever bothered that much over me! You should think yourself lucky, gel, instead of sitting there looking like you've found a farthing and lost a tanner.'

'I know all that, so stop fussing! I'll write back to him when I can decide what to say.'

'Well, make sure you do it soon. He'll wonder what's been keeping you all this time, especially when you were making such cow-eyes at him that first night.'

'I was not!'

Dolly grinned, cheered by the sparkle returning to Gracie's eyes.

'Not much! You were practically ready to drop — well, I'd better not say any more, for fear of scandalizing the old ducks in the ward,' she said, chuckling. 'When are they letting you out of here, anyway?' she added, turning the conversation neatly before Gracie could blast her for making such insinuations.

'In another week, I hope. I have to practise walking again, since my leg's been weakened by having it bandaged all this time.'

'Get that letter in the post to Charlie boy, then. You don't want him to go off you and find some other girl to cuddle up with on a dark night, do you?' Dolly advised. 'Promise me now.'

'All right, slave-driver, I promise!'

And despite her jitters she knew she felt considerably better at having Dolly chivvying her to do what she knew she should. The only problem was in finding exactly the right words to say to Charlie.

★ ★ ★

It took a lot of thought that evening, while she chewed a pencil and surveyed the half-dozen discarded pieces of paper surrounding her. She might have sounded resolute before, but her nerves were getting the better of her again. What could she say to him? She didn't really know him. She thought she had had glimpses of him now and again since that first magical night that had ended so terribly . . . in the park, on a street, on a tram . . . but she was willing to admit that it was only because she had *wanted* to see him so much that she had turned the image of every dark-haired, good-looking man into Charlie . . .

In the end, she kept it simple. He had a right to know why she had ignored his invitation to the theatre and the complimentary ticket he had sent her. He had a right not to feel snubbed. So she wrote as simply as she knew how.

Dear Charlie, she wrote, after agonizing whether or not she should be more formal, and deciding that was plain ridiculous . . .

Thank you for your letter and the ticket to the Roxy show. I was very happy to hear from you again; and I certainly am the Gracie Brown you remember — though perhaps not quite as you remember her.

She paused for another chew at the pencil. Was that too stupid for words? Was it too pompous, putting herself in the third person?

Furious at herself for her constant indecision, she plunged on, refusing to screw up any more pieces of writing paper, and to say whatever came to mind.

I've been in an accident recently. You may have seen the account in the newspaper about the excursion train that was derailed on the way to Margate a few weeks ago, though I suppose it's old news by now. Well, me and my friend Dolly were on that train, and landed up in hospital. Dolly's back in London now, and I hope to be going home in about a week. I had a badly crushed leg, and at one time the doctors thought I might have to have it taken off.

He'd know how to spell the word amputated, but she didn't, and she hated the sound of it anyway, so she left it at that. He might as well know her for what she was, just

324

a seamstress with no great education, and if she carried on like this, then any minute now she'd be feeling so sorry for herself she wouldn't be sending the bleedin' letter at all, she thought, with a burst of Dolly's bravado.

But now they assure me I'll be as good as new apart from a few scars, and once I've mastered walking properly again, I'll be able to dance again too.

Was that being too forward? Was it asking him to remember, the way she did, how they had once danced so close together that they could have been wearing the same skin . . . ? Her eyes misted, and she dashed the tears away.

But she had to say the rest. Before he saw her and his eyes widened in shock and then turned away, she had to say it.

I had a facial injury too. Flying glass, they said. But they promised that the scar on the side of my cheek will fade eventually, and as long as I let my hair grow a bit, I'm sure I'll be able to hide it.

No, no, no! Angrily, she scratched out the last sentence. It sounded as if she was pleading for sympathy, and she was too proud to settle for sympathy when what she yearned for was love.

So as soon as I'm able, I'll turn up at the Roxy one of these fine nights, and look forward to seeing you backstage as you suggest.

She signed it quickly: *Gracie Brown*, and without even stopping to read it through, she stuffed it in the envelope Sister had given her and addressed it to *Charlie Morrison, c/o the Roxy Theatre*. Then, taking the bull by the horns, she limped along to Sister's office and asked her to post it for her.

'I don't normally act as unofficial postman, miss,' Sister said pointedly, 'but I'm glad to see you making use of those legs, so I'll do it for you tomorrow, even though you'll probably be back home before the letter arrives.'

'That's all right,' Gracie said hastily. 'Just as long as it gets there.'

The sister smiled more tolerantly. 'Your young man, is it?'

'Sort of,' Gracie mumbled, and hobbled back to the ward as fast as she could, wishing with all her heart that it was true.

18

It felt strange to be back in the flat, as though she had been away for months instead of a few weeks. At first she was completely disorientated. It was as if she was in an alien environment, with a need to wander through the rooms and touch all her things to make them seem familiar again.

The Fosters made a great fuss of her, insisting on sending a dish of stew upstairs for her evening meal, so that she wouldn't have to bother herself, and also a bunch of flowers to brighten up the flat, which touched her deeply.

Eventually she looked at the small pile of letters waiting for her. They were mostly answers to her advert in the newspaper and asking if she could get in touch with a view to some work, which was cheering. The minute she recognized Charlie's handwriting on one of the envelopes, her heart leapt, and she tore it open eagerly. The letter had obviously crossed with hers, since it was obvious that when he wrote it he hadn't yet heard about her accident.

Dear Gracie, she read,

I hope I haven't offended you by sending you the ticket for our show. I hope you'll be able to use it one evening, and that you'll take special note of a certain song in the show, written by yours truly. Yes, I'm actually a songwriter now, as well as a saxophone player, and I'd like to know what you think of my efforts. We danced so well together, and I sensed that you had a feel for the music, the way I did. I hope you're doing well with your new career, and that Gracie's Glad Rags will be a huge success.

Sincerely yours,
Charlie.

Gracie read the letter several times before deciding what to make of it. On the one hand she was overjoyed that he was following up his first letter with a second one, and that he hoped she would go to the show at the Roxy. On the other hand, she couldn't decide if it was merely a polite letter to an acquaintance. And the way he had ended the letter with 'Sincerely yours' was another thing. Did he mean he was actually *hers*, or was this just a formal way of closing a letter?

'I'm such a idiot,' she finally burst out,

exasperated at herself. 'The obvious thing is to go to the theatre and find out.'

She read the letter again, wondering about the song he had written, and consumed with a fervent wish to hear it. It would be wonderful, of course. Music was in his heart and soul. She remembered the way he had almost caressed the saxophone as he played it, his sensitive fingers finding the notes, loving them, producing magic with his touch, and giving the music all the attention a man would give a woman.

She shivered, wondering if there was more of Dolly's wanton lust in her than she realized. But what if there was? She was young and alive, thank God, and it was the most natural thing in the world for two people in love to desire one another too. *If* he loved her, and *if* he desired her.

She made some tea with shaking hands, knowing she had a compulsion to go to the theatre as soon as she felt able, if only to be polite, though that was far from her real reason. She needed to see his reaction when he saw her. She needed to be sure he wouldn't be repulsed when he saw how the scar on her cheeks hadn't faded very much yet, and how she still had a little problem keeping her balance when the wayward, weakened leg threatened to let her down if she wasn't careful. She wasn't ready for dancing yet . . .

★ ★ ★

Dolly turned up a few evenings later, looking perkier than ever, which could only mean one thing.

'You'll never guess what!'

'Yes I will,' Gracie said. 'You've got a new chap.'

Dolly laughed. 'Not exactly. But there's a new bloke in the packing department at Lawson's who keeps giving me the eye. He's ever so good-looking, Gracie, and I'm sure he fancies me — oh and in case I forget to tell you, your face is looking much better now, and you look nearly as good as new.' She finished without pausing for breath.

'Thank you, I'm sure. So who is this paragon? Are you sure he's not spoken for already if he's Mister Wonderful?'

'Quite sure,' Dolly declared. 'His name's Len and with any luck we're going to the flicks one Saturday night.'

'What do you mean — with any luck?'

'Well, he hasn't actually asked me yet, but I'm working on it,' she said with a wink. 'So how are you settling back in the old routine?

Have you finished those bridesmaid dresses yet?'

'As a matter of fact, I have. I suddenly realized how time was moving on, and it also made me feel much better to be doing something with my hands again. They're ready now, and I'm going to deliver them to Mrs Barnes-Gilbert as soon as I've done a bit more walking.'

'If you want to take them on Sunday afternoon, I'll come with you for moral support,' Dolly offered. 'I wouldn't mind seeing how the other half lives.'

'I'd like that, Dolly, just in case I start wobbling all over the place.'

'You won't do that, you ninny. But what else has been happening that I don't know about? Has Charlie been to see you?'

'Of course not. Why would he?'

She hesitated. She was pathetically grateful that Dolly would be going on the tram with her to Mrs Barnes-Gilbert's place, because she didn't feel confident enough to go out very far on her own just yet — but it was another thing to risk suggesting that she came with her to the Roxy too. Once she got up the courage, this was one place where Gracie wanted to go alone. It wouldn't matter that there were hundreds of other folk in the theatre. As far as she was concerned there would be only her and Charlie.

Dolly soon twigged. 'I bet you've heard from him again, haven't you? I can tell there's something going on, Gracie. What's he said this time?'

Gracie sighed. It was hardly a love-letter, and there was no need to keep the contents from Dolly.

'Tell me what you think.' She handed it over and Dolly read it quickly.

'Well, he ain't exactly forthcoming, is he? And it's no more than what was said in that newspaper about him being a songwriter. I s'pose he thought you didn't know about that.'

'I s'pose he thought I didn't know about the girl hanging on to him, either!'

'Bleedin' hell, Gracie, sometimes I give up on you, really I do. Do you want him or don't you? The truth now!'

Gracie smiled, and regardless of the scar on her cheek she looked so luminously beautiful that Dolly could only stare at her, speechless for once.

'Want him? Of *course* I *want* him. I've hardly been able to think of anything else but him for months if you must know!'

'I do know,' Dolly said drily. 'So what are you waiting for? What you need to do now is go to the bleedin' Roxy like he says, sit in the front row and listen to this special song he's written. Then go backstage, and for goodness' sake tell him you like his song, whatever you think of it. Chaps like to hear a bit of flattery. You don't want to call yourself Gracie's Glad Rags for nothing, neither. You get togged up in your best bib and tucker, and you won't give that other girl a snowball's chance in hell.'

Gracie was laughing by the time Dolly had finished with her so-worldly advice.

'Oh Dolly, you do me a power of good.'

'Never mind all that. Are you going to do as I say, or do I wash my hands of you?' Dolly said determinedly.

'Of course I am. Would I be daft enough to ignore the advice of an expert?' Gracie laughed wildly as they hugged one another.

★ ★ ★

On Sunday Dolly was suitably in awe of Mrs Barnes-Gilbert's mansion, as she called it. The maid took her below stairs for a cuppa while Gracie was shown into the sunny conservatory where Mrs Barnes-Gilbert was arranging some flowers. As soon as Gracie was announced she turned at once.

'My dear girl, how good it is to see you looking so well after your terrible ordeal. I was so concerned for you. Do sit down and Hester will bring us some tea while you tell me how you're feeling.'

Gracie gulped at such a warm reception, resisting the involuntary need to put her hand to her cheek to cover the scar.

'I'm much better, thank you,' she murmured. 'My leg has healed and providing I don't stand on it for too long, it feels perfectly well. It's only — '

The lady put her hand over Gracie's.

'If you're worried about the small blemish on your cheek, Gracie, you shouldn't. It doesn't detract a bit from your lovely face, and some discreetly applied powder will cover it. There are people who have far worse things to worry about than a little scar, my dear.'

'Yes, I know.'

She spoke humbly, wondering if this was a mild criticism of her vanity. And then, to her sheer horror, emotion got the better of her, and before she knew it she was blubbering, and Mrs Barnes-Gilbert had put her arms around her, and Gracie's tears were threatening to ruin her lovely silk afternoon dress.

'Oh, my Lord, I'm so sorry, ma'am. Whatever must you think of me?' she gasped, mortified, but the lady wouldn't let her pull away.

'Don't be so silly, my dear. You've been

through an ordeal and the shock of such events has a habit of coming back to us at the most inopportune times. We're all human, Gracie, and trite though it seems, a good hot strong cup of tea often does wonders to raise the spirits.'

Gracie was vaguely aware of the maid bringing in the tray, and would have laughed had she seen Dolly's comical expression a few minutes later, on being told that madam was actually cuddling the young woman, for all the world as if she was a close relative.

But Gracie knew none of that until later. All she knew was that this kind lady was comforting her, and it was probably true that there was still a bit of shock in her as a result of the train crash. It explained a lot of things, including her unpredictable moods, and her indecision about Charlie. As if Mrs Barnes-Gilbert was a mind-reader, she mentioned him.

'I'm sure your young man has been wonderfully supportive, hasn't he?'

Gracie couldn't recall that she had ever mentioned a young man, but she nodded anyway. There were some things you couldn't confide to a stranger, even such a kindly one.

'Oh yes.'

'Then the rest of the world doesn't matter, does it? Now then, I'm looking forward to seeing the bridesmaid dresses as soon as we've finished our tea,' she said with a smile, reminding Gracie of why she was here.

By the time she and Dolly returned to the flat, there was a fat fee in her purse, and the promise of more work for her once the wedding was over. And Dolly was all agog at how the other half lived.

'You really fell on your feet there, gel. Getting a patron like that is worth more than all the reg'lar money old Lawson pays. She'll tell her friends what a find you are, and you'll be well set up.'

'I suppose I will.'

'Well, blimey, don't go overboard, will you? Ain't you pleased?' Dolly said.

'Of course I'm pleased. It's just that sometimes, when you've got what you've always wanted, you're not so sure it's what you wanted after all,' Gracie said without thinking.

Dolly looked at her as if she had two heads. 'You're daft, that's what you are. I wouldn't mind being as independent as you are, though if Len comes up to scratch, maybe I'll end up being Mrs Len and never have to work again.' She finished with a hoot of laughter, just to cheer Gracie up.

And if Charlie comes up to scratch, maybe I'll end up being Mrs Charlie Morrison, and live happily ever after, Gracie thought. And pigs might fly.

'Just be careful. You know what I mean,' she warned Dolly hastily, pushing the treacherously seductive thoughts out of her head. They had never really surfaced before, but to be Charlie's wife would surely be the best, the most precious way of all to spend the rest of her life. It was completely impractical to think that way, of course, because they would need to get to know one another first — and who knew whether that spark still remained at all?

'Don't worry. I'm never getting caught like that again,' Dolly said, but by then, Gracie wasn't listening as she bent to pick up the note that had been pushed under her door, and ripped it open.

Not again, she thought despairingly. How many more times were they going to miss one another? And should she take this as a dire omen that they were simply not meant to be after all?

'What is it?' Dolly said hearing her intake of breath.

'He was here,' Gracie stuttered. 'Charlie. This afternoon. He was here, and I was out.' She wouldn't weep, even though she felt as though all the fates were conspiring against her.

'Well, at least it shows he's keen, don't it?' Dolly said.

'Or that he's almost giving up on me. He says the management will only hold the front-row seat for two more weeks, so he hopes I'll make use of the ticket, but if not, he'll understand. What does he understand?'

'Perhaps that you're being an idiot. If you want him, you've got to let him know it. Blokes like to be told as much as we do. Turn up at the Roxy the minute you can before that other girl gets her claws in him once and for all. Go for it, gel!'

* * *

Gracie wondered if Charlie really had looked for her every night since sending her the ticket. Watching the empty front-row seat, and wondering why she never turned up. Thinking he had offended her. Thinking she wasn't interested in him. Thinking she didn't remember, didn't care. She toyed with the idea of sending a note to the Roxy telling him she'd be there on Saturday night, and then decided against it. She needed to see his reaction when he realized the front-row seat was occupied. Then she would know if his feelings for her were real, or if she had been imagining them all this time.

She dreamed of him all that week, when she was asleep and when she was awake. When she took daily walks in the park to help strengthen her leg as she had been told to do at the hospital, and when she had her late-night cup of cocoa, curled up in an armchair in her dressing-gown. Whenever she looked at the stars through her bedroom window, and whenever she awoke to a new day, knowing that Saturday was coming closer.

The week seemed endless and yet gone in a flash. And then it was here. She followed Dolly's advice, and dressed in her Sunday best, cream-coloured dress and buttoned shoes and matching cloche hat, a string of amber beads around her neck.

She had let her dramatic red hair grow longer, so that when she pulled out small tresses of it to frame her face, it hid much of the scar, which she had duly powdered to follow Mrs Barnes-Gilbert's suggestion. A pinch of rouge put some much-needed colour into her cheeks, and when at last she was ready she drew on her cream chamois gloves and gazed critically at herself in her mirror.

But she knew she was looking the absolute best that she could, and whatever happened from now on was up to fate. Apart from the collywobbles in her stomach whenever she thought of how momentous this evening might turn out to be, she was ready to face the world. In particular, she was ready to face Charlie at last. Almost, anyway.

'My goodness, but don't you look a picture tonight, Miss Brown!' she heard Mrs Foster say as she went carefully down the stairs on the high-heeled shoes. 'Are you going somewhere special?'

'To the theatre,' she said, thinking it was the best thing anyone could have said to her, considering the state of her nerves.

'Well, I hope whoever is taking you, realizes he's got the belle of the ball, dear,' the woman said generously.

'Thank you, Mrs Foster,' Gracie said, smiling, and not for one minute did she think of putting her right on whoever was taking her.

The older woman's obvious admiration boosted her courage, and as she went into the street and thought about taking a tram, a taxi cruised alongside her, clearly wondering if she was a fare.

And recklessly, she thought, why not? Why ever not? This was a night for turning up in style, unruffled, cool and serene, like the images on the silver screen she admired so much.

'The Roxy theatre, please,' she told the

taxi-driver, and slid inside the vehicle as if she had been born to it.

It took less than half an hour to arrive at the front of the theatre, where people without tickets were already queuing outside, and the lucky ones who had booked in advance swept through the foyer like royalty. Gracie wasn't quite that confident, but it certainly felt good to be one of the favoured ones as she handed over her ticket, and was shown to the centre seat in the very front row.

As in most theatres the band was kept well out of sight in the orchestra pit during the performance, but they were clearly visible as they came in and took their seats.

Her hands were becoming increasingly damp inside her chamois gloves. She took the gloves off and put them inside her little evening bag, hardly able to look up. And then she saw him.

Charlie was right in front of her, the saxophone in his hand, looking so dark and elegant and wonderful in his evening clothes that she felt her heart stop for a moment. He was concentrating on moving quickly into his allotted place, so that he didn't see her immediately, and then he looked directly at her, seconds before the lights dimmed, but the smile that illuminated his face was worth every moment of anxiety she had felt all these months.

She had bought a programme on the way in, but even if she had been able to read it, she couldn't have said what was in it. Her stomach felt too topsy-turvy for that. She only knew that there was a special scene in the second act with a song that was called *Someone I once knew*, written by Charlie Morrison. She waited for it as if her life depended on it.

As the leading male singer came on to centre stage, the band became muted, and his voice was accompanied mainly by the haunting sound of a saxophone.

'There's someone I once knew . . . just for a moment, just for an hour . . . but her memory lingers in my heart, like her fragrance and grace . . .

Does she remember, the way I do, the way we danced on one magical night? The way we almost fell in love? And as sure as there are stars above, I'll never stop searching . . . for that someone I once knew . . . '

There were other words, but amid the thudding of her heart, Gracie heard only those, praying desperately that there was a hidden meaning in that phrase 'fragrance and grace.' Was that word meant to speak directly to her?

As the song ended, she was aware of the thunderous applause for Charlie's music. For one brief moment, he stood up to acknowledge the applause, and his eyes sought hers as she had known they would.

The rest of the show passed in a haze for Gracie. She was on the brink of finding out for sure if she had been imagining all this time that the man she had almost fallen in love with really existed, or if the dream had been no more than a fantasy. She knew he was *real*, but had that night at the Palais really been as significant as she had believed?

Beset with nerves again, she could hardly wait for the final curtain, and in exasperation, she wondered just how many encores the cast was going to have before the band played the national anthem.

At last they did so, the cast standing to attention like the audience, and she realized again that Charlie was a true musician. He was probably going places, so why would he ever want a working girl trying to make an independent life for herself?

As the house lights went up, she tried to pull on her gloves, but they simply wouldn't fit on to her damp hands, so she put them back in her evening bag and wondered what to do next. She was half tempted to scurry out of the place, knowing that backstage would be full of theatre people, excited and happy that another show was over, and she would feel like an unwanted bun at a feast. While she was still hesitating, one of the theatre ushers approached her.

'Miss Brown, will you come this way, please?' he said, and she knew there was no turning back.

She followed him mutely to the rear of the theatre and the large room backstage where the noise was deafening, as the cast and band congratulated one another on another superb performance. Glasses of wine were handed round; the smell of greasepaint and perfume was overwhelming; the glitter of the stage costumes making Gracie feel like a pale shadow in comparison, and it was all so very sophisticated that she could have slunk away at once.

'Gracie, at last!' she heard Charlie's voice say, and then he was beside her, his arms around her, his mouth kissing her lightly on the cheek. It was the scarred cheek, she registered, though he didn't seem to notice. In any case, it was little more than an air kiss, the kind that theatre people made, or so she was told. It didn't mean a thing, and almost instantly he was dragged away.

'Have a glass of wine, love,' Gracie heard a female voice say, and found herself looking directly into the eyes of Joyce, the singer. 'Thank God you've finally arrived. Our boy would have died from a severe case of heartache if you hadn't turned up after all.'

'Would he?' Gracie said, taking a too-large gulp of the wine and feeling her head spin.

'God, yes. He's totally besotted, you know, and I suppose you realize that his song was dedicated to you? Once we heard it, we knew the rest of us didn't stand a chance, so here's to you, kid.'

She raised her glass to Gracie as if to wish her luck, and then turned back to the handsome leading man. In seconds Charlie was back beside Gracie again, pushing his way through the mass of congratulations.

'I'm sorry. It's always like this at the end of a show. What did you think of it? Did it come up to your expectations?'

'The show or the song?' Gracie murmured.

She was out of her depth. Her so-elegant outfit, combined with the fire of her hair, seemed so ordinary now, compared with the glittering stage costumes all around her. She was being jostled in all directions, and to the uninitiated the release of artistic tension at the end of a good show was almost terrifying.

Charlie laughed, but she could see a spark of unease come into his eyes.

'The song, of course. What did you think I meant?'

'It was lovely.'

'Lovely,' he said abruptly. 'Is that all it meant to you?'

'Was it supposed to mean anything else?' she said, wondering what was happening to them. She had waited so long for this meeting, and she presumed he had wanted it too, since he had contacted her and sent her the ticket. And here they were, acting like the strangers they really were, instead of being on the brink of something far more. Her eyes shimmered as she tried to hide the sick hurt she felt, but he saw, and he knew. He spoke more gently.

'I haven't even asked how you are. I was so overwhelmed at seeing you it hardly seemed necessary because you look so beautiful, exactly as I remembered.'

'Do I?' she asked shakily.

His soft touch on her scar was as gentle as a butterfly's breath.

'*Exactly*,' he said. 'Look, give me five minutes to change, and then we'll get out of this crush and go somewhere quiet for supper. Will you wait?'

Did he think she was going to turn and run the minute he left her with all these people? Her chin lifted.

'Of course I'll wait,' she said, and he could make what he wanted to of that. Hadn't she already waited for him all her life?

★ ★ ★

A short while later, sitting beside him in the new motor car he had recently acquired, Gracie became tongue-tied again. The motor smelled of leather and newness, and its opulence seemed to mark out how far he had come since she had met him, such a relatively short time ago.

But they were no longer the same people, she thought in a mild panic. How could she ever have thought that they could just move back into each other's lives as if nothing had happened? She had lost her mother and her father in tragic circumstances, but she had managed to become independent in a small way, doing the job she loved best. Then there was the trauma of the train crash ... and her injuries that had badly undermined her new-found confidence for a while ... even if Charlie didn't seem to notice.

While his career had gone ahead in leaps and bounds. A saxophone player in a band had seemed glamorous enough to her, but to be a songwriter and have his songs sung on the wireless and on gramophone records, and to have the world at his feet, was something she couldn't even imagine.

'I've missed you,' he said suddenly. 'You have no idea how many times I've thought I saw you, almost turned to speak to you, to call out your name, only to realize that it wasn't you.'

'Have you?' she said, startled, and turning to look at him in the dimness of the car's interior. 'How strange.'

He gave a short laugh. 'Strange? Because I thought I'd found somebody special, and didn't want to lose her? Is that something you'd call strange?'

Gracie caught her breath, unsure whether or not there was a note of bitterness in his voice now. As if he really cared.

Play it cool, Dolly advised, even though she never took her own advice — but Gracie knew that there were times when it was far more important to say what was in your mind, and in your heart.

'No, not strange in that way. It's strange, because you can't imagine how many times I thought I saw you too. I know it sounds silly, but every time I heard a band playing in the park I hoped it would be you.'

She paused and then plunged on recklessly: 'But I suppose you won't be doing that any more now, will you? Not now you're such a star.'

For a moment his hand left the steering wheel and pressed hers.

'Gracie, if you ever think I'm getting too big for my boots, and too important to play in the park, you have my permission to tell me so.'

'You think we'll be seeing each other again then?' she said, her heart beginning to beat a good deal faster than before.

'You can count on that. I'm not going to lose you now. I need inspiration for all these songs I'm going to write, and you're the only one to give it to me. How do you think I wrote the one you heard tonight if it wasn't because you've filled my heart ever since that night at the old Palais?'

It was weird to be having such an intimate conversation in a car while they drove to the late-night supper club. Weird and wonderful. And for Gracie, with the night full of a million stars, it was the stuff of dreams, of romantic movies with dashing heroes and lovely young heroines.

When he finally stopped the car Charlie put his arms around her.

'We are going to see one another again after tonight, aren't we, Gracie?' he said. 'You're not going to be so elusive again, are you?'

'Yes. Oh, and no,' she said in confusion, answering both questions at once.

He laughed. 'Well, thank goodness for that. And by the way, my mother is constantly asking me when she's going to meet my young lady. I kept telling her I didn't have one, but you know what mothers are. She'll never take no for an answer. So will you come? Sunday afternoon tea seems like a very good start to me. Tomorrow, next week, whenever you say. I don't want to rush you into anything, but I'm not losing you now that I've found you.'

Gracie caught her breath. Everyone knew that being invited for Sunday afternoon tea at the home of a young man meant that his intentions were serious. It was the socially accepted thing. Everyone knew that, even if she and Charlie must also know that they needed time to get to know one another properly, before — if — the miracle happened, and there was a happy-ever-after ending after all.

'I would love to come to Sunday afternoon tea and meet your mother,' she said huskily, seconds before his mouth was kissing hers for the first time, regardless of who might be watching outside the supper club.

They broke apart at last, laughing a little self-consciously at being so blatant in a public place, but more so because of the sheer magic of being together. Gracie found herself offering up a silent prayer to whatever twist of fate had brought them together, for in those moments she had become very aware that Charlie's heartbeats had matched the rhythm of her own. It was the music of the heart, she thought joyfully . . . the music that never ended.

THE END

We do hope that you have enjoyed reading this large print book.

Did you know that all of our titles are available for purchase?

We publish a wide range of high quality large print books including:
Romances, Mysteries, Classics
General Fiction
Non Fiction and Westerns

Special interest titles available in large print are:
The Little Oxford Dictionary
Music Book
Song Book
Hymn Book
Service Book

Also available from us courtesy of Oxford University Press:
Young Readers' Dictionary
(large print edition)
Young Readers' Thesaurus
(large print edition)

For further information or a free brochure, please contact us at:
Ulverscroft Large Print Books Ltd.,
The Green, Bradgate Road, Anstey,
Leicester, LE7 7FU, England.
Tel: (00 44) 0116 236 4325
Fax: (00 44) 0116 234 0205

Other titles published by
The House of Ulverscroft:

A PERFECT MARRIAGE

Jean Saunders

Robert Jarvis dies from a heart attack, leaving his wife Margaret a widow at forty-two. Family and friends rally round, but their attentions only serve to stifle her, and with increasing suspicions that her marriage had not been as perfect as it had appeared to be, Margaret longs to get away from it all. Six months later she revisits Guernsey, the scene of her honeymoon twenty-five years earlier. There she meets and becomes attracted to the confident Philip Lefarge, but after a night of torrid passion, Margaret is filled with guilt and indecision . . .

DEADLY SUSPICIONS

Jean Saunders

The discovery of a mutilated hand had closed the investigation into the disappearance of sixteen-year-old Steven Leng. Now, ten years later, the victim's mother is still determined to find out what really happened to her son. She contacts private investigator Alexandra Best, who discovers more about the incident in the woods that originally sparked off the mystery. Alex becomes convinced that Steven was murdered and her investigations lead her to the Followers, a religious group that appeared to fascinate Steven. Alex treads a dangerous trail that finally leads to a dramatic denouement.